THE
SUMMER
OF THE
SHARK

ALEXANDER CARR

© 2024 Alexander Carr. The Summer of the Shark. All rights reserved.

No part of this publication may be reproduced, distributed or transmitted in any form or by any means, including photocopying, recording or other electronic or mechanical methods, without the prior written permission of the author, except as permitted by U.S. copyright law.

This is a work of fiction. Unless otherwise indicated, all the names, characters, businesses, places, events and incidents in this book are either the product of the author's imagination or used in a fictitious manner. Any resemblance to actual persons, living or dead, or actual events is purely coincidental.

For Janie

CHAPTER ONE

SATURDAY, 7TH JULY
The Wreck of the Medusa,
Off Newquay, Cornwall

The two divers rolled backwards off the side of the boat and swam to the marker buoy before following the shotline down to the wreck below. The unusually hot, calm weather, meant that conditions for diving were excellent and the wreck of the *Medusa* soon appeared beneath them.

As they swam down to the keel, they disturbed hundreds of bib that sheltered in the rusting hulk. The main steam engine had fallen to starboard and amongst the bent tubes, a conger eel stared out to see what dared disturb it in its protected lair. The propeller shaft emerged from the remains of the engine room, and they followed it to the rear of the hull to the point where it had snapped. And, a few metres further out, lay the remains of the propeller itself and the rudder.

The two divers had spent almost forty minutes exploring

the wreck when Ed, the leader, checked his dive watch and signalled to his fellow diver, Matt, that they should start their ascent. Finding the shotline, they moved up slowly, with Ed constantly checking the dive computer on his wrist. They paused at six metres down for their final three-minute safety stop.

Ed suddenly felt Matt touch his arm, pointing to his left. As he looked up, he saw a large, dark shape emerging from the gloom. For a split second he thought it must be some form of submersible, but then the reality suddenly dawned on him. The demonic smile on its jaw and the fins on the creature's top and side immediately defined it. Fuck, Ed thought, it's bloody massive.

Both divers froze with fear, incapable of moving as the huge shark swam towards them. On its current course Ed was sure it would crash into them. But then, at the very last second, it gave an almost imperceptible swing of its tail and started to move past, but so close that he could have reached out and touched its pectoral fin.

He could clearly see the individual rows of vicious teeth in the shark's mouth and the shark's black, lifeless eye as it looked directly at him. The numerous scars and abrasions on its massive, sleek body marked the reality of a long life lived in the deep. A large, ragged wound had torn into the trailing edge of its dorsal fin. And, finally, clearly outlined before him was the defining grey colouring of its upper body and the white below.

It seemed to take a lifetime to pass them, but they watched, terrified, as it moved effortlessly into the darkness and disappeared. Without even glancing at their watches, they immediately struck out for the surface. Bursting out of the water, they threw their flippers on to the dive boat and raced up the steps so quickly that they virtually threw themselves onto the deck. Pat, the boat captain, helped them remove their tanks and, for a moment they sat in silence. Pulling their masks off, they suddenly burst into adrenaline fuelled laughter.

'Thank Christ for that,' Pat said, taken aback by their silence. 'You two look like you've just seen a ghost.'

'Not a ghost,' Ed replied. 'We've just had a visit from the Grim Reaper.' He paused. 'And lived to tell the tale.'

12 DAYS EARLIER...

CHAPTER TWO

MONDAY, 25TH JUNE
Bentham Hall, Shropshire

Nick Martin looked down at the video link on his screen. In a studio in London, the veteran broadcaster Caro Johnson prepared to introduce him to the audience of her morning show on National Radio.

'My next guest really doesn't need any introduction. His film star looks and velvet smooth voice have assured his place as the go to presenter not only on British wildlife film and television but also across the world. Nick Martin, welcome to the show.'

'Thank you Caro for that embarrassingly generous introduction,' Nick replied.

'Well, it's true!' Caro responded. 'So, what are you up to at present?'

'Straight after this broadcast I'm driving up to the northwest coast of Scotland to continue researching for a new series for Channel 4 on the hidden secrets of the British coastline. I think it's due to go out early next year.'

'We'll all look forward to that. Nick, you've been a familiar face on our televisions for a number of years now, so let's go back. How did it all start?'

'I think that a huge amount of luck and being in the right place at the right time would sum it up perfectly.' Nick said.

'Tell us more.'

'Well after uni I did a bit of travelling in what people used to call their 'gap year'. I was staying with an old school mate, Charlie, who lived with his parents in Australia. His dad was running one of the big TV News channels and very kindly offered me a three month training placement, as long as I could get a temporary work visa.'

'How did that turn out?'

'Well there was a bit of a delay getting the visa sorted out, so I eventually started at the beginning of September. The placement was absolutely brilliant, a great experience,' Nick explained. 'Initially I did everything from making the coffee to assisting on pre- and post-production work. After a couple of weeks they even allowed me to help write scripts, though I'm not sure how much re-writing went on! For the last month I worked with the outside broadcast teams reporting on everything from kangaroos getting stuck in garden fences to events in parliament. I got to see how the real experts did it.'

'So what was the defining moment that put you on the path to where you are now?'

'One weekend in early November some of Charlie's friends invited us to spend a few days surfing with them a bit further down the coast. It was all pretty basic, camper vans and tents and so on, but what they didn't tell us was that one of the group would be the Australian Prime Minister's son, Harry Radcliffe, who had a protection officer with him due to some online death threats.'

'Not exactly like a weekend surfing off the Cornish coast then?'

'No, just a bit different! On the last morning, a few of the guys decided to go for a final surf. Charlie and I were feeling a bit rough after overdoing it the night before, so we thought we'd stay dry and video the guys riding the waves. I noticed Harry lying on his board waiting to catch a wave and started focusing on him. I'd literally just zoomed in when he was suddenly lifted into the air as a massive great white erupted from the water taking both Harry and his board in its mouth, before crashing back into the sea, dragging him under. He disappeared for what seemed ages but, in reality, was probably only a couple of seconds. I remember thinking 'how the hell is he going to survive that', but he miraculously reappeared, still holding onto his board and no shark attached.'

'What happened next?'

'A couple of the surfers, raced over to him and helped him back to shore. His protection officer had sprinted down to the beach shouting into his phone, and ran into the water to help drag Harry out.'

'How did he look?' asked Caro.

'Absolutely white, poor bloke. He must have been in a hell of a lot of pain. When I looked at my phone, I realised I'd still been filming. He looked up at me and said, "I hope that you got that?". I nodded and a pained grin lit up his face. "Well don't stop filming. I may want to show that to my kids one day." Look, I'm in awe of the guy. You could see the blood coming out of the lacerations on his wetsuit. He didn't complain once. When we got him off his board, there was a huge imprint of the shark's teeth on the underside, proving just how big the shark was. An ambulance soon turned up, along with a couple of police cars. The paramedics stabilised him, put in various drips and rushed him off to hospital where he spent a few days in intensive care.'

'That all sounds terrifying. What happened to all the footage that you took?'

'Charlie told me later that he'd been filming *me* most of the time because I'd been giving a running commentary on events as they unfolded - I had no idea I'd been doing that. So Charlie phoned his dad and told his PA to get him out of whatever meeting he was in if he wanted the biggest news story of the year. Within five minutes we'd sent over all the video and they put out quite a lot of it unedited. His dad said he liked the urgency of it all.'

'I seem to remember the film shot round the world and featured in almost every news broadcast in every continent for the next twenty-four hours,' Caro said. 'And you became an instant news star.'

'I'm not so sure that Harry would agree with that. Whenever I see him now, he gives me a hard time and says I owe my entire career to him.'

'Well he certainly played his part! So how did this lead on to where you are today?' Caro asked.

'I returned to England a couple of weeks later and got a message from David Hunter, who was the Head of BBC's Natural History Unit in Bristol. He'd seen the shark attack report and told me that he'd liked what he'd seen and asked me about my future job plans were. I told him I had this dream of working in television. To my utter surprise, he invited me to go and see him and, ultimately, offered me a job. So that's where it all started.'

'That was twenty-five years ago. You now have your own media and production company, Live World Films, which you started with your wife Sophie. You've done series for the BBC as well as collaborating with the Discovery Channel, National Geographic and NBC Universe, to name but a few. A pretty impressive list. Which has been your favourite series to date?'

'That's a really tough question.' Nick paused. 'If I had to choose one, it would probably be *Shark Week* in the US that I presented a few years ago. As you know, sharks are my special interest, and it was great to have the opportunity to dive with them and work alongside some really great people.'

'Now, you're very much involved with the protection and conservation of sharks across the globe. Tell us a bit about your work.'

'I work with a number of charities, but one of the most important goals for me is the eradication of the appalling shark finning trade.'

'For the benefit of those listeners who don't know what shark finning is, please could you explain a bit more about it?'

'Shark finning entails cutting off some or all of a shark's fins, usually while the shark is still alive, and then dumping the animal back into the sea to die a slow, agonising death. The fins are mainly used for shark fin soup, which is an East Asian dish, traditionally associated with wealth and prosperity. The sad reality is that shark fins don't actually have any taste and as many as seventy million sharks are killed each year for what is, in effect, vanity.'

'That's appalling,'

'And it's unsustainable,' Nick added. 'Not only are we decimating shark populations across the globe, but sharks have low reproductive rates making repopulation increasingly difficult.'

'So if people want to find out more and perhaps contribute to the charities working in this field, where should they look?'

'If they just go to our website at LiveWorldFilms.com they'll find all the information they need there.'

Caroline glanced at the studio clock. 'I'm afraid we're almost out of time, but before we end, please can you answer a question I know many listeners, as well as me, would love to ask… are there great white sharks in British waters?'

'I'm certain we do get occasional visitors to our shores and it's only a matter of time before one of them is recorded on film or video to prove the case,' Nick replied. 'Look, everything is right for them. Marine conditions off our coast are not dissimilar to those found off Africa, or the east coast of America and we have an abundant seal population. If Sunfish and Barracuda have been found off our shores, as they have, then why not great whites which are far more adaptable?'

'So you think it's more a matter of when, than if?'

'Yes I do, and, personally, I can't wait for that to happen.'

'I'm sure we all agree with you on that except perhaps some nervous swimmers or surfers! Nick, thank you so much for taking the time to be with us on National Radio today. Good luck with your trip to Scotland. I hope you find something new and interesting for your next series.'

'It's been a pleasure,' Nick said. 'And I never cease to be amazed by what the Scottish coast can reveal.'

NICK REMOVED HIS HEADPHONES, turned off the screen and walked out of the sound proofed studio into the Live World office beyond. The office was in a converted seventeenth century barn, complete with enormous beams from which designer lights hung. Nick, over 6 feet tall, had to bend down as he went through the old door opening.

'That seemed to go all right.'

Nick looked up. The voice from across the office belonged to Jill Higham, Nick's personal assistant who, along with her husband Peter, had worked with him for over fifteen years. Like Nick, Jill was also in her mid-forties, but, unlike him, she was stylishly dressed and could pass for a woman ten years younger. 'Though it's a pity you didn't find the time to comment on all the wonderful women in your life who've made it possible… not that I'm desperate for approval or anything.' Becky and Mima, the two younger mainstays in the office smiled in agreement with Jill.

'I just didn't want to embarrass you all,' joked Nick.

'Some hope.' Jill said. 'Now, you'd better get on your way, otherwise you won't get up to Ullapool until the early hours. Pete's got the itinerary and everything else you need. Have a good fact finding trip and don't forget to bring back some smoked salmon.'

'As if I'd forget. As ever, thanks for all your help. I'll see you in a few days.' Nick waved goodbye and made his way across the cobbled courtyard to the main house. He entered into the spacious kitchen, where a large, four door Aga took pride of place. His mother in law, Beth, and his wife, Sophie were sitting at the kitchen table looking at something on her laptop.

'Ah here he is, the man with "film star looks and a velvet smooth voice",' Sophie said. 'I wish someone had told me about that before I married you.'

'Too cruel,' Nick said, feigning offence. 'It was a bit cringey, wasn't it? There again, she does have great taste.'

'More like bad eyesight,' Sophie responded. 'Talking of taste, Mum's put together a wonderful picnic lunch for you and Pete. Probably enough for dinner as well, if you don't want to waste time finding somewhere to eat en route to Ullapool. It's in the blue cold bag in the car.'

Nick walked over to Beth and gave her a peck on the cheek. 'You spoil me, my favourite mother-in-law. Thank you.'

'I'm the only one you've got, so that's not hard,' she replied giving him a hug. 'Have a good trip. We'll look forward to hearing all about it whenever you get back.'

'Thanks. Where are the children?' Nick asked.

'I think the girls are in the stable,' Sophie said. 'The last time I saw the boys, they were outside trying to get Pete to smuggle them into the car. I'll come out with you.'

As they walked outside Nick shouted to the girls that he was off. Two heads belonging to Milla, aged fifteen and Heli, fourteen, suddenly popped up over the stable door. Both girls were tall for their age and, to Nick's growing consternation, already looking like the young women they were becoming.

'Yup, okay, see you, Dad' and disappeared back inside.

'Love you too,' Nick said, pretending to be upset.

'I'm afraid they're so used to you heading off, it's not a big deal anymore.' Sophie said. 'But at least they're doing something useful for a change, mucking out the stable instead of having their heads stuck into their phones.'

'That's true. Now, where are the twins?' Nick asked. 'Charlie, Fred, where are you?'

'Hiding behind the front seats,' said Jill's husband Pete, emerging from the front of the car. Pete, a former marine, was even taller than Nick and built like a rugby prop forward. 'Come on you two, out of there.'

The eleven-year-old twins, Charlie and Fred, scrambled out of the car and sprinted across the garden and shouted 'Bye Dad, bye Pete' as they disappeared.

Nick chuckled to himself and looked down as Molly, his

cocker spaniel, wandered over and rubbed against his leg. 'At least someone's making a fuss.'

'Come here,' Sophie said, giving Nick a big hug. 'Take care and don't lead Pete astray will you?'

'More like the other way round,' Nick replied as he climbed into the car. 'I'll call you tomorrow.'

'Yes, okay. Bye Pete,' Sophie called out and got a wave in return as the car pulled away down the drive.

CHAPTER THREE

TUESDAY, 26TH JUNE
Ardmair Beach Holiday Cottages,
Ullapool, Ross & Cromarty, Scottish Highlands

Christopher Warren lifted the last kayak off the trailer and carried it to the water's edge. He looked at his watch and walked back to the picturesque waterside lodge in which he and his adult children had just spent their first night.

He opened the door. 'Ben, Emma, let's get going. We should have been on the water ages ago.'

'Coming Dad,' he heard his son reply as he turned to take in the breath taking view across the still waters of the bay to the mountains, their summits still covered in light cloud.

He closed his eyes momentarily and sighed.

'If only you could see this Gilly,' he whispered softly to himself.

The family kayaking holiday had been planned with his wife, Gilly, a couple of years before. Her sudden and unexpected death from a heart attack six months later had meant that the plans were put on hold. Enough time had now elapsed for them to go ahead with the trip in her memory .

'It's going to get really hot out there. I hope you've used some Factor 50 and got clothes to cover up if necessary,' Christopher warned.

'Dad, we're not kids anymore,' complained Ben, a strapping twenty-four-year-old trainee accountant, as he and his sister walked out of the cottage to join their father. 'Come on then, let's get these boats in the water.'

To the east, the sun was starting to climb over the hills into the clear blue sky as they dragged their kayaks the last few feet into the water. The sheltered sea in Badentarbet Bay was as calm as any they had seen.

'Remind me, how far are we going today?' asked Emma, an attractive, blond haired, twenty one year old with an athletic physique.

'I don't think we'll be out too long. Shall we see how we go and try to get back here mid-afternoon?'

'Sounds good to me,' Ben said and Emma nodded in agreement. 'How far is it to this Horse Island you mentioned last night?'

'Oh, I should think about three hours. Let's just head up the coast and take a look.'

'By then I'll be starving so we can pull up on a beach and have some of those lovely biscuits I saw you hiding into your rucksack, Dad,' Emma said as she pushed her boat out into the water. 'Let's stop this chatter and get going. I've got a feeling this could be quite a trip.'

THREE MILES ALONG THE COAST, Nick and Pete were walking along the Ullapool harbour wall. They were to meet the local representative of the Scottish Marine Protection Agency. They'd arrived at Harbour View, their charming B&B, shortly after midnight and Nick was thinking they could have done without the early start this morning.

'This looks like our man,' Pete said as a squat, solid looking man dressed in a yellow safety jacket climbed up onto the sea wall from an orange rib and held out his hand in greeting as they approached.

'Good morning gentlemen,' said the stranger.' 'I hope you managed to get a bit of rest after your journey yesterday. I'm David Scott. Sorry about the surname, but I suppose it fits the role.'

'Good to meet you, David. Nick and Pete.' Nick did the introductions. 'Thanks for agreeing to take us out today.'

'Ah, not at all, it's a real pleasure to have you with us. Now if you're ready, we'll get on our way'.

They all stepped carefully down into the rib and David introduced the skipper, Angus, a broad shouldered man with long, red hair. David explained that Angus had been 'working on these waters since he was a young lad.'

'My dad was a fisherman as was his father before him,' explained Angus with a west coast lilt to his voice. 'I'd hoped to follow in his shoes but I'm afraid there's just not enough fish anymore to be able to make a decent living.'

'So what do you do now?' Nick asked.

'Well, during the summer months I mainly take tourists out on day trips around the Isles and in the winter I also do a bit of plastering.'

'Crikey, couldn't be more different,' Pete said.

'True,' Angus said, 'but I do okay. I enjoy working with David and his team throughout the year.'

'Right, gentlemen,' David interrupted, reaching down into a compartment by his right leg, 'if you could just put these lifejackets on, we'll be on our way. Now, I understand you want to take a look at Gruinard Island. Have I got that right?'

'Yep,' Nick said. 'As part of a new TV series that we're putting together, we're looking for British coastal locations with a different story to tell.'

'Well Gruinard certainly has that,' David replied as the rib pulled away from the harbour wall into open water. 'Do you know much about its history?'

'I've done a bit of research but I'm not sure Pete has,' Nick said. 'David, would you mind going over it in case we've missed something?'

'Of course,' David said, clearly pleased to have the chance to share his knowledge. 'Back in World War Two, British government scientists had become very worried about intelligence they were receiving. The Nazis were developing chemicals for possible biological warfare. As a result, it was decided that scientists working at the biological weapons laboratory at Porton Down should carry out tests of a particularly nasty bacterium called Anthrax. And they chose Gruinard Island for the experiment. So, in 1942, a number of bombs were detonated over the island and a cloud of deadly brown dust drifted down onto a flock of unsuspecting sheep with the inevitable result that all the sheep perished. The spores in the soil also made Gruinard uninhabitable for some five decades.'

'Am I right in thinking there was some sort of protest group that took action in the 1980s?' asked Nick.

'Yes, I think that it was in the early 1980s. A protest group that went by the rather menacing name of The Dark Harvest Commando started demanding that the government decontaminate the island. They brought it to everyone's attention by sending a pack of the island's soil to Porton Down, accompanied by the threat to send other parcels around the country. It certainly seemed to work because in 1986 the government at last began the clean-up operation which then took four years to complete. I'm pleased to report that since 2007 there hasn't been a single case of Anthrax among the test flock of sheep they left on the island.'

'That's really interesting, thank you David,' Nick said. 'I think I'd like to do a bit more research into The Dark Harvest. They sound a very interesting group of people.'

'Not a bad idea. It won't be too long before we get there. In fact, you'll start to see the island as soon as we get round the headland, so I'll leave you in peace for a few minutes. Forgive me while I sort out some paperwork that I've been putting to one side for a couple of days.'

'Of course,' Nick said. 'We'll leave you to it.'

CHRISTOPHER'S FORECAST had been right. It was now eleven o'clock and the hot sun was high above them. All three kayakers were now wearing protective hats and sunglasses to reflect the dazzling light being reflected off the water.

They'd pulled up on the beach on Horse Island for brief rest and, to Emma's delight, to polish off the biscuits and rehydrate.

Half an hour later, Christopher suggested they should start to head back. Studying his map, he pointed to a small island towards the southwest. 'I think we'll go via that lovely little island you can see over there. We should get back to Ardmair Beach around mid-afternoon. How does that sound?'

'Fine by me,' Ben said. 'One thing is for sure - I'm going to feel knackered tonight.'

'Wimp,' Emma said and smiled as she headed off towards the boats.

They had been paddling for about half an hour when Ben pointed out a large fin cutting through the surface of the otherwise millpond calm water, about 200 metres away to their right.

'What do you think that is Dad?' Ben asked. 'A basking shark? They must be quite common around here and it's certainly big enough.'

Christopher wasn't so sure. Over the years he'd experienced several interactions with basking sharks while kayaking, mainly off the Cornish coast, but this looked different. He seemed to remember that the triangular dorsal fin on the basking sharks he had seen were more rounded on the apex, whereas this one was more pointed. He also remembered that basking sharks' tails often protruded above the water as they fed. This one didn't.

'Have you got your GoPro turned on, Dad?' Ben asked.

'Not yet but it's a good idea,' replied Christopher and leaned forward to adjust the static camera attached to the top of his kayak.

'What about the one with a head strap?' Emma asked.

'It's too hot to be wearing that.' Christopher said, still attending to the fixed camera.

'Daddy, what's the point of having it if you're not going to use it to record moments like these?' Emma complained.

Christopher could never let his daughter down and, a couple of minutes later, had both cameras up and running.

'God look,' Emma said pointing at the fin. 'It's moved much closer.'

'Okay, let's just keep paddling,' Christopher said, trying hard to maintain a calm appearance but secretly worried that the tremor in his voice might reveal his true concern.

The fin was now only forty metres away. They could clearly see its true size and the jagged, trailing edge on the dorsal fin which had a large part missing.

'Jesus, it's massive,' Emma said. 'Looks like it might have had a collision with a boat prop or something.'

'Ben, let's both move in towards Emma.' Christopher said growing anxious about the danger that was unfolding.

As they did so, the fin turned and started to move towards them. When it was just twenty metres away, it slipped under the surface of the water without causing a ripple.

'Watch out, Ben. It's coming straight at you,' Christopher shouted.

'No kidding, Dad,' Ben said, his faltering voice betraying his fear.

Through the crystal clear water, they watched as this magnificent creature's enormous, sleek, dark grey, body slid silently first under Ben's kayak and then Emma's before surfacing about ten metres to Christopher's left.

'Wow,' Emma shouted, letting out some of her nervous energy. 'That was incredible. It's huge.'

'Yep, must be at least six metres' Christopher said, 'and I'm pretty sure that's a great white shark.'

'That's just what I was thinking,' Emma said.

'What, here in UK waters?' Ben said. 'Well, whatever it is, it's impressive but bloody scary.'

They watched the shark continue to move away to the left of the kayaks and then disappear beneath the surface once again.

'Where the hell is it?' Ben asked.

'I don't know,' said Christopher, 'but I think we should keep moving and look to see where it surfaces once more. I don't think it's being aggressive - it just seems to be very curious.'

They continued paddling and after five minutes or so they'd had no further sightings.

'Well, it looks like it's lost interest…'

At that very moment the shark broke surface directly under Emma's kayak. The dorsal fin appeared next to Emma's face and she let out an involuntary scream. As the shark's massive body moved forward it lifted her kayak clear out of the water, tipping it over to the left, throwing Emma into the water. As she slipped momentarily beneath the surface, she managed to turn to her right in time to see the shark's massive tail slam against the boat only a metre away from her head but then keep moving slowly away.

As her head reappeared above the surface, she heard both her father and Ben desperately shouting, 'Emma!'

'I'm fine,' she shouted. 'Can you just hold my boat for me? Dad grab my paddle.'

The men manoeuvred their kayaks tightly alongside hers and held it steady as Emma climbed up awkwardly from the back. She slowly moved forward until she could get her legs back into the cockpit and then slid onto her seat.

'Are you alright?' Christopher asked, clearly shaken.

But Emma just had a huge smile on her face. 'Wasn't that just bloody amazing? Thank God it didn't come back to see what had fallen in the water.'

'Look, it's just come back up again to the surface,' Ben said pointing at the fin which had reappeared no more than forty metres in front of them. Then suddenly, from behind them, they heard a loud voice.

'Are you all OK?'

The three of them turned round and were shocked to see a large, blue and white painted fishing boat just a few metres away.

CHAPTER FOUR

TUESDAY, 26TH JUNE
Gruinard Island, Scottish Highlands

Nick watched as Pete reached under the bench and pulled out his camera case and backpack. Pete lifted the Canon FX Pro camcorder from its case and started to set it up in preparation for recording footage of the approach to the island. He didn't have long to wait. As they turned south round the headland, the outline of the treeless Gruinard came into view. Twenty minutes later, the rib came to a halt on a long, stone covered beach with the grass covered island stretching into the distance beyond.

'Welcome to Anthrax Island,' David said. Nick and Pete looked at him with concerned faces.

'Don't worry,' he said. 'It's safe and we don't need hazmat suits anymore. Let's get ashore and I can show you around, not that there's a huge amount to see.'

Half an hour later, David's prediction proved to be true. Apart from a crumbling stone bothy, all they could see in the distance were acres of lush grass and thick bracken.

They struggled through an area of spongy sphagnum moss on their way to the 'summit' of the island, *An Eilid*, The Hind. Here they had a stunning, uninterrupted 360° view of the mountains to the east on the mainland, the Hebrides to the west and the Summer Isles to the north, all set against a perfect clear blue sky.

They made their way back down a different way via the northern slope. As they reached the stone covered beach, Nick caught a familiar smell on the wind. He looked at Pete who nodded in acknowledgement and they followed the scent to what Nick had expected to find – the body of a dead grey seal lying on the water's edge. As they got closer, a cloud of flies took to the air from the rotting corpse revealing a huge bite mark where the flesh had been ripped from the body. Nothing remained of the seal's guts, just an empty void.

'Bloody hell,' Pete said. 'Have you ever seen a bite mark that big on a seal in British waters? What the hell could have done that?'

'Just what I was thinking,' Nick agreed. 'It's far too big for any British shark and the bite mark just doesn't look right for orca. Can you take some film of me lying alongside so we can get an idea of scale?'

David Scott stood to one side with an astonished look on his face as Nick lay down next to the rotting corpse.

'So, if it wasn't a shark found in our waters that did that, then what the hell was it?' David asked.

'That, my friend, is the million-dollar question,' Nick replied.

CHAPTER FIVE

TUESDAY, 26TH JUNE
Carn nan Sgeir, Summer Isles,
Ross & Cromarty, Scottish Highlands

Calum McLeod was returning home after an early start to visit the numerous lobster pots he had placed in the waters surrounding the isles. Lobster numbers were declining every year and the meagre return from today's catch would barely help to cover the running costs of his boat, the *Sorcha*. This was powered by a very quiet hydrogen engine that all small, inshore fishermen were now obliged to run.

As he passed by the rocky outcrop of Carn nan Sgeir, he spotted three kayaks in the distance. As he got closer, he also noticed a large triangular fin moving slowly through the water not far from the paddlers. Taking out his binoculars, he examined the fin and could see both its pointed apex and the damaged trailing edge. It resembled nothing he'd come across in his twenty-five years working on the sea. It certainly looked like a shark but was so much larger than any he had seen before.

He nervously watched as it disappeared under the boats only to reappear on their far side and then saw it slip below the surface not far away. He waited to see where it might breach again and decided to approach the kayaks to offer help. As he turned the *Sorcha* towards them, he saw the shark suddenly surface directly under the middle boat, tipping the kayaker into the water. He was relieved to see that they had managed to climb back on safely, but he was concerned that the shark continued to circle them at a distance. He called out as he approached them. Their shocked reactions showed that they clearly hadn't heard the quiet boat come up behind them.

'Bloody hell,' a very wet Emma screamed. 'That's enough shocks for one day.'

'Sorry. I forget how quiet this engine can be,' Calum said. 'Look, I've been watching you for the last ten minutes and saw what that big fish did to you. Can I suggest that we get you out of the water for the time being? I've got a feeling you might not be so lucky next time.'

'That'd be great, thank you,' Christopher said, very relieved.

'Okay, I'm Calum.' He looked at Ben. 'Let's get you out of the water first and you can then help me pull the other boats on board?'

'Sure,' replied Ben. 'I'm Ben, this is my Dad, Christopher, and this very wet person is my sister Emma.'

Emma shot Ben a filthy look and said to Calum, 'Sorry, I never look my best after I've just been tossed into the sea by a great white shark.'

'A great white? You might be right but what the hell it's doing in these waters? Anyway, hello to you all. Ben, let's get going before our friend out there decides to take a closer look at you.'

Ben manoeuvred his kayak against the side of *Sorcha*, handed his paddle to Calum and lifted himself over the side. With Calum's help they lifted his kayak out the water and stored it safely on the far side of the deck. They repeated this with Emma and her boat.

Meanwhile, Christopher kept a watchful eye on the shark's movements. It had swum closer and, when only thirty metres from them, slipped below the surface once more.

'Hurry up Dad,' Ben said. 'I can't see the shark anymore.'

Christopher moved his boat into position and handed his paddle to Calum. As he started to stand, Emma screamed. 'Daddy look out!'

The shark burst from the water, wrapping its massive jaws around the front of Christopher's kayak and slamming it against the side of the *Sorcha*. Christopher was thrown off balance. He desperately reached for something to grab onto but couldn't avoid falling into the water in the narrow gap between the kayak and the fishing boat. As he went under, the noise as the shark shook and tossed the kayak around as it were a child's toy was deafening.

Christopher froze, mesmerised by the raw power of this magnificent creature. For a split second, he felt an irrational urge to reach out and touch it. His reverie was broken by two strong arms reaching down and pulling him clear of the water and onto the deck. As he got up, Emma threw her arms around him.

'Daddy, Daddy, are you alright?'

'I will be when you stop squeezing the life out of me and let me breathe,' Christopher said, secretly enjoying his daughter's concern.

They all looked stared in awe as the shark continued to test out the existence of any edible qualities in the kayak's composite shell, shaking it from side to side and causing the sea to explode with foam. It finally lost interest and rolled over briefly onto its back as it turned away, showing the full length of its white under belly, before heading off south.

'Well, one thing is for certain,' said Emma, '*that* is a female.'

'How on Earth can you tell that?' Ben asked.

'A marine biology degree helps,' Emma replied.

'Very impressive,' said Calum. 'Shall we get what's left of that shark's toy back on board and see what damage that wee girl has done?'

As they lifted the mangled boat on board, the damage was easy to see. The first three feet of the kayak was just a crumpled mess of acrylic and fibreglass, unrecognisable from its original form.

'One thing's for sure,' Christopher joked, 'I won't be using that again this holiday. Good job we brought Mum's old kayak with us, just in case of an eventuality like this.'

'What do you mean *like this*?' Emma mocked. 'As if you had planned on the possibility of having your kayak wrecked by an inquisitive great white shark!'

Calum was looking at the wreckage of the kayak. He turned, disappeared into the wheelhouse and emerged brandishing a pair of pliers.

'Fancy a memento?' he asked. He pushed the pliers down into the damaged area, tugged and held up the pliers revealing a large shark's tooth.

'Wow.' Emma shouted. 'That tooth will definitely prove, once and for all, that it was a great white. Simply, bloody amazing.'

Calum passed the tooth to Christopher for safekeeping and turned back to the wheelhouse once more. 'I need to get this boat and my meagre catch back to port. Where are you staying?'

'At Ardmoir Beach,' Christopher replied.

'Nice place. Can I suggest we go back to Ullapool first and I'll organise someone to give you a lift to pick up your car and, presumably, trailer?'

'That would be great Calum,' Christopher said. 'I really don't know what we would have done if you hadn't come along.' The others nodded and muttered their agreement.

'Och, it was nothing. Perhaps you should take off your wet garments and hang them over the kayaks to dry a bit in the sun? I'm just going to call ahead on the radio and let them know what happened. You never know, there may be someone who wants to speak to you about it.'

CHAPTER SIX

TUESDAY, 26TH JUNE
Approaching Ullapool, Ross & Cromarty,
Scottish Highlands

On their rib, David and his guests could see in the distance the distinctive pattern of platforms and floats that supported the nets below which kept hundreds of thousands of young salmon in place. David explained that salmon farming was still proving to be a contentious subject locally.

At the wheel, Angus finished the conversation he'd been having on his radio for the last couple of minutes.

'Right, gentlemen, I've got some news I think might interest you.' Angus smiled as he continued. 'I've just been talking to the harbour master. It appears a group of kayakers had a rather intense meeting with what they claim was a great white shark. It happened about an hour or so ago not far from here. They were picked up by a local lobster fisherman, and are heading back to port as we speak.'

'That's incredible,' Nick said. 'I'd like to know why they thought it was a great white - there's never been a proven sighting before in UK waters. If they're right, it would certainly explain the size of the wound on the seal we found back on Gruinard. Were there any more details?'

'He couldn't tell me much but he did reckon that it had made a real mess of one of the kayaks. At the speed we're going, we'll be arriving shortly after them.'

Angus' calculation was right. They pulled up alongside the harbour wall just as the kayaks were being unloaded from the fishing boat docked thirty metres further along.

'Angus, David, thank you both very much for your time and your company. It's much appreciated,' Nick said and Pete nodded in agreement. 'We've got plenty of material to work on and I hope to see you again later in the year, when we come back with a full production crew. If you're free, that is.'

Angus smiled. 'I'll make sure I am. Just give me a bit of notice.'

'Same for me,' David added. 'I'd be delighted to help in any way I can.'

'That's great, thanks again. Hope to see you soon,' Nick replied. 'Pete, got everything together?' Pete nodded. 'Okay, let's go and find out what those lucky people can tell us about their great white encounter.'

They approached the fishing boat as two men were lifting the last of the kayaks onto the harbour wall.

'Excuse me,' Nick said. 'Sorry to trouble you but am I right in thinking you had a rather interesting encounter with a shark earlier this morning? I would love to hear about it. Let me introduce myself. I'm Nick Martin and this is my colleague, Peter Higham.'

'I think we all know who you are,' Emma said. 'I'm Emma Warren, this is my dad Christopher and my brother

Ben, and that lovely man in the boat is Calum who came to our rescue.' They all shook hands. 'I apologise for looking like a bedraggled scarecrow but I wasn't planning to be tossed into the sea by a great white.'

'That's exactly why I'd love to hear what happened out there,' Nick said, glancing down at the damaged kayak. 'Wow! Now that was definitely done by a seriously big fish. It would be great to have a chat with you. It looks like you all could do with a drink. How about going for a quick coffee or something? How does that sound?'

'Thanks Nick, that's very kind of you. I think we're all ready for coffee,' Christopher replied.

'I'm sorry,' Calum said, 'but I'm afraid I can't join you. I've got to get these lobsters packed in ice as soon as possible and sent off to the market. I'll be around later or tomorrow if there's anything else I can help with. You're going to hear a remarkable story. And it's all true.'

'Thanks,' Nick said. 'Perhaps we'll see you tomorrow. Can you recommend somewhere where we can grab a coffee please?'

'Yes, there's a decent place a couple of hundred metres down there,' Calum said pointing to the buildings over to their left. 'You can leave your kayaks here. I'll make sure they're looked after for you. If you give me an hour or so, I'll be able to give you a lift back to Ardmoir to collect your trailer.'

'Don't worry about that,' Pete said. 'I'm sure we can help out when we're finished.'

'In that case, nice to meet you all and I hope that the coffee's up to your expectations.'

The three kayakers thanked Calum again and headed off with Nick and Peter.

. . .

The cafe was in a white painted building which had been recently converted from a shop. The staff were surprised when Nick walked in, immediately recognising a face they had seen many times on television. They quickly pushed a couple of tables together to accommodate the large group.

After ordering the drinks, Nick spotted a delicious range of homemade cakes in a chilled counter display and ordered a selection for the group.

As they waited for their orders to arrive, Nick turned to the three kayakers.

'Can you tell me why you chose this location for your trip and just what happened to you out there this morning?'

Emma could see that her father hesitated to reply, so took up the story with Ben helping out.

Although desperate to ask questions, Nick managed to hold back. But when the drinks and cakes arrived and everyone got stuck in, he thought the time was right.

'Thanks all three of you. That was quite an experience. Is it okay if I ask a few questions? The obvious one is what made you think it was a great white? Porbeagles look very similar to great whites and are commonly found in British waters.'

'Well, I think I can give you three reasons why we feel sure it was a great white,' Emma replied. 'Firstly, porbeagles grow up to a maximum size of about twelve feet. The shark we met was at least seventeen feet long. Secondly, we've got film from two Go Pros that will provide you with the visual proof you need and finally, we have also got this. Daddy?'

Christopher reached into his pocket and pulled out a still wet handkerchief. He opened it on the table to reveal the shark's tooth.

'Calum pulled this out of the front of my kayak where the shark had its bit of fun,' explained Christopher.

Nick let out an unconscious whistle of excitement as he

picked the tooth up and examined it closely. The triangular shape and serrated edges were very familiar to him.

'I have seen many great white shark's teeth over the years, and I'm 99.9% sure that this is one. It's also probably the biggest I've ever seen. This is a stunning find and I hope it will provide the proof that these remarkable creatures do swim in our seas. But to be certain, we'd need to have a DNA test carried out. Can I ask a big favour? Would you allow me to send this off analysis? I can promise it'll be returned safely to you.'

'Of course,' Emma said. 'We'll help in whatever way we can. One further thing, it's a female.'

'Can I ask how you're so sure about that?'

'Well I've just finished a Marine Biology degree at Southampton. Part of the course centred on the role of larger pelagic fish in the ocean's ecosystem. Sharks were a major topic.'

Nick's eyes lit up and he gave a small nod of appreciation. 'Emma, that's really helpful and I'd love to talk to you about it because, as you may know, sharks are my particular interest. But you also mentioned Go Pro cameras. I don't suppose you have them with you by any chance?'

'Yes, they're in my backpack,' Christopher replied and delved down into the bag at his feet. 'Here you are.'

He placed the two units on the table and Pete selected one.

'I'm sure I've got a cable in my bag that will fit these,' Pete said with a smile. 'If it's alright with you, I can download them onto my laptop and see what you filmed.'

'Yes, of course,' Christopher replied. 'We'd love to see what's on them.'

'Brilliant. While Pete's doing his stuff, would anyone like another drink or anything else?' Nick asked.

'Another cake for me please,' Pete said without looking up from the screen in front of him.

'Ooh, me too please,' Emma added with a guilty grin.

A full round of drinks and cakes arrived just as Pete finished downloading the files from the second camera.

'Right,' Pete said. 'Let's see what we have on this one.'

The first film was from the camera Christopher had worn on a head band. It clearly showed the shark's fin in the distance and followed it as it dived under first Ben's kayak, then Emma's and Christopher's, before returning to the surface some distance to the left. Nick was amazed at the quality of the pictures and the clarity. The sound track revealed the family's conversations and added to the dramatic impact when the shark unexpectedly surfaced under Emma's kayak. Even though she knew what was going to happen, Emma still jumped in her seat.

'Jeez,' Nick exclaimed. 'I wasn't expecting that.'

'Nor was I,' Emma added. 'Can't say I look very elegant climbing back onto my boat, though.'

'Who would in those circumstances?' Nick smiled at Emma. 'I'd just want my legs out of the water as fast as I could.'

The film showed Calum's arrival and the transfer of Ben and Emma's kayaks onto the fishing boat. Just as Christopher stood up in his boat, his head was thrown to the side as the shark crashed into his boat. The camera caught the shark as it tossed the kayak around in its massive jaws. Then, suddenly, Christopher was above water being hauled into the boat by Calum and Ben. He managed to get back to his feet in time to record the moment the shark stopped its frenzied thrashing and moved slowly away, turning over onto its back to reveal its white underside.

'Emma, you were absolutely right,' Nick agreed. 'That is

definitely a female - one of the biggest great whites I've ever seen. Christopher, your kayak is about fourteen feet long?'

Christopher nodded.

'In that case I would say that she is at least eighteen feet long, possibly nineteen feet.'

'That's huge,' Pete commented. 'Almost the size of Deep Blue which is probably the largest shark ever filmed in the wild. Shall we have a look at what the second camera shows us?'

Pete clicked on the file icon and showed the picture from the forward-facing camera that was fixed to Christopher's kayak just in front of the cockpit.

'I think it's going to start with some pretty dull sea views,' Christopher said. 'Can I suggest that you scroll through to where the shark decides to have a nibble of my kayak.'

Pete did as he suggested. The screen was suddenly filled with the shark's huge head and jaws and the foaming sea as it threw the kayak around like a toy.

Nick let out the breath he'd been holding. 'You just can't appreciate how powerful they are until you see something like that close up. You've got some amazing footage and I'm sure Pete would love to edit that together for you.'

'It would be my pleasure,' said Pete, looking at his phone. 'I don't want to alarm you, but your encounter's already trending on the internet.'

They all checked their phones. Sure enough, the simplest search found headlines like *Great White shark attack off Scottish coast* and various others referring to *Jaws*.

'How the hell did they get to hear that so soon?' asked Ben.

'I would suspect that the Coast Guard and other government agencies will have been informed and no doubt someone leaked the story from there,' Nick suggested. 'This is a huge story and every newspaper, TV and radio station will be sending reporters and film crews to do some location reports. That means that they'll be looking for you.'

'But we just came here for a quiet holiday, not to be the centre of some media scrum,' Christopher said, anxious that their holiday could be ruined.

Nick sympathised. 'Look, can I make a suggestion that might get you out of all this with just an hour or so of your time? I know what the media want. Let's face it, I'm one of them. They're definitely going to be here tomorrow in their droves. We can't stop that. I think we should arrange a press conference here tomorrow and get your input out of the way as soon as possible, with the least interference for you. Once they've seen you, heard your story and seen the film – sorry Pete a lot for you to do – they'll have what they want and you can get back to enjoying your holiday. I know it's not perfect, but I honestly think it's the best option. You don't have to worry, we'll do all the organisation. How does that sound?'

Christopher turned to his children. 'What do you two think?'

Emma and Ben nodded to each other.

'Yes, let's go for it,' Emma said. 'Though I'm not sure what I'll feel like in front of the cameras.'

'Okay, we'll be guided by you,' Christopher said, if a little hesitantly.

'Don't worry, you'll be great. Let's plan for a two p.m. kick off. I've just got to call my office and start making the arrangements. Then I'll drive you back to your holiday cottage or wherever it is you're staying in.'

'That would be great, thanks,' said Ben. 'I can come back with the trailer and pick up the kayaks.'

Pete looked up from his phone. 'I think I've found the perfect place for tomorrow's press conference. It's a hotel just a few hundred metres along the sea front and it has a conference facility for a hundred people. So while you're taking these lovely people back, I'll go and see if they can fit us in. I may be able to negotiate a special deal because they'll have the amazing Mr Nick Martin in the house.'

Nick was the only one not to laugh. 'Enough of that, thank you Pete,' he said, a smile breaking out on his face. 'Of course, if *you* can't get a good deal then you could ask your wife to give them a call. She can always talk someone into giving her a discount. Right, five minutes and we'll be on our way.'

CHAPTER SEVEN

WEDNESDAY, 27TH JUNE
The Regent Hotel, Ullapool

Ullapool had never seen anything like it. The streets were packed like a bank holiday weekend, not with normal tourists' cars but with large vans and trucks carrying enormous satellite dishes on their roofs. Every hotel room was booked and every boat in the harbour commandeered by camera crews and photographers desperately hoping to get a glimpse of *the* shark. All eager to be able share the experience that was the main topic of every news headline, not just in the UK. The story of a great white shark attack on a group of kayakers had caught the attention of the world's media.

Nick was in an unused catering room with a shuttered bar, separated from the conference room by a fire-proof door. Opening the door cautiously, he peered into the conference room where the press were gathered. Having Nick's name linked to the event meant even more media outlets had sent reporters than normal and he guessed that the number of people in the room exceeded the nominal one hundred limit.

The door behind him opened and the Warren family walked in, almost unrecognisable in smarter clothes. It was Emma who was going to catch everyone's eye. No longer the self-acclaimed *'scarecrow'*, she looked stunning as her long blonde hair fell over her shoulders and her white blouse helped to emphasise her deep tan.

Nick greeted them all, complimenting them on 'scrubbing up so well' and then made a point of telling Emma how different her 'scarecrow look' was today.

'I'll take that as a compliment then,' she said.

'Please do.' Nick said. 'Look, before we go in, let me run you through it. I'll do a brief introduction and explain why I'm here and then I'll leave it to you to tell your story along with the film. Pete has done an amazing editing job on it overnight. We'll ask for any questions to be held back until they've seen the film. How does that sound?'

'Yes, fine, but I think I'll leave it to Ben and Emma, if that's alright with you?' Christopher said, a slight tremor in his voice betraying his nerves.

'Of course. Whatever feels right for you. Okay, if you're ready, let's go and do this,' Nick said and then turned to Ben and Emma. 'Remember to speak up and enjoy yourselves. *You* are the stars of the show.'

As they entered the conference room all the cameras were on Nick; however, as soon as the family took their places behind the white covered linen table on the raised platform, the cameras picked up on Emma and moved their focus to her.

Nick stood up and addressed the assembled media. 'I'm delighted to welcome you all here today to mark this very important event in the history of British marine life. For many years there has been a widely held belief that great white sharks have been frequent visitors to our shores, with numerous sightings but no definitive physical or photographic proof to back up those beliefs. Well, today I can confirm that, at last, we have both and, for that, we must be grateful to the Warren family, Christopher, Nick and Emma, who will tell you their own story in a minute.'

'In case you're wondering, I'm only here due to a very fortuitous bit of planning, doing research for a new series. It was purely by chance that I was introduced to these three wonderful people, shortly after their "*meeting*" with the great white.' Muffled laughter filled the room. 'So today is totally about them and I'm only here to chair this press conference. The family will tell their story first and then we have some actual film of what took place. Can I ask, therefore, that you keep your questions until after the film has run? By the way, we'll be giving you an access code so you will be able to download the film before it's released on the internet. Right, I'll hand over to Ben and Emma to tell you how they came to be here, and to describe their amazing experience.'

Despite their nerves, both proved to be naturals and Nick could see that the audience were truly engaged by what they were hearing; however, it was when the film appeared on the giant television screen that they really started to take interest. Nick watched with amusement as almost everyone in the room jumped when the shark suddenly surfaced under Emma's kayak and even the hardened journo's laughed with slight embarrassment at their own reaction.

As soon as the film ended, Nick stood up again. 'Okay, you've now seen this beautiful shark for yourselves. It's a female, between eighteen and nineteen feet in length and weighing about two tons, which makes it one of the largest ever recorded on film. But we still have one more piece of evidence to show you. Christopher please can you let everyone see what's on the table in front of you?'

As Christopher held up the shark's tooth, a hundred cameras zoomed in and flashes filled the room.

'This tooth was retrieved from Christopher's kayak after the shark had finished playing with it. It's a perfect example of a great white tooth and provides the final physical proof that we needed. I can tell you that, immediately after this conference, the tooth will be sent for DNA analysis and independent examination by leading specialists. Now, has anyone got a question for the family please? Can I ask you to wait until you've been nominated and then state your name and who you represent? Right, first question – yes the lady in red at the front.'

'Thank you Nick. Good afternoon everyone. My name is Rosie Goode and I'm from the *Daily Globe*. We've all been enthralled by your story and the film of your amazing experience. Can I ask Emma first, what would your mother have made of it all, and also what went through your mind when the shark attacked your kayak?'

'Well Mummy would have bloody loved it,' Emma answered confidently. The entire room burst into laughter, relieving the slight tension in the air. 'She had a real interest in whale and shark conservation and, to be honest, if she'd been there, she would probably have leapt into the water to give the shark a big hug.'

More ripples of laughter passed round the room.

'As to what went through my mind - I would imagine just the same as anyone whose kayak had just been used as a scratching post by a huge shark and then been tipped into the water … bloody shocked! Having said that, as soon as I hit the water, the reality of the situation caught up with me and I was *rather* relieved to see the shark's tail moving away from the boat. Once I'd climbed back onto my kayak, I remember a feeling of euphoria taking over.'

Before Nick could ask for further questions, Emma continued.

'Before I finish, please can I just ask you all to avoid describing what happened to us yesterday as an *attack*. To me, the word *attack* suggests a deliberate action intended to cause harm. This shark was just being inquisitive, and I think she was probably also having a bit of fun. One thing's for sure, if that two-ton, eighteen foot shark had intended to *attack* me, then I sincerely doubt I would be here to discuss it with you today! Oh, and if you need a headline that doesn't refer to *that* 1970's film, then how about *Shark Dumps Blonde*?'

Nick joined in the laughter and, having selected the next questioner, looked over at Pete who gave a surreptitious thumbs up. Nick knew exactly Pete meant. Emma was proving to be a natural in front of both the camera and the audience - amusing yet confident enough to make a well-judged serious point. Perhaps she could be a useful addition to the team at Live World?

After nearly an hour of questions, Nick asked for a final contribution. A hand went up.

'Yes, the gentleman at the back.'

'Simon Jones, *Capital Tribune*. Thank you Nick and my question is actually for you. Am I right in thinking you're an advisor to the government on maritime and coastal safety?'

'Yes, that's correct, but only on an informal, ad hoc basis. I'm afraid to say that the biggest problem so far has been a swarm of jelly fish off Skegness.'

'Not exactly life threatening!' Simon said. 'So let me put to you the possible future scenario of this enormous shark prowling off a crowded beach in the UK and the danger this would represent to thousands of holidaymakers. What would you do? ' He paused and smiled. 'And let's face it, we've all seen what can happen in *Jaws*.'

The audience laughed and Nick couldn't help but smile too.

'Can I remind you that, despite how exciting the film was, the *Jaws'* depiction of the great white was purely fictional and doesn't apply in any way to this latest visitor to our shores. This shark doesn't seek out humans - the Warrens just happened to be in the same area of water where it was swimming. And remember what Emma said about the shark appearing to be playful and not showing any intention to attack her. That is the reality of the great white.'

'In that case, how do you explain the mess it made of the kayak?'

'Well even sharks are allowed to have a bit of fun. Look, I'm not downplaying any potential threat. I can assure you that I will do my best to ensure that the government looks at every development and encourage them to act accordingly. Anyway, it's quite possible this old girl will just disappear from our shores as quickly as she appeared.'

Nick looked at his watch.

'I'm aware many of you have copy to submit and reports to prepare for this evening's news programmes, so we'll let you get on with your serious work after having enjoyed the presentation here this afternoon.'

'Thank you all for coming but most importantly our thanks must go to the Warren family, without whom none of this would have been possible. They've given up their holiday time to be with you today, so can I please ask you to respect their privacy and allow them the opportunity to enjoy the rest of their stay uninterrupted? To all of you who have had to make the long trek here today, have a safe journey home. Thank you.'

The Warrens got up and accompanied Nick back into the adjoining closed bar room.

'Well that seemed to go well,' Ben said.

'I have got to say you were all absolutely brilliant and I don't think it could have gone better,' Nick assured them. 'They all loved your story and the film was the clincher. Did you see the way they all jumped when the shark surfaced under your kayak, Emma? It's always enjoyable to watch thick skinned hacks giggling with embarrassment.'

'I think that my sis went down rather well with the photographers in the audience,' Ben quipped. 'We might be seeing her face plastered across the newspapers tomorrow.'

'You could be right there,' Nick agreed, smiling at Emma.

'Oh shut up you two. Talk about embarrassing,' Emma said.

'Nick, we were wondering if you and Pete would like to join us for dinner tonight at our humble lodge?' Christopher asked. 'I can't promise haute cuisine but I'm sure we can knock together something edible for you and find a drinkable bottle of wine or two.'

'That would be great,' Nick said, 'and I think there may be a few things of interest to discuss. What time would you like us there? We won't stay too late because we've decided to travel back tomorrow and that means an early start.'

'In that case, come for a drink at seven and we'll take it from there.'

'We'll look forward to it,' Nick replied. 'I'd better go back in next door and help Pete clear up our gear. See you later.'

Once they'd packed away the camera and the rest of Pete's equipment, they said their thanks to all the hotel staff who'd helped to run the event. They then went back to their

B&B for a quick rest before heading out to the Warren's for dinner.

Back in his room, Nick checked his phone. There were a couple of messages from Jill and a missed call from Sophie. He called Jill first to ask if there were any urgent business matters needing attention.

'Nothing that can't wait till you get back,' said Jill. 'We all watched the live press conference. That poor family certainly had a scary time, and the film really brought it to life. Very exciting.'

'That was all down to Pete's clever editing. You know he stayed up most of the night putting it together?'

'Indeed I do because he called me at 2 a.m. to tell me,' Jill explained. 'Anyway, what I want to say is, who was that fantastic girl? I mean she just took over the event and had everyone eating out of her hand. Beauty, brains and a total natural in front of the camera, it's just not fair.'

'Yes, I know,' Nick agreed. 'They've kindly asked us to dinner tonight and I'm going to ask about her future plans.'

'Well, if you're thinking about her joining us, then she gets a thumbs up from me. When are you thinking about coming back?'

'We've decided that we have enough background material to work with, so we're going to head off early tomorrow. Hopefully we'll get home sometime during the evening.'

'OK have a good journey. I'll give Pete a call to see how knackered he's feeling after pulling an all-nighter.'

Nick dialled Sophie and asked how things were with the children.

'Yes, all good,' she said. 'They're currently making their own pizzas with Mum next door in the kitchen. You've never heard such a racket. She's definitely a saint. How did you feel the press conference went? We all thought it was a great success. Even the twins were fascinated.'

'Miracles will never cease,' Nick said. 'It felt like it went really well. I think the family all dealt with the press brilliantly and, let's face it, journalists always love a good story backed up by an exciting bit of film.'

'Well there's been an explosion of interest on social media. I'm not sure who's been getting the most coverage though, the shark or that remarkable young woman. Emma, was it? You've been talking about finding a younger presenter for ages, and I think she would definitely be worth considering for that role.'

'Interesting you should say that. Pete and I were discussing it only a short while ago and Jill also suggested the same thing. Anyway, we're having dinner with them tonight, so I'll try and sound her out.'

'Well don't go in all guns blazing like you normally do,' Sophie warned. 'Just do it gently and give her the chance to think about it.'

IT WAS SUCH a warm evening that they ate outside. Nick and Pete had arrived with a chilled bottle of champagne they'd managed to buy from the hotel. This had slipped down very agreeably as they looked out at the setting sun across the bay and discussed the life changing events of the past two days.

Dinner was an enormous bowl of pasta with a delicious beef ragout sauce that Emma and Ben prepared, accompanied by a bottle of rich, fruity Italian Zinfandel from the Puglia region.

As they cleared away the plates after dinner, Nick asked Emma about her future plans.

'To be quite honest, I don't really have any. I've had a few goes at trying to find work with a marine conservation group but had no luck with that so far. So I'm a bit stuck.'

Nick smiled. 'Well, I have to tell you that not only were Pete and I really impressed by your performance at the press conference, but also everyone back at the Live World offices. That includes Pete's wife, Jill, who runs the business on a day to day basis and also Sophie, my wife, and they are both very hard to impress. We've had a talk amongst ourselves and wonder whether you would consider coming to join us at Live World? It would be on a trial basis initially to see how we all get on and whether you can put up with us. What do you think?'

Emma was clearly taken aback. She stared at Nick for a moment, shocked. Eventually she said; 'Bloody hell, you know how to put someone on the back foot, don't you? The answer is, of course, I'd love to have the chance to work with you. It's the offer of a lifetime. But what sort of role were you thinking about?'

'We all think that, with some training, you could do a brilliant job at presenting. Yes, you've got all the qualities needed but, equally importantly, you also have background knowledge from your degree. I've been looking for someone to help share the burden with me for some time now. I think we need a younger face to offer a fresh perspective and to appeal to a new, younger audience. How does that sound to you?'

Emma's face lit up. 'It sounds wonderful. You really think I could do it? Hold on, can I just check I haven't just entered some alternative reality and this isn't all a fantasy?'

'No, believe me, it's real and we all feel you would fit the role perfectly,' Nick said. 'So, if you're still saying yes, shall we go and join the others and you can tell them what we've just discussed?'

CHAPTER EIGHT

FRIDAY, 29TH JUNE
Bentham Hall, Shropshire

Nick had got up early and taken the ever eager Molly for a long walk across the fields to ease some of the stiffness from the previous day's long drive home. As he walked through the back door of the house, he took off his boots, and the spaniel immediately made a playful grab for one of them and disappeared with it into the kitchen.

'Come here you little bugger,' he shouted as the dog's tail disappeared through the door.

'I'd gladly come to you,' came a voice from the kitchen, 'but I'm not sure I like to be called *you little bugger*!'

Sophie's mother, Beth, smiled at Nick as he walked in the kitchen. 'I'll tell you what, come and give me a hug and I'll forget what you just said!'

Nick was happy to do what he was told. He counted himself fortunate to have such a good relationship with his mother-in-law. She had sadly lost her husband several years before and had moved to live with them in a separate 'granny' flat. She was fun to have around, was brilliant with the children, and seemed to have endless reserves of energy. But the best thing was that she adored Nick - he felt the same way about her.

He asked her how things had been over the past few days.

'Oh, the same as usual. Boys running riot, girls moody as hell, ponies refusing to come in, dog demanding attention and your wife missing you hugely. Plus ça change'

'Well at least I didn't miss anything then,' Nick replied as he bent down to retrieve the proffered boot from the dog. 'Is there enough of that lovely fresh fruit for me to grab a bowlful?'

'Of course. There's yogurt as well.' Nick picked up a spoon and helped himself. Beth added, 'I bet you had a rather more exciting trip than you'd expected. And congratulations on that press conference. It was amazing to see what that family went through with the shark. What an experience and that lovely young woman was very brave. I understand we might be seeing more of her?'

'Yes, she's coming down early next week and we'll take from there. My feeling is she'll fit in perfectly. I think you'll get on well with her, and you'll have a lot in common.'

'Of course by that you mean she shares my classic good looks? No, don't say anything, I'll take that as a yes. Were there any more sightings of the shark? From what we saw on the news, it seemed like the world and his wife were out on the water looking for it.'

'No more sightings.' Nick replied, enjoying his first spoonful of fruit. 'In fact the fisherman who rescued the Warren family sent me a message to say that a pod of orca had been seen a few miles away to the north, which would certainly discourage the shark from hanging around. I would be surprised if we do get more sightings.'

'Well don't be so sure that she hasn't just moved away from that area,' Beth said, as she turned to the sink to wash the knife she'd been using. 'I think that old girl might have a soft spot for British waters. After all, with so many seals around our coast, it must seem like a fast food counter for great whites!'

'You could well be right. We'll have to wait and see.'

They both looked up when they heard footsteps approaching in the hall and smiled as Sophie came into the kitchen.

'Hi Mum,' she said, walking up to Nick and giving him a kiss. 'You were up early. I thought you might sleep in for a bit.'

'No, too much to do, I'm afraid. In fact I'd better get over to the barn and show my face otherwise I'll have Jill calling me a part-timer!'

'Don't forget to give her the smoked salmon,' Sophie reminded him. 'Or you'll be in serious trouble!'

'Oh crikey, thanks, I'd forgotten. Is it in the fridge?' Nick said as he opened the dishwasher and stacked his bowl inside.

'Yeah. A couple of things before you go. We need to sort out what's got to be taken down to Dowrtreven, who's going to go in which car and what time you want to leave on Thursday? Also, have you spoken to your sister to find out what their plans are? In fact, we need to talk about everything really.'

Dowrtreven was the house in Cornwall on the Helford River where Nick and his twin sister, Alice, had grown up. They'd inherited the house twenty years earlier when their parents had both tragically been killed in a car crash. They set aside two weeks every year to holiday there, with their families, two weeks which the adults and children on both sides absolutely loved.

'No, sorry, I haven't called her yet but I promise I will this afternoon when I've had a moment to think,' Nick said, opening the fridge to retrieve the pack of smoked salmon. 'Let's sit down this evening and go through everything.'

'That would be good. Mum and I are taking the boys swimming later, and possibly the girls if they feel like it but, to be honest, I'm not holding out too much hope. Anyway, we'll be back by one if you fancy a bit of lunch?'

'Thanks, that sounds great. Have fun!' Nick said and as he headed out of the door, his mobile rang. He quickly looked at the caller display and accepted the call.

'Minister, how lovely to hear from you.' The 'Minister' was the Rt. Hon Jamie Stoddard, Secretary of State for Transport and a childhood friend of Nick's. Jamie's parents had lived a couple of miles away along the Helford River and he and Nick had gone to school together. Jamie was now often talked about as a future Prime Minister.

'Good morning Nick and less of the Minister bollocks please!' Jamie replied. 'Are you still in Scotland?'

'No, got back late last night.'

'Hope you're not too knackered. I have to say, like everyone else, I was amazed by the kayakers' film, not to mention the press conference. That young woman has certainly made an impression.'

'That *young woman* is called Emma, and I'm delighted to say she'll be joining us at LiveWorld. She's due to arrive here tomorrow. By the way, we're off down to Dowrtreven later in the week. Are you around?'

'Excellent. I'm hoping to get down for a few days next week to the constituency office. Bella and the children are down there already, so we must get together.'

'That would be great,' Nick said walking over to the stable and gave the pony a rub on the nose. 'Give us a call once you know what you're doing and come over for lunch'.

'Excellent, thank you. Now the reason for calling is actually official business. Don't worry, nothing to be concerned about,' Jamie assured him. 'As you may know, my responsibilities as Secretary of State for Transport include the Coastguard and Maritime Agencies. The appearance of this shark is causing a ripple in No.10 and I want to make sure that I'm ahead of the game, just in case. What are your thoughts?'

Nick's thoughts were interrupted by the pony rubbing up against his shoulder. He almost lost his balance.

'Bloody hell. Sorry, nearly got knocked over by the girls' pony. I fully understand your concern. At present there's no reason to be overly concerned. But you're right, we need to be prepared. The shark might just disappear, but if she doesn't, we'd need to look carefully at her movements, track them and try to predict where she might turn up.'

'Well there's not a great deal we can do until then,' Jamie said. 'In the meantime, I'll look at what we need to put in place and get back to you in a few days. Is that OK?

'Of course. Speak then. Bye.'

Nick gave the pony a final pat and walked across the yard to the barn.

IN THE OFFICE, Jill was busily typing at her keyboard and studying the screen in front of her. She looked up as she heard him enter.

'Ah, the Wanderer returns,' she said.

'And, even better, he comes bearing gifts!' Nick said as he handed the side of smoked salmon to Jill. 'It comes from a small family smokery near Ullapool. Pete and I tried some in the shop - it's a really strong smoke, just as you like it.'

'That's very kind. I can't wait to have some with the

bread I baked last night. Before I forget,' Jill said, searching her desk for a piece of paper. She handed an A4 sheet to him. 'We had an email overnight from a shark conservation group, who work mainly off the east coast of the States around New Jersey. They saw the film from Scotland and are pretty sure that the damage to the shark's dorsal fin is a match for a female great white they've had on their records for over 20 years.'

'God, she's a long way from home,' he said, letting out a small whistle of surprise while looking at the email. 'There again, great whites have been known to make enormous journeys. Years ago, a tagged South African shark was tracked all the way to New Zealand, a journey of over 11,000 miles.'

'That's amazing.' .

'What's more amazing is that it didn't hang around long, turned around and swam back again.'

'So, a short 3,000 mile swim across the Atlantic is nothing.' Jill said as Nick walked across to his desk and added the email to the pile of papers already awaiting his attention.

'Now, what have you got lined up for me?' Nick asked.

'Right, here's a list of things you've got to go through as soon as possible.' Jill walked over and handed a clear plastic folder to him. 'Key things are, firstly, to review the latest edit that Si and Lins finished on the Kenyan lions' film yesterday. We need to get that over to BBC Bristol asap. Next, and probably most importantly in terms of time, is for us to sit down and discuss a progressive training plan for Emma. I've put a few ideas together and a provisional calendar, but it needs your input. We could also do with Sophie working on this.'

Nick quickly looked through the file. 'This looks like a really comprehensive plan, thank you. As soon as I've reviewed the edit, let's go through the plan in detail. I'm going to have lunch with the family, so I'll get Sophie to have a look at it afterwards and get her thoughts.'

'Okay, that would be good.'

They both turned as the office door opened. Mima and Beck walked in and greeted them both with a cheery 'Good morning' and a 'welcome home' to Nick.

'There's a large bar of chocolate on your desk,' he said, pointing across to their workstation.

'Oh perfect, thank you,' Becky said, racing over to the desks and making a grab for the chocolate.

'Hey greedy, that's for both of us,' Mima said. 'Thank you Nick, we'll *both* enjoy that with our coffee later. And Jill, of course.'

'That's what I like to hear,' Jill said and turning back to Nick. 'Now, you'd better get into the edit suite and review the film. Then we can also quickly go through the various emails that need your attention.'

'Will do,' he said walking towards the edit suite. 'I'll see you all soon,' and disappeared inside.

FOUR HOURS LATER, Nick walked across to the house to join the family for lunch. Nick could hear the sound of children laughing and shouting in the kitchen and was greeted with a loud, 'Daddy,' from them all as he appeared through the door.

'Well that was a lovely welcome, thank you everyone,' Nick said, struggling to move as the twins wrapped themselves around his legs. He gently peeled them off, ruffled their hair affectionately, whilst acknowledging Beth and Sophie across the kitchen. He gave both his daughters a big hug and kiss. At fifteen and fourteen respectively, Milla and Heli were both tall for their age and growing up fast - a fact that Nick was still finding a little hard to come to terms with.

'I don't suppose anyone missed me then?' Nick asked, hopefully.

'Nope, been far too busy,' Milla said, hugging her father tightly. 'But we did watch your press conference and saw the shark knock that woman into the water. She was so brave about it – I would have been terrified!'

'I've got some news for you. That woman name is Emma and she's coming down here on Monday to start working for me'.

'That's great.' Heli exclaimed. 'We'll be able to ask her all about it.'

'Come on, everyone, sit down please and we can have some lunch,' Sophie said firmly. The children responded eagerly. Beth spooned large helpings of homemade macaroni cheese onto plates and Nick and Sophie passed them round. As soon as the adults had sat down, the children tucked in enthusiastically.

The noise grew as the children competed to tell Nick what they had been up to whilst he was away. They had just finished eating when Pete arrived.

'My apologies,' Pete said. 'I didn't realise you were still having lunch.'

'Hi Pete,' Nick said. 'Don't worry, we've finished. What's up?'

'Well there's something that I think you all might like to see. Can I use the internet connection on your TV?'

'Yes, of course,' Nick replied.

'Won't be long, I promise,' Pete said as he typed on the keyboard. 'Somebody found this bit of film somewhere on the web last night and it's already been watched over 20,000 times!'

On the screen a page appeared with the title '*Shark girl gets her prey*'.

'It's a clip from last year's Women's Universities' Rugby European Cup Final between France and England. Bear with me, I promise you'll want to see this, even though it's in French and the camera work isn't great. It shows the last two minutes of the game and England are leading by just two points, so basically whoever scores next will win the title. Here we go.'

The clip started. The French side are launching attack after attack around the England 22 metre line but are being repelled by the England team. But then the scrum half passes the ball to her left finding the French lock forward - by far the largest player on the pitch. With a powerful run she breaks through two flailing tackles leaving only one England player – the smaller winger - between her, the try line and victory. The French commentator is screaming by this stage, obviously convinced that victory is theirs. But instead of using space and running round the winger, the French forward chooses to power through her on her way to the line. A big mistake.

As the French player dips her shoulder to absorb the impact, the English player crouches and springs up with force so that her shoulder contacts her opponent just under the ribs. Not only does she stop the French player in her tracks but the winger uses her momentum to drive her back almost five metres. The English forwards pile in, the ball comes back on their side and, as time is up, is kicked into touch and the match won.

The film ends with the English winger being mobbed by the rest of her team and as the camera zooms in, her face can be seen clearly.

'Bloody hell,' Nick said and Sophie looked at him disapprovingly, 'That's Emma! She never mentioned she was a rugby international.'

'She's obviously far too modest to brag about it,' suggested Beth. 'Perhaps you should ask her to send over her CV in case there is anything else you should know about her before she comes down.'

'*Anyone* would be proud to have made such an amazing tackle.' Pete said. 'Anyway, sorry to have interrupted but I thought you'd all want to see what our new colleague was capable of.'

'I hope she won't need to use those skills in her new role,' said Sophie.

'And on that subject,' Nick said, looking at Sophie. 'Have you got time to go through the draft induction and training schedule that Jill's putting together for Emma. I'd really welcome your input.'

'Of course. I'll come over as soon as we've cleared up the kitchen.'

'Don't worry, I'll do that,' Beth said. 'You go and deal with that schedule. She'll be here in a couple of days and you need to have everything in place.'

'Thanks Mum,' Sophie said and turning to the children, she added, 'And you lot, give your grandma a hand please.'

A general groan from the kitchen could just be heard as Sophie accompanied Nick across the yard to the Live World office.

Nick, Sophie and Jill sat round a meeting table as they went through the training plan in depth.

'I think we need to have another look at what you've got planned for Emma when we go down to Cornwall on Thursday,' Sophie suggested. 'If she's going to be such an integral part of this company, then we all need to get to know her well, and soon. Rather than leave her here to fend for herself, I think we should ask her to join us for a few days so we get the chance to see her away from the office. What do you both think?'

Nick and Jill nodded in agreement.

'I'm afraid that our two cars are going to be jam packed,' Sophie pointed out. 'So would it be possible, Jill, for you and Pete to bring her down with you in your motorhome on Friday?'

'Of course, 'Jill said. 'We'd be delighted to have the chance to get to know her better on the journey down, though she may not agree once she sees Pete's driving!'

'Are you still planning to do some research work while you're down there, Nick?' Sophie asked

'Yes, I'd planned to and it would be useful for Emma to be involved with that,'

'So please could you give her a call after the meeting and see if she's happy with what we've discussed.' Sophie said. 'Perhaps you could also ask her to send through her CV at the same time?'

Nick smiled to himself. He knew that sometimes it was best to acknowledge that Sophie could still run this company better than him, even on a part time basis.

CHAPTER NINE

WEDNESDAY, 4TH JULY
Porthdinllaen, Morfa Nefyn,
North Wales

Gillian Roberts was a very happy woman.
Every year, at the beginning of July, her daughter brought her only grandchild, Emily, age six, to stay. Gillian was delighted to have the chance, not only to spend time with her daughter, Zoe, without her overbearing husband, but also to re-establish her close bond with her granddaughter.

Gillian's house was a white painted, former sailmaker's cottage, perfectly positioned right on the beach at Porthdinllaen. She had bought it five years earlier from a charming London couple who had found the Welsh second home tax to be unsustainable. Even though the access via the National Trust owned golf course could be a bit of a nuisance, it was worth it to be able to enjoy the cottage's wonderful position and views that it offered. The cottage was at the far end of the row of converted, former working buildings, a hundred metres along from the famous Ty Coch Inn. The cottage's small terrace directly overlooked the beach where hundreds of people were still enjoying the sun and the warm water.

Gillian, an active, 60 year old widow, walked through the sitting room and onto the terrace that abutted the beach. Zoe and Emily were sitting at the table, Emily busily drawing a picture of the bay with crayons.

'Come and look at my picture Nanna,' Emily said enthusiastically. 'Look, I've drawn lots of people. That one is the man who catches those big crabs.'

'Oh, it's beautiful, darling,' Gillian said. 'And that does look like Mr Hughes, the crab man. Now, it's almost four o'clock. Shall we have a little walk and see if the seals are waiting for us? We might even see that seal pup again.'

'Yes, yes, yes,' Emily replied loudly. 'But only if I can film them with your phone again Mummy.'

'Oh alright,' Zoe said, getting up from the table and walking into the cottage to fetch Emily's shoes.

It took another ten minutes to finally get Emily ready for the outing. They climbed the steps down from the terrace and turned left along the beach. As they walked past the Ty Coch, a few customers, who had clearly enjoyed their afternoon at the pub, shouted out a friendly greeting. Gillian smiled at them and took Emily's hand, guiding her past as they walked along the narrow path at the bottom of the cliff.

Five minutes later, they reached the Porthdinllaen Lifeboat Station and began the climb up the gentle slope to the top. On arrival, they carefully looked left before walking across the golf course, past the green with its yellow flag and down to the tip of the peninsula. As they reached it they could see four heads bobbing up and down in the water.

'Look Nanna, there are four of them and see, one of them is a baby,' Emily said.

'Oh yes,' Gillian said looking down at the water. 'Do you remember what we call a baby seal?'

'It's a pup, isn't it?' Emily replied confidently as Gillian nodded. 'Can I have your phone now Mummy so I can film them?'

'Of course you can,' Zoe replied taking out her phone.

She handed it to Emily and explained once more how to point it and keep the image centrally on the screen.

'Oh dear,' Emily said as she looked at the screen. 'There's only one left.'

Zoe looked up and saw that the three adults had disappeared but the grey seal pup was still there. 'Oh yes. That's a pity but you've still got the pup there. Just try to keep it in the middle of the screen. Yes, that's good. Well done.'

Zoe turned to speak to her mother just as a golf ball landed far too close to them for comfort. They both glared back angrily down the golf course.

'I never feel safe near the course,' Gillian said. 'Half of them don't seem to know where they're hitting those balls.'

Emily started to cry.

'What's wrong?' Gillian asked.

'The big fish came and took the baby seal away and there's nothing to film now.'

The adults looked at each other quizzically.

'Oh dear, that's sad news,' Zoe said. 'What was the big fish doing?'

'It took the pup in its mouth and carried it away. Now there's nothing there.'

'Let's have a look at the film and see what took the pup, shall we?' Zoe said.

Emily handed the phone to her mother. Zoe scrolled back to the point where Emily's unsteady hand had taken over the filming. Despite Emily's shaky filming, she was able to see the pup clearly enough. Suddenly, without any warning, a huge shark's head appeared above the surface, its massive jaws closed on the tiny seal pup before disappearing under the water again, barely causing a ripple on the surface.

'See Mummy, the big fish did take it.'

'Yes darling, you were right. Poor little pup.'

Zoe looked across at Gillian, hoping that her mother would understand the concerned look on her face.

'Now, Granny is going to find you a sweet and I'm going to have another look at what happened to that poor seal pup.'

'Yes, come on Emily.' Gillian said encouragingly. 'I'm sure that I've got something delicious in my bag for you.'

As Gillian searched in her bag, Zoe watched the action again. She could tell the shark was huge because, by comparison, the pup looked so tiny. Zoe watched the action again a couple of times. On the third viewing she noticed the shark's dorsal fin had appeared above the water as the shark bit down on the pup. Although she couldn't be sure, she thought she could make out a jagged cut on the trailing edge. Hadn't she seen that, or something similar on the film about the kayakers in Scotland? *Oh god*, she thought, *a great white shark and people in the water only a few hundred metres away?*

She anxiously turned to her mother and said.

'Mum, we need to head back and I need to get down to the Life Boat station immediately. Can you manage Emily down the slope on your own? I'll meet you outside the station.'

Gillian could hear the urgency in her daughter's voice and knew immediately that something was seriously wrong. 'Yes, of course. What's the problem love?'

'I really think the shark that took the seal pup might have been the same great white that we saw in that footage of the kayakers from Scotland. I've got to get to the lifeboat station and warn them because lives may be at risk.'

With that she sprinted away across the golf course and scrambled down the cliff. When she reached the building, she pulled open the door. The Lifeboat stood directly in front her seemingly filling the entire space. Zoe shouted for help. A startled female crew member shouted a response and quickly appeared around the side of the boat.

'Hi, I'm Bethan Thomas. I'm the coxswain on the lifeboat. What's the problem?'

Zoe explained and showed Bethan the film on her camera.

'Bloody hell,' Bethan remarked as she saw the shark. 'It's massive. I think you're right, it does look like the shark they saw in Scotland. Okay, we need to ensure that it's not going anywhere near the beach. I'm going to call in another crew member and get the rib out on the water as soon as possible. I also need to call this in to HQ so that they can plan accordingly. Look, thank you for getting to us so quickly. You're going to have to leave this with us to deal with. Are you just here for the day?'

Zoe explained that she was staying with her mother and where the cottage was.

'I know it well. Could you possibly send me that film please? If you bring it up on your screen, I'll enter my own mobile for you. I'll then send it on for my bosses to see.' Zoe prepared her phone, handed it to Bethan, and her phone pinged seconds later to show it had arrived.

'Brilliant. Leave it with us and we'll be out on the water as soon as my colleague gets here which should be in the next 10 minutes or so.'

Zoe said goodbye and went outside to find her mother and Emily waiting for her. She explained her conversation with Bethan and what the plan of action was.

'I just hope they can warn the people on the beach in time,' Zoe said and they set off along the narrow coastal path back to the cottage.

By the time they reached the beach, they could see the orange RNLI rib starting to patrol the bay, turning back any swimmers and people on paddle boards.

'I wonder what the locals will make of this,' Gillian remarked as they walked past the pub again. 'There again, it might put day trippers off for a while, which I wouldn't mind one bit.'

'Unfortunately, I'm afraid that it might have the opposite effect. Let's just hope that they can scare the shark away and that no one gets injured,' Zoe said as they arrived back at the cottage.

'I'll get Emily's tea ready.' Zoe said. 'Are you alright to look after her for a while, Mum?'

'Of course. I'd love to,' Gillian replied and lifted Emily on to her lap as Zoe disappeared into the house

Grandmother and granddaughter sat on the terrace and hugged each other. They watched the swimmers shouting and running out of the water, heeding the warnings that had started to percolate along the beach. Visitors began to leave for the day, half hoping to see something dramatic as they made their way but, at the same time, relieved that they were safe.

'Was that shark bad for what it did to the pup Nanna?' Emily asked.

'No it wasn't. All animals have to eat and it's just a bit sad that sometimes it's the pretty young ones that get caught while the bigger, older ones get away.'

'Well, in that case, I hope the shark doesn't get caught by something bigger too.'

'That's a nice thing to say,' Gillian smiled and gave her granddaughter an extra big, loving hug.

CHAPTER TEN

FRIDAY, 6TH JULY
Dowrtreven,
Helford River, Cornwall

In Cornwall, Nick sat at his office computer and, ran through the film of the Welsh sighting on his screen. Reports of the event hadn't been picked up by the news outlets until Thursday morning, by which time Nick and the family had already started their long journey south.

Jill had called him en route to suggest he should look at the link she'd sent him. Fortunately, he'd been able to do so when they stopped for a planned break at a motorway service area. He also took the chance to read a few of the reports that were appearing on various news outlets. Nick agreed with them. He felt it was almost definitely the great white seen in Scotland. But, as ever, he wanted to be certain and this was what he was now studying carefully on his screen.

The clarity wasn't ideal. He copied a single frame of the film showing the shark's dorsal fin and then enhanced the picture utilising specialist software that they had installed on their company mainframe. Within seconds, the image became more clearly defined. He then compared this to the clear picture they already had on file from the Warren's film. The unusual damage to the shark's fin was identical in both pictures. This was the same shark.

Nick thought for a moment about the location of the second sighting. He had visited Morfa Nefyn in his youth and knew how close the attack on the seal pup had been to the beach full of holiday makers just a few hundred metres away. He debated whether this had been a lucky escape or had the shark been so focused on its natural food source that the noise and activity of a beach presented too much of a risk?

Nick studied the map of the UK on his office wall. He calculated that if the shark continued its journey south and at the same rate of progress, it could easily have already reached the north coast of Cornwall. With the heat of the British summer attracting huge numbers to Cornwall's beaches, the presence of a great white could prove to be a real problem.

His musings were interrupted when his sister, Alice, put her head round the door.

'Hi bro. We're all going to have breakfast. Sophie was wondering if you are going to join us?'

'I can recognise a command when I get one,' Nick joked as he accompanied Alice outside to the terrace where, unusually, all the children were already dressed and sitting at the long dining table. Both families had arrived in Cornwall the previous day

'Morning everyone,' he said to the assembled children. In return he only received the odd grunt of recognition from his own family but a more enthusiastic, 'Good morning' from his thirteen year old niece, Georgie, and eleven year old nephew, Josh .

'Dad, when's Emma arriving?' asked his son, Fred.

'She's coming down with Pete and Jill and they're hoping to be with us by lunch time,' Nick replied.

'Great!' Charlie shouted, turning to his cousins. 'Just wait till you meet her. She's the one we were talking about. She was the one who was knocked out of her kayak by the great white shark.'

'*And* she's a rugby international,' Fred added.

Amid the excited chatter, Nick joined his brother-in-law, John, at the adjacent table.

'I feel sorry for her already,' said John, smiling. 'I hope she's not going to get too overwhelmed with all the hero worship!'

Nick assured him that Emma would be able to cope. He enjoyed a very good relationship with his brother-in-law, a successful equine vet, and always looked forward to spending time with him on family holidays.

'Nick, I've got an apology to make. I've been asked to be on duty at Newton Abbott racecourse tomorrow - it's a bit of a favour for a friend. So I'm afraid I won't be here most of the day to help you with the children.'

'John, that's not a problem,' Nick said. 'I think we've just about got enough adults to keep the terrorists at bay.'

They both stood up as Beth appeared on the terrace carrying a large tray.

'I'll make sure I'm back for dinner though,' John added, speaking in an unnecessarily loud voice. 'I wouldn't want to miss any of Beth's fabulous cooking.'

'I heard that,' Beth said, placing the large tray on their table. 'John, you're my favourite *almost* son-in-law.'

'Heh!' Nick said pointedly. 'What about me?'

'A bit of flattery about my cooking wouldn't go amiss!'

Beth bent down and gave Nick a peck on the cheek. 'I'm only kidding.'

Beth walked round the table to give John gave a quick hug.

'Good morning to you both. Now, there's lots to bring out from the kitchen, so please could you two men go and see what your hard working wives have got ready for you.'

As everyone was enjoying their breakfast, Nick's phone rang.

'Daddy, you always say no phones at the table,' Heli complained.

'Sorry, you're absolutely right but I'm afraid I must answer this,' Nick said leaving the table. 'Jamie, how are you?'

'All good thanks,' Jamie said. 'Are you down at Dowrtreven?'

'Yes, we arrived yesterday. Alice and John are here too.'

'Excellent. I'm travelling down on next Wednesday. It would be good to get together at some point, but let's leave that to the girls to arrange? Look, sorry to be a bit brisk but I've got rather a lot on. I'm sure you will have seen the footage from North Wales. What are your thoughts?'

Nick had walked across to the wall overlooking the river and watched as pair of mallards landed directly in front of him. 'By my reckoning, I think she could be off the north Cornish coast by now.'

'Really, so soon?' Jamie responded, sounding slightly alarmed. 'In that case I need to move into action immediately. I've been looking to put together a team of people who can advise and be ready to take action should the need arise. On the operational side I've already got the CEO of the Coastguard, the RNLI Chief Exec and the Police and Crime Commissioner for Devon and Cornwall. On the advisory side I would very much like you to join me and I was thinking about asking Professor Andrew Wallace from Southampton University as well. What do you think?'

'Jamie, of course I'd be delighted to help in any way I can. Andy Wallace is a top guy with a huge amount of knowledge about shark behaviour. You really couldn't get a better man.'

'That's good. I'm delighted you're on board and that you agree about Andrew Wallace. I'm expecting a call from him shortly.' Jamie hesitated for a moment. 'A word of warning - the junior Minister who has direct responsibility for the Coastguard and Maritime agencies is Nigel LeGrand. I'm sure you'll have heard of him. A bit of a right wing firebrand, but the PM seems to think he has something special to offer. He kindly decided to foist him on me following the reshuffle. He's just about bearable but a lot of people think that he's a bit of a legend in his own mind. Anyway, he'll be in charge of the advisory committee and any flak will be coming his way. I hope you still feel able to contribute. We need to get moving on this pretty quickly, so can you do a video call early next week, say Monday at 9.30 a.m.? I'll sit in on this one but he'll take the chair for any future meetings.'

'Yes, still happy to help in whatever way I can. Monday is good for me.'

'I'll confirm that later today and thanks once again. Please send my love to Sophie and Alice. And not forgetting the wonderful Beth as well. Hope to see you all soon. Bye.'

As Nick returned to the terrace, Sophie asked him who he'd been speaking to.

'That was our future Prime Minister, or Jamie Stoddard as he prefers to be known.'

'How is he?' Sophie asked.

'Yes, he's good,' Nick replied as he sat down at the table. 'He's travelling down next week. Bella and the children are already here.'

'It would be lovely to see them all,' Sophie said. 'I think I'd better give Bella a call over the weekend and sort a date out with her. It would be good to catch up and I'm sure Jamie has more important things to do than arrange the social calendar for his family. I presume that wasn't the reason for his call?'

'No, something a bit more important than that,' Nick said and explained about his new role on the advisory committee.

'I can see how having a great white around might present a bit of a problem,' Sophie said. 'But I wouldn't like to be Jamie if it ultimately came down to closing beaches. With the south west seaside towns as busy as they are at this time of year, that's a lot of potential voters you could really upset.'

'Let's hope that's not going to prove to be necessary,' Nick said reaching for the coffee pot. 'There are plenty of seals around that coastline to keep that old lady busy and away from the beaches. And don't worry about Jamie, he's made sure he stays out of the firing line if the proverbial hits the fan. He's already passed on responsibility for the committee and any decision making to a junior minister, that ghastly man Nigel Legrand. Like I said, Jamie is showing all the necessary skills to be a future PM.'

CHAPTER ELEVEN

FRIDAY, 6TH JULY
Dowrtreven,
Helford River, Cornwall

'Here we are,' Pete said as he turned the motorhome off the narrow lane and onto a gravel drive. A small slate sign announced the property to be *Dowrtreven*.

Emma was surprised to find that she was a little nervous. Perhaps it was the fact that she would be meeting Nick and Sophie's extended family for the first time? Pete and Jill had helped put her mind at rest by telling her how lovely they all were and how easy they were to get on with.

Her thoughts were interrupted when the campervan pulled up outside the impressive stone built house and a small army of children rushed out to meet her.

Slightly shocked but delighted, she opened the door and called out, 'Hello everyone!' However, her voice was drowned out by what seemed to be each member of the welcoming committee desperately trying to introduce their cousins.

'Hello Georgie, hello Josh. Lovely to meet you both. I hope we get the chance to say a proper hello later.'

Jill and Peter had also got out of the vehicle and, momentarily, the children's attention was turned to them.

Emma turned as a familiar voice behind her said, 'Welcome to Dowrtreven, Emma. Sorry about the raucous welcome.'

Sophie walked up to her and gave her a kiss on each cheek and also welcomed Jill and Peter.

'Emma, let me introduce Nick's sister Alice.'

'Lovely to meet you at last, Emma,' Alice said and shook Emma's hand. 'We've heard a lot about you.'

'Oh dear,' Emma replied. 'Should I be worried?'

'Not at all!' Alice laughed. 'Though I should warn you that the children haven't stopped talking about you, so your hero status is firmly established. Come on, let's go and join the others on the terrace.'

'Oh, my bags.' Emma turned back towards the motorhome.

'Don't you worry,' Pete said. 'I'll bring them in for you.'

'Thank you, Pete. You're a star,' Emma said, smiling to herself when she thought she saw Pete blushing slightly.

Emma followed Alice and Sophie into the house. They passed through a large, family sitting room with a TV, numerous sofas, chairs and lounging cushions scattered on the floor. They emerged onto the terrace through French doors and the view over the Helford River opened up before them. Centuries' old trees lining the steep river banks opposite were reflected in the slow moving river below.

'Oh my god,' Emma exclaimed. 'It's absolutely beautiful. What a fantastic house to have grown up in.'

'We were very lucky,' Alice replied. 'And we're also very fortunate to have it now for our children to enjoy.'

They went down some steps to the lower terrace where Nick welcomed her and introduced his brother-in-law.

'How was the journey?' John asked. 'I hear Pete's driving can be rather exciting at times.'

'I was sitting well back in the campervan so I couldn't say,' Emma replied diplomatically. 'But I remember Jill complaining about wanting to arrive with all body parts intact.'

'I share her pain.' Nick laughed. 'Now, let's show you to your room. It isn't quite The Savoy, but we do have hot and cold running water.'

Emma pointed to the river behind her. 'Well, there's water to jump into, so really a bed is all I need.'

'The perfect guest,' Sophie said. 'But don't worry, we do include clean sheets as well.'

They turned back to the house to be greeted by Beth. She was carrying a large tray of cutlery and glasses which she put down on the long table.

'Emma, my dear. How lovely to see you. Welcome to sunny Cornwall.' Emma crossed the terrace to Beth.

'It's lovely to be here and to get such a warm welcome. I've just seen that you've even got your own beach. How amazing. I can't wait to do some exploring.'

'Well before you do all that, we're going to have some lunch, if you can manage it after that long journey',

'I'm always hungry,' Emma said, her hands moving unintentionally to her waist. 'My mother was always shocked by how much I could eat. I seem to be one of those lucky people who can eat without putting lots of weight on.'

'You lucky thing,' Beth said, looking down at her own slightly larger waist. 'If only that was the case with me.' Beth turned to speak to the two men.

'Right, come on you men. Have you shown Emma her

room yet?' Nick was about to reply but Beth continued. 'Well get a move on, please. Then can you and John come and show your faces in the kitchen or we won't be starting lunch before 3 p.m.'

Nick groaned, made some joking aside about mother-in-laws and took Emma into the house.

AFTER LUNCH, Emma eventually managed to drag herself away from the demands of the children by promising to go swimming with them later. She joined Nick and Jill at the next table.

'Have you told Nick what we discussed on the way down?' Jill asked her as she sat down.

'No, not yet. I'm afraid I don't seem to have had much of a chance!' Emma replied looking nervously from one to the other.

'What's this?' Nick asked, his eyebrow raised quizzically.

'Emma's come up with a project idea that Pete and I think could really work,' Jill explained.

'That sounds interesting. Come on Emma, tell me about it.'

'Okay,' Emma cleared her throat and placed her hands together on the table. 'Well, as we've all seen, there's been a huge amount of interest in the appearance of the shark. Unbelievably, our kayak film has now been watched almost half a million times. Oh and by the way, Dad says a big thank you for enabling him to get some income from it. Even the Welsh seal pup clip has already had over a hundred thousand viewings.'

'You're right, the numbers have been incredible,' said Nick, nodding in agreement.

'And there could still be more sightings, more interactions,' Emma continued. 'I was thinking we could take advantage of this huge interest and perhaps consider producing a one hour special that looks back across these great white events. Obviously this would mean interviewing all those involved to hear about their experiences. I think we could also look at it from the shark's point of view and try to explain why it behaved as it did in each incident.'

'I think that's a great idea and it would give you the perfect opportunity to get in front of the camera.'

'Oh no,' Emma replied immediately, and looking anxiously first at Nick, and then at Jill. 'I didn't mean I should do it.'

'Why not?' Nick asked, smiling at her reaction. 'That's the reason we've brought you on board. You've come up with the concept and I think you should see it through. What do you think Jill?'

'I agree entirely,' Jill said. 'Emma, you've definitely got the ability to bring this off and let's face it, you've got first-hand experience of coming face to face with this great white.'

Emma looked uncomfortable at the idea. 'But I've got no experience in presenting or interviewing.'

'As we discussed at your induction meeting, we can arrange some external training for your presentational skills,' Jill said. 'Not that I think you'll need much. As far as I'm concerned, interviewing is all about getting on with people and getting them to talk, which you're really good at. Look, we're all here to help and advise as needed. I think Nick is right. It's a golden opportunity for you.'

At the next door table, there was a sudden scraping of chairs as the boys left the table and disappeared indoors.

'Look, thank you for your confidence in my ability. I'm

not sure you're right but I'm willing to give it a go, if you are.'

'Brilliant,' Nick said. 'That's our next project sorted. We just need are a few more sightings or interactions and you'll be able to make a start.'

CHAPTER TWELVE

SATURDAY, 7TH JULY
Newquay Harbour, Cornwall

Pat Mahony said goodbye to Ed and Matt and waited till they had walked a good distance from his boat before using his phone. He scrolled through his contact list and selected the number of his good friend, a reporter on the Cornish Gazette. The phone only rang twice before it was answered.

'Dave Turroch.'

'Dave, it's Pat Mahony. How are you doing?'

'Pat, I'm doing well thanks mate. Busy, as always. Now, to what do I owe the honour of this call?'

'Well, I've got the story of the century for you, if you want it. It'll cost you a few pints mind.'

'If it's as good as you say, I'll be buying more than a few. Why don't we meet at The Falcon in half an hour?'

'Perfect,' Pat said. 'And be warned, I've got a hell of a thirst on me!'

'Nothing new there then. See you soon.'

Pat finished sorting his gear and headed off to the Harbour Master's office where he explained to the Master, Jack Trevithick, what the two divers had seen.

'Bloody hell,' Jack said. 'You just wouldn't think it was possible around here, would you? I'd better get onto the Coastguard and let them know pronto.'

Feeling happy he'd done his duty as a good citizen, Pat moved off to The Falcon where Dave Turroch stood at the bar. A pint of Pat's favourite local bitter was waiting for him.

'So, what's this story that you think's going to make me famous?' Dave asked, handing the pint to Pat.

'Just let me take the head off this,' Pat said, downing the pint in one. 'Looks like I'll need a refill to help my memory.'

'Alright, you bugger, but this had better be good,' Dave said, handing Pat's glass to the barman for a refill.

'Oh it is, that I can promise you,' Pat said and started to tell Dave the full story that the two divers had recounted during the journey back to the harbour.

'And this is kosher?' Dave asked.

'Absolutely. Them two boys told me they were marines, stationed nearby and I reckon they were officers. They didn't need to embellish their story. One thing I forgot. When they got back on the boat - and, believe me, they were in a right bloody hurry to get out the water – they said they'd just come face to face with the *Grim Reaper*, and I thought that was a bloody good name for a killer shark!'

'I reckon you're right there,' Dave said, already imagining the headlines for his article. 'Look, I'd better get off and get this piece written before some bastard at the Coastguard gives the story away.'

'What about my beer?' Pat asked.

Dave opened his wallet and pulled out a bunch of notes. 'Here's fifty quid. That should keep you going for a couple hours.'

With that, Dave was out the door and heading back to his house to write the article of a lifetime.

CHAPTER THIRTEEN

SATURDAY, 7TH JULY
Dowtreven,
Helford River, Cornwall

Emma had kept her promise, spending more than an hour playing with the children in the river. Seeing her in a swimsuit persuaded even the older girls to join in. Pete and Jill had then decided to join in the river fun. Shrieks of joy and laughter filled the air. Encouraged by Jill, the children jumped all over Pete trying, but failing, to duck him under water.

Emma joined the others for tea on the terrace and was checking her social media when she came across recently posted headlines.

'Nick, you've got to see this,' she said, showing him her screen.

'Grim Reaper stalks Cornish shores'
'Grim Reaper terror close to Cornish beach'
And from the red top papers –
'Fin Reaper shock'

'Jaws for thought'

Nick stared at the screen with increasing fascination as he scrolled through headlines

'What the hell has brought this about?' He asked.

'It appears a couple of marines were diving on a wreck not far from Newquay this morning and came face to face with our favourite great white,' Emma explained.

'I should think that was a pretty terrifying experience,' Beth said.

'How did they know it was our shark?' Nick asked.

'It doesn't say here.' Emma quickly scanned the article. 'No, nothing more about that. It just says the two marines were believed to be officers stationed at RM Stonehouse, Plymouth. Apparently it's the HQ of 3 Commando Brigade.'

'We really need to have a quick chat with them to confirm what they saw,' Nick said. 'We might have a problem getting hold of them though. I bet every journalist in the land is calling the switchboard at Stonehouse.'

Sophie was walking towards the house to make more tea, but stopped and turned as she remembered something.

'Didn't we meet the Commanding Officer and his wife when we had dinner with the Coldwells at Christmas?' Sophie asked. 'What was his name? Something Lowell? A bit of a strange christian name?'

'Yes, well remembered Sophie,' Nick said. 'Xavier, wasn't it?'

Sophie nodded and Nick turned to Emma.

'Please can you find the number for RN Stonehouse - I'll see if being a minor celeb has its benefits.'

Emma found the number and the other adults watched on in silence as Nick dialled it. He stood up and paced impatiently round the terrace. After ringing out for over a minute, his call was answered.

'RN Stonehouse. How can I help you?'

'Lt Colonel Lowell please?'

'Is he expecting your call, sir?'

'No, I don't think so, but please tell him it's Nick Martin calling. We met at Christmas.'

'Okay, thank you, sir. I'll try his line.'

Nick continued to prowl around the upper and lower terraces before pausing by the wall and staring out across the river. After another minute of waiting, he was relieved to hear a strong voice break through the silence,

'Xavier Lowell speaking.'

'Xavier, this is Nick Martin. You may remember we met at Christmas?'

'Indeed I do, Nick. Nice to speak to you again. We've seen you quite a bit on television recently. Would this call, by any chance, be related to another sighting of that huge shark?'

'I'm afraid that you've got it in one, Xavier. I understand a couple of your fine young officers had an interesting meeting this morning with our shark. I was wondering if it would be possible to have a quick chat with them. I'd very much like to find out exactly what they saw and, above all, to check that it matches what was seen in the Scottish incident.'

'Well, it would appear that you and the rest of the world's media would like to speak to them!' Xavier joked. 'Look, I know your reasons are professional and not for cheap headlines like some others, so this is what I'll do. Can you give me your email address? I'll then get them to send you a video call link for 9.30am tomorrow. That should give you enough time to clear your head and for them to get in a couple of hours' fitness work. Don't keep them on for too long, please. They're due back in training with their men. How does that sound?'

Nick turned and held up his thumb to Emma and the other adults sitting at the table behind him.

'Absolutely brilliant, thank you. Are you around over the next week or two? Perhaps we can get together for dinner?'

'That's very kind of you but I'm afraid we're setting off on deployment overseas very soon and I just can't get away before then. Give me your email address and I'll set up the meeting. By the way, their names are Ed Richards and Matt Jackson, both captains and both bloody good officers. They'll also be heading off abroad with the rest of the regiment. You can definitely trust what they tell you.'

Nick gave Xavier the email details and thanked him for his help before ending the call.

'That was impressive,' Emma said. 'Once people have met you, they don't forget you!'

Nick laughed and shrugged his shoulders as he rejoined the others at the table

'You know, on the odd occasion it helps to have a face and a voice that people recognise. You're going to find that out soon enough Emma, if you haven't begun to already.'

'I think I can wait thanks,' Emma replied.

'We'll see,' Nick said with a knowing smile. 'I want you to be in on that call tomorrow. If we're going ahead with your new project, you'll have to interview those two at some point.'

'No problem,' Emma said, and this time it was she who had the knowing smile. 'Two, fit marines' officers – there's a chance I might just enjoy it!'

CHAPTER FOURTEEN

SUNDAY, 8TH JULY
Nick's Office, Dowrtreven,
Helford River, Cornwall

Emma clicked on the connect button and the faces of the marines' officers appeared on the screen. Both had regulation short haircuts and were wearing standard combat shirts. Judging by the bed in the background and the dress uniform hanging on the back of the door, it appeared they were sitting in one of their rooms in the barracks.

'Good morning, gentlemen. Thanks very much for taking time out of your busy schedule to talk to us this morning. Let me introduce Emma Warren - you may recognise her? She's in an elite group of only two people to get as close to the shark as you did. And I'm Nick Martin.'

The dark haired officer spoke first. 'Well, sir, it's a pleasure to meet you, if remotely, and we do indeed recognise Ms Warren. Of course, not only for her achievements in the water, but also on the rugby field.'

'Come on guys.' Emma laughed. 'Don't hold that

against me! And can we drop the Sir and Ms bit please? Call me Emma and him Nick.'

'Thank you,' the blonde haired officer said. 'I'm Ed Richards and this is Matt Jackson.' Ed raised his hand and sheepishly pointed over his shoulder. 'Can I just apologise for what you're seeing behind us? I'm afraid we're having to use Matt's room to get some privacy - tidiness isn't one of his greatest strengths.'

Matt made his mouth to speak but Nick got in first.

'It's good to meet you both and don't worry about the room. We're in my office and, as you can probably see for yourselves, there's barely room to swing a cat in here.' Nick said. 'I'm delighted to say that Emma has now joined our production company, so that's why she's with me today. I understand that you're a bit limited for time, so do you mind if we crack on?'

'No problem,' Matt said. 'Fire away.'

'Could you quickly take us through events as they happened?

'Yes, of course,' Matt said and started to smile. 'But, just before we do that, we have something to reveal to you that hasn't leaked out yet. I'll let Ed tell you.'

'I had a video camera attached to my chest during the dive.' Ed explained. 'You see, the thing is that, in the excitement that followed the dive, we completely forgot to look at it. This meant the boat skipper, who was probably the source of the story getting out, was totally unaware that we had some film of what went on. That's why, so far, no one knows anything about it. Anyway, we think you might like to watch the clip that covers the appearance of the shark. I'm afraid, that once it got close up, the focus wasn't perfect.'

'God yes, we'd love to see it,' Nick said excitedly. He looked at Emma who nodded enthusiastically in agreement.

'The file's quite large so would you mind if we sent it to you after our call?'

'Yes, that would be brilliant.' Nick said. 'But in the meantime, we'd love to hear your story.'

'No problem,' Ed said.

The two marines took it in turns to take them through from diving over the wreck to ending up back on the dive boat. Nick glanced at Emma as they spoke, and smiled to himself. She was clearly enjoying listening the marines tell their story but he noticed that she seemed to pay particular attention whenever Ed was speaking.

When they'd finished, Nick said. 'That's a great story and well told, thank you. How close were you to the shark?'

'Well, if we'd reached out we could have touched its pectoral fin,' Ed said lifting his arm to demonstrate the action. 'But to be honest, we were both so bloody terrified we couldn't move!'

'I'm not surprised,' Nick sympathised. 'The only times I've been in the sea with a great white, there's been a metal cage between us. Even with the cage there, I have to admit I was both exhilarated and crapping myself at the same time!'

'What was interesting was the huge number of scars all over its body,' Matt added, leaning in closer to the camera. 'I seem to remember reading you thought the old girl was possibly over fifty years old. Well the abundance of scars would certainly seem to support that.'

'That's interesting. Could you see the damage to the dorsal fin?'

'Yes, we could,' Matt said. 'In fact, it was one of the first things we discussed when we got back onto the boat. We both realised this could be the same shark that threw Emma into the sea. By the way, just how scary was that Emma?'

Emma was momentarily taken aback by the question. 'Well, as you can imagine, it was a bit of a shock when this huge dorsal fin appeared next to me!' The marines both smiled. 'But to be honest, we'd been watching the shark for quite a while. Somehow, it wasn't really as scary as you'd expect when I ended up in the water with her. In fact, once I got back into my kayak, I felt quite euphoric – I almost wanted to jump back in again to repeat experience. Adrenaline, maybe?'

'Not at all,' Ed said with a broad grin. 'We can understand that because once we'd got back on the boat, we just couldn't stop laughing, could we?' Ed turned to his partner for agreement. 'As you said, it's just the most brilliant adrenaline rush, isn't it?'

Nick sat back, taking in the conversation of three young people who'd shared a unique life experience. He'd been through many himself over the past twenty odd years, but he still rather envied them that unique first occasion.

'Nick, apologies for us gabbling on while you're sitting there,' Ed said.

'Not a problem,' Nick said raising a hand in reassurance. 'I'm actually quite envious of your experiences. Only too well I remember my first really heavy adrenaline moment. It was on Australia's north coast when a fifteen foot saltwater crocodile unexpectedly jumped out of the water across our boat, almost tipping us into the water. It then tried to grab hold of me.'

'Bloody hell,' Emma said under her breath and looked at Nick, astonished.

'Fortunately our guide reacted quickly and hit it in the eye with the his paddle. It slipped back into the water empty mouthed. I was just frozen to the spot and was still unable to move for what seemed like an age afterwards. What I do remember clearly is that it got to within a couple of feet of me and the smell of its breath was disgusting!'

'Now *that* is some story,' Matt said in admiration.

'Yes,' said Nick. 'It was a real brown trouser moment. And I mean real!'

'Aww, too much information,' Emma screeched and screwed up her face in disgust. She turned back to the screen. 'Now you guys, we're hoping to put together a programme covering all the recent events linked to this incredible shark. Would you mind if, at some time in the future, I came up to your place and filmed an interview of your experience?'

'We'd love to help in any way we can,' Ed said, enthusiastically. Nick tried to keep a straight face as he watched Ed's reaction. 'And we'd also love to show you round our base, so you can see what we marines actually get up to.'

'Now that sounds like fun.' Emma said smiling at the screen. 'If could you send over both your emails, I promise to be in touch. We understood from the Colonel that you'll disappearing for a while on deployment. I won't ask where you're going, but do you have any idea how long you're likely to be away?'

'I'm afraid we're not sure about that yet, but at least a couple of months,' Matt said.

'That long? I was hoping to get something together before then.'

'Well, we're likely to get time off at some stage.' Ed said looking to Matt for confirmation. 'As long as we can get a decent connection, would you be happy to record an interview online like we're doing now?'

'Yes, that would be great,' Emma said, raising a thumb to indicate her agreement. 'Perhaps I can still visit you at a later date for a more in depth interview?'

'Fine by us,' Ed said. 'We'll look forward to that.'

Matt looked at his watch and nudged Ed.

'Right, apologies, but I'm afraid we'd better be going.' Matt said.

'It's been great meeting you both,' Ed said, pushing his chair back from the desk. 'Emma, we look forward to seeing you over here sometime in the near future.'

Emma nodded and smiled at the screen. 'I'll look forward to it and thank you both for all your help.'

'I second that,' added Nick. 'Many thanks and good luck wherever it is you are about to be sent.'

'I think we'll need it!' Ed said and laughed. 'We'll transfer that file over in a minute. Bye.'

'Yes, bye,' Emma said and her smile slowly disappeared as the screen went blank.

'Nice guys,' Nick said as he stood up and stretched. 'I'm sure you'll enjoy going up for that interview. I thought Ed was charming,' Nick winked at Emma.

'Stop that,' Emma said, trying to cover her embarrassment by poking him on the arm. 'But yes, it would be interesting to see for myself what sort of life those marines have.'

Within a couple of minutes, an email arrived from the marines, saying how much they'd enjoyed the meeting and including their email addresses. Attached to the email was the file containing the divers' film. It took a while to download. Emma opened it on the screen and sat back to watch the action

The clip opened with the two divers at their final stop. Ed's hand and dive watch appeared and suddenly the picture changed as Ed turned to his left. Through the gloom they could make out the shark, moving slowly towards them. As Matt explained earlier, it seemed like it would crash in to them. But at the last moment it veered off to their right and the camera captured the head and bulk of the body as it slid past, disappearing into the gloom once more.

Their anxiety was clearly apparent in the speed of their swim to the surface and clambering aboard the boat.

'That's a great piece of film,' Emma said. 'They really

should get that online for the world to see. Shall I send them the link you gave Dad? They deserve to make a few pounds for having gone through that.'

'Yes, please do that and send my thanks.'

'Consider it done,' Emma said, as she started to type on the keyboard.

CHAPTER FIFTEEN

SUNDAY, 8TH JULY
Tesco Superstore, Gloucester

Anne Neal studied her shopping list. 'Just get another pack of baked beans for me will you love?'

Her husband, Kevin, sighed quietly to himself and moved round the shopping trolley to access the shelf. But before he could get there, his seven year old son, Rees, had already grabbed a pack and put it in the trolley. Kevin ruffled Reece's hair. 'You're too quick for me.'

Shopping in Tesco was just about the worst way that Kevin could imagine spending an hour of his life. Anne had asked him to help her with the 'holiday shop' and he was determined to make sure that nothing, not even accompanying his wife to Tesco, was going to spoil the prospect of their Cornish holiday, only a day away now. The thought of spending a week with Rees was his idea of heaven. Kevin hadn't really been sure he wanted a family, but as soon as he had held the small bundle in his arms and looked into those big, innocent eyes, he'd known that his life had suddenly changed permanently for the better.

With the shopping packed away, they drove out of the car park and headed for home, a new build house on the outskirts of Gloucester.

'Dad,' Rees asked from the back seat, 'what's it going to be like in Cornwall?'

'You won't believe it,' Kevin replied. 'The sea's nice and warm and there are waves that you can dive into. There's a huge beach and the sand is perfect for making sandcastles.'

'And the sun is going to be really hot,' Jill added. 'I think we'd better stay in the shade between twelve and two. We'll need to rub in lots of factor 50.'

'Mummy's right, we've got to be careful. Don't forget we bought that blow up crocodile boat for you to sit on and I can pull you up and down the shore.'

'Can we go now?'

'Sorry son, it's got to be tomorrow. We'll be getting up at four o'clock to avoid the holiday queues. That way we should be on the beach by late morning.'

'Cool,' said the seven year old and his parents stole a glance at each other and smiled.

CHAPTER SIXTEEN

MONDAY, 9TH JULY
The Shore Thing,
5 miles off Newquay, Cornwall

Sean Howell loved this time of year. His shark fishing charter company, *Reel Business*, was fully booked for the next five months and the summer weather was certainly playing its part. Clear blue skies and a gentle breeze – perfect for pulling in the punters.

And today was no different. He had three guests on today's charter. Andy and Baz had been out with him a couple of times before but the third, Gary, was, by his own admission, a complete novice.

They'd expressed an interest in catching blue sharks and, fortunately, this year had already proved to be a good one for catching them. He'd explained to the guests that, while blue sharks were, by nature, ocean wanderers, they arrived in UK waters when the mackerel started to shoal in June. On their best day so far this year, they'd caught eighteen blue sharks along with several other common sharks. He reminded the guests that he operated a strict catch and release policy.

They had started out early and had already stopped to gather some fresh bait. Dropping strings of feathered hooks over the side, it wasn't long before the mackerel in the depths below seized the lures and were reeled back on board and stored to be used as bait for later in the day. After half an hour, Sean was happy they had enough and he started up the *Shore Thing's* motor to continue the trip out to a location where he was confident they'd find some sharks.

Sean was reassured to see his guests relaxed, talking animatedly and joking amongst themselves. Occasionally, they stopped to marvel as they watched gannets diving at speed into the sea to catch their prey.

The boat made good time through the calm sea and, after another hour, Sean cut the engines. The Cornish coast was now barely visible on the horizon. Sean went to the large plastic bin in the cockpit, filled two mesh bags with its stinking contents and walked out to the main deck.

'Jesus!' Gary exclaimed as the stench hit him. 'What the bloody hell is that?'

Sean smiled. He got the same reaction from new guests every time he produced the bags.

'What I've got here's what we call Rubby Dubby. Basically it's minced up fish with some bran and fish oil. You might find the smell quite disgusting, sharks find it irresistible.'

Sean hung a bag of Rubby Dubby over each side of the boat, just suspended in the water.

'Right, gentlemen,' Sean said, getting their full attention. 'It's time to do what you've come here for - fish for sharks. We'll have three rods out, all at different depths and distances to make sure we don't get any tangled lines. You'll be taking it in turns to try to land a fish. Gary, I suggest you go second. You can watch how your friends work the catch and learn a bit from that.'

Sean took out a couple of old ice cream sticks from his pocket and hid them in his hand with just the tip protruding.

'Andy and Baz, pick a stick. The longest gets first go.'

Baz punched the air when his stick was the winner. Sean showed the guests how to bait the curved hooks on each line with the mackerel. Having done so, they watched how he took each rod in turn, carefully positioned it, and then paid out the weighted line, which was then allowed to drop down into the sea below, drifting away from the boat with the current.

All four men stood on the deck looking out across the vast expanse of sea and sky, waiting patiently for the first fish to bite. After about thirty minutes, the audible ratchet on the middle reel started to issue its click, click, click warning as a fish played with the bait. Then, suddenly, there was a heart-stopping scream as the fish took the bait and swam off at speed. Baz was on it in a second, pushing the lever drag to strike, allowing the line to fully tighten, then firmly setting the hook in the fish's mouth with three sharp jabs of the rod.

'Don't rush it,' Sean shouted. 'Enjoy the moment. Remember to keep the rod bent to maintain the pressure.'

After half an hour of a muscle stretching battle, Baz had brought the shark to the side of the boat. Sean decided it was too small to bring on board to weigh. He released the barbless hook from its mouth and watched it slip away. Although disappointed, Baz had fished shark enough times to understand Sean's decision.

'Don't worry,' Sean said, 'There'll be plenty more for you and much bigger than that one. Good one to get you warmed up with though! Right, Gary, your turn to land a whopper!'

CHAPTER SEVENTEEN

MONDAY, 9TH JULY
Nick's Office, Dowrtreven,
Helford River, Cornwall

Jamie Stoddard, Secretary of State for Transport, opened the first video meeting of the Advisory Group. After welcoming the attendees and thanking them for their participation, he introduced each attendee individually, outlining their qualifications and the reasons for their inclusion in the group. He handed over to Nigel LeGrand to chair the meeting.

Nick noticed that, despite the hot weather, Legrand still insisted on wearing his trade mark three piece pinstripe suit. He'd also positioned himself in a rather self-important manner in front of a large oil painting. His boss, on the other hand, wore a simple open neck blue shirt and sat in front of what appeared to be a young child's painting of a seal. What a difference, thought Nick.

LeGrand immediately addressed the focal point of the agenda.

'As we're all aware, there has been a number of sightings and interactions with a large great white shark off our coast. It's presumed that it, or should I say, she, is still somewhere off the Cornish coast. As I outlined in the brief I sent to you, there are two points we have to consider. Firstly, we need to establish what possible threat such a large fish might represent and, secondly, what actions we need to take now to prevent that threat becoming a reality. I hope you all have received the brief?'

On the screen, four heads nodded in confirmation.

'Good. Andrew and Nick. You're both shark experts, so please could you give us your initial risk assessment at this point? Professor, would you go first?'

Nick smiled as the face of his friend Andrew Wallace appeared in the middle of the screen. He always thought Andrew looked like a typical professor - balding, scruffy clothes and glasses perched on the top of his head. But, as Nick knew perfectly well, this professor really knew his subject and was considered one of the world's leading shark experts.

'Yes, of course, thank you, Minister.' Andrew paused, pushing his glasses down onto his nose and continuing: 'Firstly, can I say that the hysterical and stereotypical reactions we've recently seen in the UK press, bear no relation to reality. Yes, great whites are apex predators but the danger they represent to humans is minimal. For example, if you look at the slide that should be appearing on your screens now, you can see that a person in the USA has a 1 in 265 million chance of being killed by a shark. There was only one death recorded there last year. In fact sharks are right at the bottom of deaths caused by animal attacks. In the USA, dogs account for thirty-four deaths a year and bees kill more people every year than sharks do. And these figures are, of course, from the USA which has a population five times that of the UK, so we really need to get this into proportion. As I will show you later, the figures are slightly higher in Australia.'

'Pardon me for interrupting, but can I just get this right?' Jamie asked. 'Those are deaths caused by *all* types of shark in the USA that you're talking about?'

'Correct.'

'What are the figures for attacks by great whites only please?'

'There were twenty seven recorded great white attacks on humans worldwide last year and only two fatalities, both in Australia.'

LeGrand appeared surprised by this but didn't wait for the professor to add further details.

'So, the risks appear to be very low,' Legrand interrupted. 'For the time being, thank you Professor. Now, Nick Martin, you've done a lot of work studying this visitor to our shores. What do you think?'

'Firstly, I completely agree with everything Andrew Wallace has said. This current image of *The Grim Reaper* is ridiculous. Great whites do not seek out humans as prey. Most interactions are purely accidental and can be attributed to the shark mistaking a surfer or swimmer for a prey such as a seal or turtle. As for this fifty year old lady, currently swimming off our shores – well, so far she hasn't shown any interest in approaching areas frequented by humans. In fact, as we saw in North Wales, she made a seal kill a few hundred metres from a beach crowded with holiday makers, but chose not to get any nearer. Also, both in Scotland and off our own Cornish coast, we've seen her ignore humans in the water, even though they were very close to her.'

'So you don't think she represents a danger to the many

people who will be using the West Country beaches over the next days and weeks?' LeGrand said.

'Look, we can only go by what we've experienced here and by the reports from shark watchers off the east coast of America. They say they have no record, at all, of this shark interacting in a threatening or dangerous manner or showing any behavioural traits that would lead them to conclude she represents a danger.'

'Right, thank you. 'LeGrand said. 'Well from what Mr Martin has just said, it would appear that we have nothing to be worried about!' A couple of the attendees smiled uncertainly at this attempt at humour. Nick remained stoney faced.

LeGrand's own smile soon disappeared. He reflected that the audience might now see this meeting as unnecessary and his own importance diminished. 'I think, however, that we would be failing in our responsibilities if we didn't at least consider a plan of action, just in case. Nick and Andrew – would you agree?'

'Absolutely,' Nick agreed. Andrew nodded his agreement. 'It's always best to assume that the worst might happen and plan accordingly.'

'Good. If we're all agreed on that, can I first ask Peter Williams, as CEO of the Coastguard, to present his suggested action plan?'

'I'd be delighted, Minister,' Peter responded. The first page of his presentation appeared on all their screens with the entitled: ***Proposals for Cross Dimensional Agency Reaction in the case of Shorebound or Near Shore Contrary Incidents.***

Nick groaned inwardly and steeled himself for what was likely to be a very dull couple of hours.

As soon as the meeting finished, Nick walked out to the terrace where Emma was busily working on her laptop.

'How did the meeting go?'

'Well that was two hours of my life I'm never going to get back,' Nick replied, sitting down next to her. 'I feel so sorry for Jamie having to work with that minister he's been stuck with - Nigel LeGrand. God, what a total pain in the arse, which also probably happens to be where he keeps his head!'

'Well he sounds like a fun person to have around,' Emma said smiling. 'Am I allowed to ask what you all decided?'

'Yes, of course. It's all going to become public knowledge soon anyway. Basically, if required, they're initially going to put in place patrols on each major beach on the north coast within ten miles of Newquay. These will involve boats, ribs and hover-skis operated by the police, coastguard and RNLI. They'll also use drones to try to spot any signs of the shark approaching a beach.'

'Are they just there to look out for any signs of the shark?'

Nick looked down at the river as a small dinghy passed by, crewed by two young teenagers who waved at him. Nick smiled and waved back.

'Yeah, they'll be doing that, but also making sure that the usual idiots don't drift out too far on lilos or anything else they have no control over. They're just trying to reduce the potential for unnecessary interaction with whatever might be out there… which makes sense.'

'That sound pretty sensible. Unfortunately, *sensible* isn't a word that describes the online coverage our girl is getting.' Emma turned her computer round, so that Nick could see the screen.

'Have you seen the number of headlines and ridiculous

articles about great white sharks that have appeared over the past couple of days? They just want to portray them as 'man killing machines'. It will be a miracle if anyone will want to go near the sea once they've read those.'

Nick quickly scanned through some of the headlines Emma had highlighted and shook his head in disgust.

'We were just discussing that during the meeting. I'm afraid the real facts about these amazing sharks just don't sell papers or get the traffic to their websites to attract the advertisers they need to survive.' Nick started to sound angry, increasingly frustrated by the rubbish he could see that social media sites, in particular, were putting out. 'The fact that great whites have probably been visiting our shores for possibly hundreds of years without any incidents isn't really of interest to them.'

'Perhaps we should put together an article that points out exactly what the facts are.'

'I agree that's what we *should* be doing.' Nick shook his head and started to pace up and down the terrace. 'However, the moronic minister has asked us to leave it to him and his department to deal with the PR side, so my hands are tied. For the time being, anyway. If he hasn't pulled his finger out in the next twenty-four hours, I'll be setting my own agenda. By the way, how are things going with your shark project?'

Emma looked through her computer notes to remind herself how far she had got.

'After a lot of difficulty, I eventually managed to get in touch with Mrs Roberts up in North Wales. To be honest, she wasn't particularly keen to appear in front of the camera. I think I eventually convinced her we'd both be new to it and she agreed to give it a go. She also gave me her daughter's contact details and I've got a phone call planned tomorrow.'

'Well done, that sounds great. How about the boys up in Scotland?'

'Have a look at these,' Emma said as she brought up some emails on her screen and showed them to Nick. 'It looks like they just can't wait to have us all up there again. From what I could tell, everyone wants to hear their stories and they haven't had a moment to themselves in the past few weeks!'

Nick nodded in agreement. 'It will be good to see them all again. Have a word with Jill and Pete and let's get a date in the diary for September when the tourist season slows down a bit.'

'OK, will do. We should get looked after pretty well wherever we go – they said it's the best summer they've had in years.'

As she spoke, the twins rushed onto the terrace.

'Emma, you've got to see this,' Fred said, putting his iPad in front of her. 'Hold on, I'll start it again.'

The video showed a snorkelling diver swimming alongside a huge tiger shark. The diver then reaches out and places her hand on the shark's nose. Instead of pulling away, the shark goes into a state of immobility, just hanging in the water.

'Isn't that amazing?' Emma said watching the screen.

'Yeah, it is,' Fred said. 'How did she do it?'

'Sharks have incredibly sensitive areas all around their heads, but especially just below their snouts.' Emma pointed to the image on the screen. 'Just there. It's full of small electroreceptors called *Ampullae of Lorenzini*, which they use to help them hunt their prey. But they're so sensitive that if they're rubbed, the shark can enter a trance like state. And that is exactly what that lady has done.'

'Wow, Charlie, we could make a shark go to sleep just by touching it.' Fred said staring open mouthed at the screen.

'But we'd have to get in the water with it first,' Charlie replied. 'And I'm definitely not doing that.'

'You would if I pushed you in!' Fred shouted , giving his brother a shove and ran towards the house chased by his twin.

'It's great they're interested,' Emma said and smiled as she watched then disappear through the door.

'Actually, they would have been even more interested if the shark had bitten her arm off.' Nick said.

'Oh God, that's gross,' Emma said, grimacing.

'Yes, that sums them up nicely,' Nick replied. 'Just wait till you've spent a bit more time with them. You'll soon see what I mean!'

CHAPTER EIGHTEEN

MONDAY, 9TH JULY
The Shore Thing,
10 miles off Newquay, Cornwall

On the side deck of *The Shore Thing*, Gary nervously waited for the familiar click, click sound of the reel indicating that a fish had finally taken the bait. It had happened several times in the last half hour, as the line drifted or a fish nibbled at the hooked mackerel. With each click, the suspense level went up another notch.

Andy and Baz tried to help Gary calm his nerves, telling the odd joke, pulling his leg about catching a great white shark, but without success. The waiting was just purgatory for him.

'Fancy a drink?' Baz asked and just as Gary was about to reply, the left hand reel with the line furthest from the boat suddenly start to scream. Gary immediately moved into place and took hold of the rod.

'Right, Gary,' Sean said calmly. 'Just remember what I

told you. Allow the lever drag to strike…you've got it, that's good.'

'OK, let the line fully tighten. Good, that's good. Now, set the hook in the fish's mouth with three sharp jabs of the rod.'

Gary pulled back three times on the rod and felt the pull as the fish fought against the hook. The reel screamed as the fish swam away at pace.

'Remember to keep that rod bent at all times,' Sean shouted, struggling to be heard over the sound of the reel. 'You need to keep the pressure on the fish, but don't be afraid to let it run for a bit.'

For the next fifty minutes, under Sean's careful guidance, Gary fought hard to bring the fish in. Fortunately, he was a big, strong man and managed to keep up with the fish without getting too tired. Both his friends filmed the action on their phones, calling out in support as he slowly won the battle.

'I'm doing my bloody best,' Gary said through gritted teeth. 'He's sure strong, this little bugger.'

Eventually, the fish began to tire and Gary started to bring it closer to the boat. As it surfaced, they could see it was a large blue shark.

'Look at the size of that,' Sean shouted excitedly. 'That's got to be a 100 pounder! Pretty bloody good for your first shark, heh? Okay, take it easy Gary. We don't want it to damage itself banging against the boat.'

Gary reeled the blue shark in very slowly. Both his mates leaned over the side with their phones to get the best picture. Just as they did so, the blue shark burst into life again. A huge shadow suddenly appeared beneath it and erupted through the surface of the water. They watched in amazement as massive jaws wrapped around the blue shark's body. The sea exploded into a mass of foam as a huge shark tossed the blue around from side to side, its teeth scything through the flesh.

Then, without warning, it turned its massive body and dived into the depths, the blue shark still in its mouth.

'Let it run,' Sean screamed. 'Don't fight that, or it'll drag you over the side and under the water. Jesus, I've never seen anything like that before!'

Gary let the reel run but then, after about ten seconds, it stopped. They all stood motionless, waiting to see what might happen next.

'Gary, I think you should just try reeling that in,' Sean said calmly. 'Slowly at first, just in case.'

Gary rotated the reel, gently at first following Sean's advice. And then, as he felt no resistance, he quickened the pace until the float appeared on the surface next to the boat, followed by the blue shark. Or rather, what was left of it.

Sean pulled the line onto the boat and they all stared at what lay on the deck before them.

All that was left was the blue shark's head and the first few inches of its body. The rest had been torn off in the frenzied attack.

Sean broke the silence. 'Well you're never going to forget your first shark, are you Gary?'

Gary was looking down at his catch and turned to look at Sean. He felt disappointed that all his energy had been spent for just the head of a shark. But there again, he thought, that was some contest.

'Well your 100lb blue turned into the hors d'oeuvre for a great white shark,' Sean joked, trying to make Gary feel better. 'Now that's a proper fishing story. You're never going to have arms wide enough to show how big that was!'

CHAPTER NINETEEN

MONDAY, 9TH JULY
Praa Sands Holiday Cabins,
South Cornwall

The journey down to Cornwall had been quicker than expected and they'd arrived at the holiday park shortly after midday. The six days at the resort had been a present from Anne's parents, who'd been staying there the previous week. They'd stayed on at the park till Monday in order to join in the 40th wedding celebrations of friends who lived nearby. Anne didn't care. Anytime away from her job as a care home worker was a blessing. The cabin was amazingly spacious with a stunning view of the bay below.

Mercifully, Rees had slept most of the way down. As a result, he was now bursting with energy and desperate to go to the beach.

In the end, Anne asked Kevin to take Rees to the beach so she could unpack in peace. Kevin had offered to bring all the stuff in from the car, but Anne said,

'No, just leave it to me. Please get Rees out of the way and I'll come down and join you as soon as I'm finished.'

Anne quickly found their swimming costumes in the luggage. Kevin and Rees were ready to head off to the beach with a yellow plastic bucket and spade that Rees' grandparents had left for him. They were about to open the cabin door when Rees said to Anne,

'We'll build a lovely sandcastle for you, Mum.'

Rees walked off with his father, proudly carrying the bucket and spade as Anne stood at the door and reminded them to use plenty of sun cream.

With the boys out of the way, Anne was able to unpack more quickly, and she was soon heading off down the lane to join them. As she reached the beach, she was pleased to see there was a Lifeguard station and relieved to find a café restaurant, so they'd be able to get out of the sun at lunchtime.

The beach was crowded and it took her a few minutes to locate where the boys had left their things. At the moment, though, they were building a sandcastle at the water's edge which the incoming tide then proceeded to wash away. Anne watched adoringly as the large figure of her husband frantically filled the bucket with sand time and again to rebuild the disintegrating walls, while the small figure of her precious boy urged his father to work faster.

She carefully unrolled her mat on the sand, applied factor 50 with care and then lay back to enjoy the sun. After half an hour, she walked down to the shore to admire their handy work.

'Oh that's lovely Rees,' Anne said and looked at her watch. 'Look, it's nearly one o'clock. We need to get you out of the sun for a while. Let's go to the café and get something to eat, shall we?'

'Great, I'm starving,' Rees said but appeared reluctant

to leave the last of the sandcastles to the destructive force of the sea. 'What's going to happen to our sandcastle?'

'You don't need to worry about that,' Kevin said, 'We'll build an even bigger one after lunch. Now, how does sausages, chips and a glass of Coke sound?'

'Brilliant!' Rees shouted and started to run back up the beach. After washing the sand off their feet under the shower at the rear of the beach, they walked over to the restaurant, found a table in the shade and placed their order.

'You did a great job building those sandcastles, Rees,' Anne said.

'It was great!' Rees replied enthusiastically and then remembered what his father had told him the day before. 'But Dad, where's my blow up crocodile boat?'

'I'm afraid it was buried under all the luggage in the back of the car, so I left it for today,' Kevin explained. 'But I'll tell you what, when we get back to the cabin tonight, I'll blow it up so it's ready to bring down to the beach tomorrow morning. How's that sound?'

'Okay. I can't wait to use it tomorrow with those waves.' Rees smiled as a waitress put a large glass of Coke in front of him. Peace was assured, if only for a short time, as he placed the multi coloured paper straw in his mouth and got stuck in.

THEY SPENT the rest of the afternoon creating all sorts of shapes with the sand and running in and out of the water. Rees enjoyed jumping over the incoming waves, shrieking with joy as he did so. By the time they got back to the cabin, it was almost 6 p.m. and Rees was totally exhausted. Kevin gave him his bath whilst Anne made Reece his tea. After tea, Kevin carried his son to bed and started to read to him from his favourite book. Within a few minutes, Rees could no longer keep his eyes open. Kevin bent down, kissed him on the forehead and quietly moved towards the door.

He was just about to turn the handle, a quiet voice behind him said, 'That was the best day ever Dad, but we still didn't blow up the crocodile.'

'I'll make sure it's done before we go to the beach tomorrow. Goodnight son.' And by the time he had closed the door, Rees was asleep.

Kevin walked into the sitting room where Anne was watching the news on the television. 'There's been another sighting of that great white shark off Cornwall,' Anne said.

Kevin sat down next to his wife on the sofa. The reporter explained a shark fisherman had had his catch stolen from the side of his boat by a great white and then warned that the film they were about to see contained scenes that some viewers might find disturbing. The action had been recorded on their phones by the other fishermen and showed the moment when a great white appeared from the depth, and mauled the helpless blue shark.

'You know, I'm so scared by this shark. I'm really worried about you and Rees being in the sea - something might happen to you.'

'Now, come on love. I think you're worrying unnecessarily,' Kevin said in a soft voice. 'Look, Newquay is on the opposite side of Cornwall from us and no shark is going to bother swimming all the way round Land's End just to get us when there are hundreds of beaches within twenty miles of where it was spotted. We're safe here, but if it makes you feel happier, I'll make sure that I don't go out any deeper than my waist. How does that sound?'

'Thanks love,' Anne replied as she cuddled up to her

husband. 'I know it sounds stupid, but I don't know what I'd do if anything happened to either of you.'

'I know, and you can be sure of one thing, I'm not going to let any shark come near our boy.' He put his big arms around Anne and gave her a big hug.

CHAPTER TWENTY

MONDAY, 9TH JULY
Dowrtreven,
Helford River, Cornwall

The excitement surrounding the shark sighting and attack ensured that even the children had joined the adults to watch the report on the six o'clock news.

'Gosh, look at the size of that!' one of the twins exclaimed as they watched the great white tear into the smaller shark. 'That little shark didn't stand a chance. Is that the same great white you saw Emma?'

'We only got a quick look at its dorsal fin during the attack, but I would say it was. Nick, what do you think?'

'I would say it's very likely,' Nick replied, nodding. 'The chances of two great whites turning up in Cornwall are pretty slim.'

'You really don't appreciate the power of a beast like that until you see it in action, filmed close up,' John said, shaking his head in disbelief at what they had all just watched. 'The sheer size of it compared to that blue shark is incredible. They said the blue was what, six feet?' Nick nodded in agreement. 'Well it looked like the great white was just having a bite out of a starter before the main course! I've never seen anything like that.'

'I can promise you, John,' Emma said. 'Seeing that old girl close up for the first time as she slipped under our kayaks was simply breath taking. She's so big it seemed to take her forever to pass underneath. It was just an incredible experience.'

'Weren't you a bit scared?' Milla asked.

Emma leant forward in her chair. 'Honestly, not really - we'd been watching her for quite a long time before she came near us. Being knocked into the water by her was a bit of a shock but, you know, I didn't think for one moment that she might turn and attack me.'

'Well, I hope we don't ever get near her or any shark in the water,' Heli said, screwing up her face. 'Sharks really scare me.'

'I don't think you need to worry about that,' Nick assured her. 'We're a long way from Newquay and, anyway, like nearly all sharks, great whites don't like river water. We'll just go swimming off our own little beach so we don't need to worry about sharks.'

CHAPTER TWENTY-ONE

TUESDAY, 10TH JULY
St Agnes, Cornwall

Kris Clark poured coffee beans into the electric grinder. He pressed down the lid, activating the motor, for eight seconds. Opening the lid carefully to avoid spilling any contents, he smelled the aroma from the freshly ground beans, placed them into a cafetiere and waited for the kettle to boil.

As he looked out the kitchen window onto his small patio garden, he stretched out his arms, and yawned. He ran his fingers through his long, blond hair. Kris, forty-three, had moved to England from his native Australia some fifteen years earlier, long enough now for him to consider this to be his real home. He lived in a small cottage on the edge of St Agnes, a beautiful village on the north coast that many people considered to be the real essence of Cornwall.

His main source of income was as a private tennis coach, working round the year at an exclusive new holiday resort near Newquay. His good looks and tall, athletic build drew him many female admirers, ensuring that his spare time, both day and night, was very limited. But his greatest love of all was surfing, and that was to be his focus on that sunny morning.

A soft bark outside indicated his dog, Ripper, wanted to come back in. He opened the door and his much loved dog ran in, jumped into its basket and sat waiting for his master to call him over. Kris had got Ripper from a dog rehoming centre a couple of years before and they'd become the best of friends. He immediately changed the dog's name from Roger – *what sort of person would call a dog that* - but didn't venture too far from the spoken sound of the name so the change wasn't too confusing. Ripper, a spaniel crossed with god knows what, had taken to the name without a problem, as he also had to Kris' training.

'Another beautiful day in paradise, Ripper. We'd better get off to beach and see what those waves are doing.'

As soon as Ripper heard the word beach, he jumped out of his basket and sprinted to the front door.

'Whoa, my little friend, give me a moment will you?' Kris said as he poured the boiling water from the kettle into the cafetiere.

Twenty minutes later, they climbed into Kris' rather beaten up electric Golf, after he'd attached his surfboard to the custom made roof rack. Ripper took up his usual place on the front seat, head leaning out of the open window, the wind blowing his ears up rather like the classic cartoon character, Dumbo the Elephant.

Although St Agnes had a good surfing beach, it was usually too crowded for Kris' liking at this time of year. To avoid the crowds, he always drove an extra couple of miles south to Chapel Porth beach, owned by the National Trust, which offered great surfing all the year round.

Kris drove down the narrow, winding approach road,

the old tin mine workings visible on the cliffs to the right. Then the view opened up to reveal the bay itself and the car park below. He never failed to be stunned by the sight of the beautiful beach and the sea. In the winter, Kris had to acknowledge it could be a pretty bleak, foreboding place; however, summer was a different story, with the beach coming to life. At high tide, it looked like a travel brochure's perfect Cornish bay with the clear blue water meeting the stretch of fine sand, framed by the backdrop of green of the cliffs. Kris had travelled the world and visited tropical beaches in Fiji and New Zealand. But he had to admit that nowhere came close to Chapel Porth for its dramatic scenery and great surf.

At high tide, not much sand remained visible, but when the tide was out, as now, it exposed miles of golden sands and 'cranking' surf for those with a bit of local knowledge.

Entering the car park, Kris recognised the cars and camper vans of a few regulars, some of whom he could see were already in the water, coaxing their boards over the incoming waves.

'Time to join them,' Kris said to Ripper, and, as he opened his door, the dog leapt out and started to run off towards the beach.

'Ripper, come here,' Kris shouted. The dog stopped and immediately ran back to his side. It waited patiently as his owner pulled on his wet suit, unstrapped the board from the roof and locked the car. The two of them then headed off to the right hand side of the beach, where the waves were always best at this time of day, joining the handful of surfers who were already enjoying the early morning surf.

COLIN AND GAIL WOODHOUSE walked slowly, hand in hand, along the golden sands of Chapel Porth bay. They had both retired two years earlier - Colin a surveyor, Gail an A&E matron - sold their house in York and bought a small, 3-bedroomed Cornish cottage of their dreams. It had the added benefit of only being a ten minute drive from this beach they had now come to love. Everyone 'back home' had told them that they would die of boredom, but, for them, every day had been like a new adventure. Early morning walks had become part of their daily routine, whatever the weather, but the beautiful clear skies of the past few weeks had made it doubly enjoyable. They were very much at ease in each other's company and had the ability to talk to each other about any subject for hours. Today was no different.

They currently found themselves discussing whether they should change the west facing wooden framed windows at the front of the cottage for more weather resilient uPVC. Colin was very much against it – *natural is best* had always been his philosophy in life – but Gail had stressed the practical viewpoint.

'We need to replace them very soon. If we use wood we'll only end up replacing them again in seven years or so. The wind, rain and salt just eat through the wood.'

Colin knew she was right but just wanted to hold his ground for a little longer before giving in, as he always did, to Gail's persuasive point of view.

Fifty metres away, a surfer and his excited, barking dog made their way to the water's edge. They had seen this surfer many times before and had often spoken to him. He had briefly introduced himself as Kris, and told them he'd come over from Australia several years ago. They had also somehow discovered he shared their liking for Indonesian food. His dog, Ripper, was sprinting ahead of Kris into the waves and tearing back out again, impatient for his owner to join him. Kris gave them a wave, shouted a quick 'Hi,' before placing his board into the water and wading into the surf.

As usual, Ripper swam alongside Kris through the first swell, lifting his head as he rode the tops of the waves. In between the peaks, Ripper paddled harder to meet the next wave in his efforts to keep up with his faster moving owner. But then, just as Kris climbed on to his board, Ripper started whining and turned back towards the shore.

'What's up Rip?' Kris shouted. 'Waves too big for you?'

Kris thought it strange because the dog usually stayed in the water until he caught a wave and surfed back into the shallows.

Oh well, he thought, dogs will be dogs, and paddled out another thirty metres. Kris exchanged a quick word of greeting with two other surfers, Rob, a New Zealander and Dan, a local. He then stopped, turning his board towards the shore and waited for the right wave

He didn't have long to wait. An experienced surfer, he was able to read the waves and he spotted one some way out, but swelling nicely. Kris paddled to gain momentum. Then, timing his mount to perfection, he stood up on his board and felt the thrill of the surge as the wave's energy carried him forward. In the short time he rode the wave, he managed to make some good turns. And then, as the shallow water of the shoreline raced to meet him, he jumped off his board only to find Ripper standing at the water's edge, whining and shivering.

'Come on Rip, this isn't like you,' Kris said clapping his hands, trying to encourage the dog back into the water, but Ripper stayed firmly where he was, unwilling to go back into the sea.

'Okay, have it your own way,' Kris said and headed back into the oncoming waves.

'Not so keen to get into the water today?' Gail said, stroking the whimpering dog. 'Oh look at you, poor thing. Don't worry Ripper, he'll be back with you soon.'

But Ripper ignored her attempts to soothe him and stared out to sea, following every move his master made. Colin also watched as the experienced surfer lay on his board and paddled out into the surf.

'That's weird,' Colin said to Gail, who was still stroking the shivering dog. 'I'm sure I just saw…'

CHAPTER TWENTY-TWO

TUESDAY, 10TH JULY
Chapel Porth Bay,
Cornwall

Kris lay on his board, pushing forward with his hands to fight against the incoming surf. Suddenly, he was conscious of a surge through the wake next to his board. He heard a muffled roar as the water exploded. It felt like he'd been hit by a bus. He was lifted clear of the water as a shark's massive jaws clamped down powerfully across his back like a giant vice, crushing him into his board. He felt the agonising pressure on his chest as his ribs were flattened. And, despite the noise of the crashing water all around him, he heard the gruesome sound of the shark's teeth grinding on the underside of the board. He knew that teeth must also be piercing his body, but the agony of his crushed bones masked any other pain.

He was tossed around and shaken violently like a rag doll. The shark dragged him below the surface and held him there for what seemed like a lifetime. Then, suddenly, everything stopped as the shark released its grip. The board rose to the surface with the terrified surfer still on it. As his head broke clear of the water, Kris desperately gasped for life giving air. He managed to look up, scared that the shark might return and continue its attack. If hunger was the shark's primary motivation, then Kris would make an easy meal.

ON THE BEACH, Colin and Gail watched in horror as the shark erupted from the water, taking the surfer and board in its mouth. The power of the strike lifted the surfer and his board clean out of the water before crashing back down. The sea exploded into a mass of foam and cascading water as the huge beast threw Kris and the board from side to side.

'Oh my god, oh my god!' Gail screamed.

Gail's screams were heard by two other surfers. They looked across to see what was happening, one of them, Dan, shouted to his mate.

'It's a shark, it's a fucking shark!'

They both paddled frantically as the shark dragged Kris under the water. As they got within a few metres, the thrashing suddenly stopped as the shark slipped away. They watched in relief as Kris, on his board, miraculously re-appeared on the surface.

I'm alive, I'm bloody well alive, Kris thought as the crushing pain subsided. Somehow, driven by the instinct for self-preservation, he tried to turn the board in order to paddle back towards the shore. Suddenly, the two surfers appeared by his side.

'Jeeez, Kris are you OK?' asked the black haired Kiwi.

Kris grunted. 'Don't worry mate, we'll get you back to dry land.'

Others on the beach rushed forward with Colin to carry the injured surfer well clear of the surf and onto the sand. Ripper desperately tried to get close to his owner. Gail, who had stood paralysed until then, suddenly came to life. She'd spent thirty-five years working in A&E. The shock that had held her in its grip only moments before, disappeared as the calm, professional instincts honed by hours of working on the medical front line, took over. Colin held onto Ripper's collar as Gail knelt down on the sand next to Kris. She took his hand in hers and spoke to him in a clear, professional voice.

'Kris, I'm Gail. We often talk on the beach. I'm an experienced nurse and I'm going to stay with you and help. Do you understand?'

'Yeah,' Kris muttered quietly. His face clearly contorted in pain as he added, 'thank you'.

'Don't worry, you're going to be OK. Right, please can you squeeze the fingers on both hands together for me? That's good. Now can you wiggle your toes? Great. Can you feel both your legs?' Kris whispered that he could. 'Well that's all good,' Gail said. She looked up at the small gathering of horrified onlookers.

'Right, please can someone try to get some blankets and towels as quickly as possible. Col, call 999.'

'On it now,' Colin said. 'Could someone just hold on to Ripper for a moment?' He passed Ripper over to a woman onlooker, and took out his phone.

Gail turned back to the surfer. 'Kris, can you tell me where the pain and discomfort are worst, luv?'

'It's my chest,' and as he spoke, he coughed up small amounts of blood. Gail tried hard to conceal her rising concern.

'Now listen,' Gail said. 'I'm worried that your ribs may be broken and damaging your lungs. I want to try and turn you onto your back so that we can take the pressure off your chest. I know that movement is going to hurt, but it'll help to stop a lot more of that pain you're experiencing. Are you okay if we do that?'

'Yeah,' Kris replied. 'Anything to stop the pain.'

By this time, people had returned with a number of towels and blankets. Gail took the largest blanket and explained to four surfers, who had joined the group, how they were going to feed the blanket gently under Kris' body and turn him.

'I know this is really hard, but can you try to lift the top half of your body first so we get this blanket underneath you. I'll count to three. Okay?'

She completed the count, Kris managed to lift the upper part of his body a couple of inches before collapsing back down as the agonising pain shot through his body. In that short time, Gail and her helpers had pushed enough blanket underneath him to be able to slide it through along the whole length of his body.

'Kris, you were amazing. We're now going to gently roll you over onto your back. It'll hurt for a short time but once it's done, I promise you'll feel a lot more comfortable. Are you ready?' Kris nodded. 'Okay, we'll start now.'

Working together, they were able to lift Kris' body in the blanket just sufficiently off the surfboard and roll him gently onto dry towels and blankets, placed on the sand next to his board.

Kris let out a loud groan but as soon as they had rolled him onto his back, the searing pain in his chest started to subside. The blood that had been collecting inside his wetsuit began to seep out around his neck and from the incisions in the suit made by the shark.

'Did you got through Col?'

He nodded, holding the phone to his ear.

Gail spoke gently to Kris. 'Right, my luv, I'm just going to speak to someone but then I'll be right back.'

Kris lifted a hand in acknowledgement. As Gail stood up, Rob and Dan took her place, kneeling down next to Kris, talking, trying to help distract him from the pain and discomfort he was feeling.

'I'll hand you over to my wife,' Colin said to the emergency call handler, as he passed phone to Gail. She moved a few metres away from the stricken surfer.

'Hi, yes of course, I'm Gail Woodhouse. Until two years ago I was a Band 8 nurse with thirty-five years' experience in A&E. Yes, I've been with him ever since he was carried out of the water. Oh, I would say, ten or so minutes since the attack. His condition? He's suffering from multiple penetrating blunt force traumatic injuries to his back and legs, some serious lacerations to his back, buttocks and thighs but no obvious signs of vascular injury. Probable numerous broken ribs, and a possible traumatic hemopneumothorax. Yes, there could be some serious internal trauma. Look, he's lost a lot of blood and is going into shock. He needs to be in hospital urgently. Yes. That would be excellent. Okay, please call me back on this number. The police? Yes, but I'll let my husband speak to them.' She handed the phone back to Colin.

Gail knelt down next to Kris and took his hand once more. 'It looks like you're going to be taking a quick ride in a helicopter. They're sending the Air Ambulance and estimate it should be with us in about fifteen minutes.'

'Thank you so much,' Kris managed to say, despite the sharp pain in his chest caused by the effort of speaking. 'Where's Ripper?'

Gail smiled and nodded to the woman who'd been

holding Ripper and making a fuss of him. As soon as she released him, Ripper rushed to his owner, and tried to lick his face.

'No Rip, lie down,' Kris said softly. The dog immediately lay down alongside his owner, his face as close as possible to Kris' head.

'Don't worry about Ripper,' Gail said. 'Colin and I will take him home with us and look after him until you're able to do so. I promise he'll get lots of walks on the beach and we'll spoil him rotten.'

Kris smiled at her, whispered a quick 'thankyou' and put his hand out to stroke his adoring dog.

'He knew something wasn't right out there,' Kris said quietly to Gail. 'That's why he wouldn't come in. You tried to tell me didn't you, Rip? If only I'd listened, heh?'

A few minutes later, somebody shouted to announce that the police had arrived and everyone turned to see a car with flashing blue lights pull on to the beach and head towards them.

The police had very soon moved the majority of the onlookers away from where Kris lay. One of the officers bent down to talk to Kris.

'Look, I'm sorry to trouble you sir but could you tell me your name, please?'

'Kris Clark,' he replied softly.

'And do you have a car nearby sir?'

Kris nodded. 'Yeah, it's a beaten up old Golf in the car park.'

'I'm going to need the keys so we can return it to where you live. Can you tell me where you left the keys?'

'They're probably in this,' Dan, the surfer, interrupted, and handing over a small waterproof bag that Kris always carried to the beach.

'That's great, thank you,' the officer said, looking inside

and finding the keys. 'Don't worry Mr Clark, we'll take care of it. Can you just tell me your address please?'

'I know it,' Dan said. The officer stood up and took out a notebook to record the details.

When Dan had finished, Gail approached the officer and explained she would be taking temporary care of his dog. The officer quickly checked that Kris was happy with this and agreed with Gail that she could collect the dog's food and bed.

Colin pointed out the sound of an approaching helicopter. Within a minute it had landed and stood on the firm, damp sand a hundred metres or so from the group. Using some towels, Gail protected Kris from the sand thrown up by the helicopter's blades. She was relieved to find a trauma specialist on board. After a quick talk with Gail and examining Kris' injuries, the specialist inserted both an IV and plasma drip. With the help of a colleague and two of the surfers, he transferred Kris onto a specialised stretcher for the trip to the hospital.

Before Kris was raised into the helicopter, Gail bent down to tell him they would visit him in hospital as soon as they were allowed.

'Thank you for everything,' Kris said, managing a smile for Gail. 'When I'm better, I promise to cook you the best Indonesian meal you've ever tasted.'

'I'll hold you to that,' Gail replied with a smile as the stretcher disappeared into the helicopter.

Colin and Gail kept Ripper as calm as they could when the helicopter took off. Ripper whined the whole time and constantly tried to break away from them to follow the chopper as it flew away.

'No, Rip, you stay here,' Gail said, stroking the dog's ears and chest until they lost sight of the helicopter.

A small crowd of people gathered round Kris' surfboard, staring in amazement at the imprints made by the shark's teeth. Several people were taking pictures on their phones but were soon interrupted by one of the police officers.

'My apologies, ladies and gentlemen,' the officer said, approaching the group. 'I'm afraid I'm going to have to take that board with me.' As he moved closer, he got his first clear view of the damage. 'Oh good lord,' he said, clearly shocked by what he had seen. 'Whatever did that must have been a monster.'

He was about to pick up the board when Kris' fellow surfer, Rob, offered to carry it for the policeman.

'That would be great, thanks. Can you just lean it against the car - I'll sort it out in a minute?'

'No problem,' Rob said and headed off across the beach to the police car.

The officer then approached Gail and Colin. 'My apologies, I didn't introduce myself earlier. I'm PC Tony Mayall. I understand you both were nearby on the beach when Mr. Clark first entered the water and that you witnessed the attack?'

'Ah, that's his name,' Gail said. 'We only knew him as Kris. Yes, that's right, we were standing on the water's edge when the shark struck.'

'OK, thank you,' the policeman replied. 'He was very lucky that someone with your medical skills was here to support him. Thank you very much for all you did until the medical team arrived.'

'That was just one bit of good fortune,' Gail said. 'It was such bad luck to be in the water when that shark swam by. The chances of that happening must have been millions to one.'

'Yeah, you're right,' the officer replied. 'I'd be very grateful if you could give me just a few minutes of your time, so I can get a witness statement from you both. Would that be alright? I don't want to put you out - I can call by your house, if that's okay with you?'

'Of course it is,' Gail said getting a nod of agreement from Colin. 'No problem at all. If we're all going to Kris' house to collect the dog's things, why don't you come straight back afterwards to our house for a cup of tea and we can do it then? We don't live very far away. I've also got some rather nice flapjack I baked last night.'

'And now you've found my weakness! That sounds perfect. I'll just check with my colleague and then we can take Mr. Clark's car to his house and follow you back.'

The officer walked back to the police car where his colleague was talking on the car radio.

Gail and Colin started to make their way over to the car park, constantly encouraging a slightly reluctant Ripper.

'Well, that was a hell of a morning, wasn't it?' Gail said to Colin. 'Not exactly the quiet life we'd planned in retirement.'

'That's a bit of an understatement!' Colin said. 'You were wonderful back there. I'm *so* proud of you.'

'Oh, I've been doing stuff like that for years,' Gail said modestly, but inwardly was glowing with pride. It was reassuring to know that she'd lost none of her innate nursing skills. 'Come on Rip, let's get you home and see if we can find a treat or two for you.'

CHAPTER TWENTY-THREE

WEDNESDAY, 11TH JULY
The English Channel,
South Cornwall

Beneath the surface of the great ocean, the shark had made an epic journey. Moving silently through the water, it had swum for many weeks unseen by man and far from land.

As it swam, it constantly moved its head from side to side, allowing its intricate array of internal senses, evolved over millions of years, to search the water. In this way it was able to detect subtle changes in pressure, adapt to the movements in the current and difference in the balance of the electrical fields.

The warm currents that had helped to carry the shark on its journey for thousands of miles, were now far behind and had been replaced by the colder, darker waters that had become its unfamiliar habitat for so long.

But, slowly. the shark began to sense a change in water

temperature. The flow of the currents was changing to something more familiar, an environment in which it instinctively felt more secure, more aware of its surroundings, more aware of the possibilities of new sources of food.

A second shark was now approaching the coast.

CHAPTER TWENTY-FOUR

WEDNESDAY, 11TH JULY
7.00am, Praa Sands Holiday Cabins,
South Cornwall

The bedroom door burst open as Rees ran in and jumped onto his parent's bed. They both cried out in surprise as the human wrecking ball jumped up and down on the bed, crushing their legs and shouting.

'Come on, Dad, get up. We've got a crocodile boat to blow up.'

Kevin opened one eye to look at the bedside clock and groaned when he saw it was only 7.00a.m. 'So much for the holiday lie in I hoped to get,' he thought.

'Yes, alright, but just be a bit quieter please,' Kevin said softly to his over excited son. 'Let's leave Mummy in bed and go and sort out your boat.'

Kevin climbed out of bed and guided his son through to the living area of the cabin. As he closed the bedroom door, he heard his wife softly murmur, 'Thank you, love.'

The sun was streaming through the large sitting room

window which overlooked the bay. Another gloriously sunny day awaited the visitors to Praa Sands.

By the time they'd unboxed the inflatable crocodile boat and blown it up with the foot pump, Kevin was feeling out of breath. Anne walked into the room and made her way to the kitchen area.

Noticing Kevin's discomfort, she said, 'Looks to me like you're going to have to do some serious training before you can join your mates on the football field next season.'

'Yeah, and lose some weight,' Kevin agreed. 'Perhaps I'll try some water aerobics when we're on the beach. Try and get these muscles toned up.'

'It's going to take a bit more than a few minutes of jumping around in the water,' Anne said with a grin. 'Perhaps you should start running each day?'

Kevin hadn't planned on doing that much exercise while on holiday and searched his mind desperately for a reason to give it a miss. 'Oh, I haven't got my running gear with me,' he said, knowing that it sounded like a feeble excuse. 'No, I'll, um, start with the water aerobics and see how I get on.'

'Whatever you say,' Anne said, starting to fill the kettle. 'It's your body. Now, please would you lay the table and we'll have breakfast together before we head off to the beach.'

'Look at this, Mummy,' Rees shouted, struggling to lift up the inflated boat twice the size he was.

'You're going to have a lot of fun with that today,' Jill enthused. 'Come and sit down at the table, please, and have some breakfast.'

While Rees tucked into his bowl of cereal, Anne quickly checked the weather app on her phone.

'The TV weather lady said last night that today was going

to be another very hot day, possibly twenty-eight degrees. It says here it's already over eighteen degrees, so I think that you're going to have wear a T-shirt in the water today Rees, and your longest shorts. We need to keep you covered up in the sun.'

'That's not fair,' Rees complained.

'If you don't then you won't be going in the sea at all, and there won't be any crocodile rides,' Kevin added. That seemed to end any further rebellion.

'I need to get some things from the shop for tea tonight,' Anne said, walking across to the bedroom. 'So I'll pop down there after breakfast and catch up with you two on the beach. Leave your stuff in the same place as yesterday. Okay?'

'Yes, of course,' Kevin said, starting to clear the table. 'Rees, bring your breakfast things over here and I'll load them in the dishwasher.'

Rees climbed down from his chair, carrying his empty bowl over to his father.

'Now, can we go down to the beach?' the young boy asked.

'Well, we've got to clean our teeth first haven't we?' Kevin said. 'Then we can pack our stuff and head off to the beach.'

'I can't wait to try out my crocodile, Dad. Today's going to be the best.'

'Don't forget, T-shirt and long shorts, Rees,' Anne reminded them from the bedroom.

'I'll make sure he's covered up,' Kevin said, shutting the door on the dishwasher and turning it on.

Fifteen minutes later, father and son were walking down the hill to the beach, each carrying one end of the large inflatable.

'This is my crocodile,' Rees said proudly to an elderly couple they passed on the way down.

'Gosh, he's a big one, isn't he?' the old man said with a smile. 'Just make sure you don't drift out to sea on it, won't you?'

'My dad will look after me' Rees replied confidently and they continued their walk. When they reached the beach, they were surprised to see that not many people had made it on to the sand yet.

'Looks like we're the early birds this morning, heh Rees?' Kevin said and looked at his watch. 'Actually, it's not even 9 o'clock yet so perhaps it's not so surprising.'

They walked past the café and said 'hello' to the two young lifeguards who were setting up their station.

'That's a helluva croc you've got there, mate. Don't go out too far with that, will you? There can be some tricky currents out there and you need to be careful.'

'We'll make sure we stay in the shallows then.' Kevin said, nodding his agreement.

'Okay. Have a great day and make sure you keep that T-shirt on,' the second lifeguard said. 'It's going to be a real hottie here today,'

'Yes, I will.' Rees said with a smile and waved goodbye.

They walked past a St John's Ambulance, parked on the beach. Two volunteers, a young woman and an older man, dressed in smart green overalls, were erecting a flag next to the vehicle. They said a cheery 'good morning' as Kevin and Rees passed by.

'Who are those people?' Rees asked.

'They're St John's Ambulance volunteers. Your Auntie Beth used to be one.'

'What do they do?'

'They help people who may have injured themselves on the beach or have spent too much time in the sun,' Kevin said looking for a suitable place to leave their bags.

'So they're a bit like doctors and nurses?'

'Yes, actually many of them are but they like to help out when they have time off.'

They eventually reached an empty part of the beach close to the spot they had chosen previous day.

'Come on,' Kevin said, 'Let's leave our stuff here and get this crocodile in the water where it belongs.'

CHAPTER TWENTY-FIVE

WEDNESDAY, 11TH JULY
Praa Sands Beach,
South Cornwall

Anne closed the front door of the cabin behind her and carried the shopping through into the kitchen. Once she had put everything away, she quickly tidied the bedroom and got ready to spend the morning on the beach.

The sun shone brightly as she made her way down the steep road to join her family. As she walked onto the sand and turned right towards the beach café, she could see Kevin pulling the crocodile boat through the water. Rees was laughing and shouting encouragement to his father to go faster. She was pleased to see that Kevin was no more than thigh high in the water, as he'd promised. Anne eventually found their pile of bags and clothes, shook out their towels and lay them on the sand.

'Hi Mum,' Rees shouted and Anne waved back. 'Come in, the water's lovely,'

'Yes, in a minute,' she called back as she rubbed sun screen lotion over her arms and legs.

Kevin was clearly having great fun with Rees and the crocodile, running up and down the beach in the shallows. As he ran, he would occasionally tilt the boat enough to make Rees think he might be tipped out, righting it again at the last moment, much to the boy's delight. He also responded to Rees' occasional cries of 'faster, go faster', though he was now beginning to find running through thigh high water more and more tiring. At least he could tell Anne he'd been doing his water aerobics.

He stopped for a moment, grateful for the break. As he rested, he felt something rough rub against his lower leg. Looking down he could see nothing in the sandy water and presumed it must have been a piece of stick or something that the current had carried with it. Then, suddenly, something crashed into his calf, so hard he almost lost his balance. He was immediately aware of a sharp, intense pain. *Jesus, what the hell was that?*

He somehow managed to steady himself using the boat for support. Blood was already beginning to discolour the water. Terrified at what he might find, Kevin reached down under the water to feel the back of his leg. Before he could do so, he was hit again so violently that he was knocked off his feet and flung forwards onto the inflatable. The agonising pain that shot up his leg made him cry out. He looked back anxiously, trying to see what had hit him. He saw a small, triangular fin momentarily break the surface a few metres away

At first Rees laughed. He thought his father was just messing about. But then he saw the shock and agony in his father's face and started to scream. With great difficulty, Kevin gently lifted his right leg out of the water, looked down and groaned. Where his thick calf should have been, all that remained was a hollow surrounded by a tangled mess of blood and flesh.

Oh fuck, oh fuck, he thought as his son threw his arms around his neck crying and screaming.

Then the awful realisation of what must have happened hit him. He knew he needed to stop anyone else getting hurt, especially his beloved son.

'Shark, shark!' he shouted. 'Get out of the water, NOW!'

Both lifeguards reacted immediately, sprinting towards the shoreline and shouting at the other swimmers. At first the other bathers seemed unable to understand what they were being told. When they looked across to where the screaming child and heard father's warnings, the reality of the situation dawned upon them. Panic took over as everyone rushed to get out of the water as fast as possible, grabbing children as they went.

On one leg, Kevin started to try to push the boat towards the safety of the beach. The life guards arrived to help him to the sand. Anne, terrified, ran into the water, grabbed Rees and carried him safely onto the beach and held him tightly in her arms.

The St John's Ambulance crew quickly appeared and produced a waterproof membrane which they placed over the sand. The lifeguards put their shoulders under Kevin's arms and half carried him the short distance before helping him to lie down on the membrane.

'What's your name please sir?' the older St John's volunteer asked.

'Kevin Neal,' he said, grimacing with pain.

'Right, Kevin, my name's Andy and this is Ros. We're going to look after you. okay? Can you just turn over onto your front for a moment? We need to take a look at this wound.'

Despite the shooting pain in his leg, Kevin rolled over. As he did so, he could see Anne, a dozen metres away, holding onto Rees, still crying as he looked at his father. It broke his heart to see his son so upset.

Kevin attempted a reassuring smile through the pain. 'Don't worry, I'll be fine,' he said.

Having examined the wound and washed it clean, Andy asked Ros to call the hospital and tell them they were about to bring in the patient.

'Kevin, you don't need me to tell you that you've got a nasty wound there. The good news is that there's no damage to an artery, so there's not that much blood loss. We can dress the wound safely here. Obviously you need to get to hospital as soon as possible. We'll take you. Is that your wife over there?'

Kevin nodded and Andy raised his hand in acknowledgement to Anne. As soon as he had packed out the wound and bandaged it for protection, he walked over to Anne.

'Hi, I'm Andy and I understand you're Kevin's wife?'

'Yes,' she said quietly. 'I'm Anne and this is Rees.'

'Hi Rees. First thing is, don't worry your daddy is going to be fine but we do need to get him to hospital.' Turning to Anne, he said. 'I think it would be a good idea if you went with him. Do you have anyone to look after Rees?'

Anne shook her head. 'No. We're staying in a cabin up the hill.'

'That's not a problem, you can both come with us in the ambulance. We'll sort out how to get you home later. Now, if you want to get your things together, we'll get Kevin into the ambulance. Alright?'

Anne nodded. She let go of Rees as she stood to her feet and then took his hand.

'I don't want to leave Daddy,' Rees said.

'We're not going to leave Daddy, love. We're just going to pack up our things so that we can go with him in the ambulance.' Anne looked back at the small crowd that had gathered round Kevin. The medics had put him on a stretcher and, with the help of a couple of volunteers, were now carrying him over to the ambulance.

'Come on, love,' Anne said to Rees. 'Let's get a move on. They'll want to head off to the hospital in a minute.'

They were soon in the back of the ambulance with Kevin, Rees hugging him and Anne holding his hand.

'You were right to be worried luv,' Kevin said, smiling at Anne. 'Those sharks are clever devils. Who'd have thought a monster shark could have stayed hidden and attacked me in such shallow water.'

'That's the worry isn't it?' Anne said, grimly.

'Yes, I know,' Kevin replied. 'On the television, they've only been talking about huge great white sharks. No one's been talking about there being another, smaller shark out there that likes the taste of human flesh.'

They looked at each other and hugged their son, both knowing the day could have turned out so much worse than it had.

CHAPTER TWENTY-SIX

WEDNESDAY, 11TH JULY
Dowrtreven, Helford River,
Cornwall

'Dad, you've got to see this,' Milla said as she ran into Nick's office without knocking. 'There's been a shark attack and a surfer's been injured.'

Nick looked up at his daughter. 'What do you mean? Where?'

'Look, I'll show you.' Milla knelt down next to Nick, putting her phone down on his desk. She played him the numerous videos and photos of the incident that had been uploaded already onto social media.

Most were images of the injured surfer, lying on the ground, the police car arriving, followed by the air ambulance. Nick was impressed at the clarity of both the videos and the photos, especially the one that showed the teeth marks on the bottom of the surfboard. He was relieved to see that the surfer was able to stroke his dog and wave to onlookers before being loaded into the helicopter.

'Does it say where this incident occurred?' Nick asked

'Yes, look there – Chapel Porth. Where's that?'

'It's a very pretty bay on the north coast. We went there years ago but you'd have been too young to remember,' Nick said, pointing out the location on the map of Cornwall that hung on his office wall. 'Please can you send a couple of those videos to me. I want to show them to Emma.'

'Of course,' Milla said. 'I'll do it now.'

'Great, thanks.' Nick picked up his own phone and got up to leave the office. 'By the way, have you seen Emma?'

'She's out on the terrace going through some stuff with Jill.'

'Okay. Thank you for bringing me up to date - much appreciated.'

'I keep telling you, that's what social media's for!' Milla teased him as she followed Nick onto the terrace.

'And that's why I've got you to look at everything for me,' Nick replied over his shoulder. He climbed down the steps to the lower terrace where the two women were totally engrossed in whatever was on the laptop's screen.

'Morning, you two,' Nick called out, approaching the table. They looked up briefly

'Nick, have you seen this?' Jill asked.

Nick moved behind them to see what Jill was referring to. It was the same video he'd been watching only a moment before.

'That's exactly what I was coming out to show *you*,' he said and started to smile.

'Well it certainly isn't what we wanted to see, is it?' Emma pointed out, raising her eyebrows.

Nick moved to the other side of the table and sat down opposite them.

'No, you're right there Emma. The proverbial is definitely going to be hitting the fan in the corridors of Whitehall. I'd imagine Mr LeGrand is currently being briefed by some poor, hapless underling.' Nick lent forward in his chair. 'Anyway, I'm not worried about him, I'm more concerned about that poor surfer. Is there an update on his condition yet?'

'Hold on a moment,' Jill said as she typed. 'Yes, there's something on the live news feed. It says the hospital's confirmed that a male patient arrived by air ambulance earlier this morning and is undergoing urgent surgery. But, it's not thought that his injuries are life threatening.'

'That's a relief,' Nick said and turned as Sophie appeared.

'I presume you're all discussing this dreadful attack?' Sophie asked. 'The poor man. How terrifying. It's now almost blanket coverage on the radio and the children are all watching it on the TV.' Sophie put her arms around Nick's shoulders. 'I suppose this means you're going to be involved in another video call soon?'

'Yes, I'm afraid you're probably right,' Nick said, looking down at a new message that had just appeared on his phone. 'Talk of the devil. It's Legrand wanting to know if we can have a video call at 12.00.'

'I'll leave you to it,' Sophie said as she started to walk back to the house. Suddenly remembering something, she stopped. 'Just one last thing. I spoke to Bella Stoddard earlier and she, Jamie and the children are coming over on Friday afternoon for a late swim and a BBQ. Hope that's alright?'

'Yes, absolutely. Looking forward to it. There'll certainly be plenty for us to talk about with the Rt. Honourable!'

As Sophie moved away, Emma looked at her phone.

'You need to get that government PR machine in action pretty quickly,' she said to Nick. 'Every awful headline you could imagine, using the worst possible metaphors, is appearing everywhere. I'm afraid that the *Grim Reaper* tag is getting particularly overused.'

Nick shrugged his shoulders. 'Unfortunately, something like this just brings out the worst in journalists. They all seem to resort to the laziest, thoughtless writing that you can imagine. I've seen it so many times before that I've given up worrying anymore.'

'What's up?' Pete said, appearing up the steps from the beach where he had been working on the rib's outboard engine. 'You all look utterly miserable. What's happened?'

'I'm sorry to say there's been a shark attack on a surfer,' Nick explained.

'Oh bloody hell. Are they alright?' Pete asked and the others nodded. 'I presume our old girl is involved?'

Pete sat down as Emma replied. 'Yes, it's almost certainly her, which isn't good news.'

'I suppose some tough restrictions will have to be put in place now, Nick?' Jill asked.

'Well, they were talking about just putting patrols around the main beaches and limiting how far people can swim out for the time being,' Nick said shaking his head. 'But now they've seen the reality of what can happen when sharks interact with humans, they may start to think differently.'

'That doesn't sound great for all those poor holiday makers, does it?' Pete said. 'Bloody glad I don't have to make that decision.' He stood up and gave Nick a discreet wink and a smile as he walked on his way to the house to wash his oily hands.

Jill laughed and then said to Pete's retreating figure. 'It's alright for some people whose only responsibility is fixing an outboard motor.'

A moment later, they were interrupted by a shout from the house.

'You lot, come and see this!' It was Pete, shouting from the sitting room doorway. 'There's been another shark attack.'

They all rushed over to the house and, as they entered the sitting room, could hear a female reporter on the television.

'…victim is a male, believed to be in his thirties. The attack happened here in the picturesque Praa Sands Bay. The victim was apparently pushing his young son through the shallows on an inflatable boat when, what was thought to be a small shark, attacked him from behind. We understand the shark struck the victim twice, biting flesh from his calf and causing a serious injury. Despite the injury, the man was able to stagger to the beach, where the wound was treated by experienced St John's Ambulance staff who happened to be in attendance. They transferred him by ambulance to the Royal Cornwall Hospital in Truro for further treatment. He was accompanied by his young son, who was fortunately unharmed in the attack, and his wife. The Royal Cornwall is where this morning's other shark victim was taken to. We hope to have further news on both patients' progress in the later bulletin. This is Gilly Bancroft, reporting from Praa Sands, South Cornwall for South West news'.

The screen then returned to the studio presenter. 'In other news…'

'That is just unbelievable,' Nick said staring in disbelief at the television. 'There are no reported injuries caused by sharks for decades and then two in one day. What the hell is happening?'

'The question is, what sort of shark could have made this attack?' Jill said, looking at Nick. 'If nobody actually saw a shark, could it possibly have been something else like, I don't know, a conger eel for instance?'

'No, I think we can exclude congers because they prefer deeper water,' Nick said as he walked over to the window and stared out. 'The strange thing is that this has all the hallmarks of a bull shark attack but what would one of those be doing in British waters?'

'More likely to have been a small mako or possibly a blue then?' Pete suggested.

Nick turned round, his back to the window. 'I think you're probably right Pete. The problem is that we've now got two coastlines that we need to worry about. This advisory group meeting's going to be fun!'

CHAPTER TWENTY-SEVEN

WEDNESDAY, 11TH JULY
10, Downing Street,
London

The PPS knocked gently on the large mahogany door before entering.

'Prime Minister. Sorry to disturb you, but I know you wanted to be updated on the situation with the shark off the Cornish coast.'

'Yes, absolutely,' the Prime Minster replied. He was still regarded as a handsome man despite being in his late sixties, but the lines on his face betrayed the rigours of his office.

'Well, I'm sorry to report there's been another attack, but this time on the south Cornwall coast.'

'What? A second attack on the same day?' the PM exclaimed loudly, taking off his glasses and stared at the rather reticent PPS.

'It would appear that a male holiday maker was

attacked in shallow water, suffering severe damage to his calf. He's being treated in hospital as we speak.'

'In shallow water?' the PM said and thought for a moment. 'So this has nothing to do with the monster on the north coast then?'

'It would appear not, sir.'

'Please get me the Secretary of State for Transport on the phone.'

'Of course, sir,' the PPS replied, slipping quietly out of the room.

THE PHONE on the PM's desk rang. He picked up the receiver and heard his PPS say, 'Secretary of State for Transport on the line, sir.'

'Thank you, put him through. Ah, Jamie, sorry to interrupt your stay in your Cornish idyll but we seem to have a growing problem with selachimorpha.'

'Sorry, Prime Minister. With what?'

'Selachimorpha – it's the Latin name for sharks. Didn't they teach you classics at your establishment?' the PM asked, smiling as he leant back in his chair and put his feet up on the desk.

'I am delighted to be able to say I gave up classics when I left prep school, Prime Minister,' Jamie said. 'The answer to your question is obviously, yes, we do appear to have a problem. I presume you're referring to the second attack this morning?'

'I certainly am Jamie and I always start to worry when there is a possibility of humans being injured.' The PM picked up a retractable biro and began to click the top up and down impatiently. 'Please can you tell me what you intend to do about this.'

'Hopefully, you will have seen the memo I sent through last week outlining our possible courses of action.'

'Unfortunately, last week, a potential shark problem didn't feature on the top ten list of national and international emergencies, so I doubt it.' The PM swung his feet off the desk and stared out of the window overlooking the garden. 'Bring me up to date.'

'I've set up an Emergency Advisory Committee including, on the operational side, the head of Devon and Cornwall police, the CEO of the Coastguard and RNLI. On the advisory side we've got Professor Andrew Wallace and also Nick Martin, who, I'm sure you know, is also an expert on sharks.'

'Yes, I've met both Wallace and Martin. Two good men to have on your side.'

'I agree. I've also appointed Nigel Legrand to chair the committee and to take on day to day responsibility for what happens both on land and at sea.'

'Excellent choice,' the PM said, and stood up, wandering round the room with the remote handset. 'So what are the next steps?'

'Well, obviously, we're going to have to restrict access to the beaches and water to a certain extent.'

That stopped the PM in his tracks. 'Be very careful about that Jamie. We don't want to upset either the locals or the holidaymakers with an election not too far away. The south west could be key for us.'

'I do understand that, Prime Minister, and I'll emphasise the point to Nigel Legrand for consideration. He's chairing the online Advisory Committee meeting at 12 o'clock.'

'Good,' the PM stood silently for a moment allowing the gravity of the situation to sink in, before adding. 'Please can you send me through, for prior approval, a summary of the measures that the committee proposes. I want look at them in detail before they are actioned. I fully appreciate that people's safety must come first, but there are other considerations that come in to play.'

'Yes, of course, Prime Minister. I'll get something across to you early this afternoon.'

CHAPTER TWENTY-EIGHT

WEDNESDAY, 11TH JULY
Nick's Office, Dowrtreven,
Helford River, Cornwall

Nick clicked on the button and joined the video conference. He was greeted by the unwelcome sight of Nigel LeGrand's face filling the screen.

'Good afternoon,' Nigel Legrand's voice boomed out from the monitor on Nick's desk. 'I think we have everyone with us now. Minister are you there?'

Jamie raised his hand in acknowledgement in the bottom corner of the screen

'Yes, good, shall we continue? Well, things appear to have moved on apace since our last meeting. Not one but two shark attacks in one day, no less. Let's deal with the attack earlier this morning on the surfer. I seem to recall, following the guidance given to us by our two *expert* advisors, we concluded there was nothing to worry about and that the great white presented no risk. Well how wrong was that?' Legrand leant in towards his camera in a slightly menacing way. 'Professor Wallace, would you care to explain how you got it so wrong?'

Silence.

'Professor did you hear me?' LeGrand said aggressively.

'Yes I did,' Andrew Wallace replied.

'In that case, would you...'

'No.'

'Could you explain why not, please?'

'I'm waiting,' Andrew said brusquely.

'Sorry, waiting for what, exactly?'

'Waiting for your apology, *exactly*.'

'For *my* apology?' LeGrand said.

'Yes and also for your apology to Nick Martin.'

'Apology for what?'

'Let me explain, since you clearly don't understand,' Andrew said, warming to the task. 'When *your* boss, the Secretary of State, invited me to be part of this committee, it was, as I understood it, purely on a voluntary, advisory basis. Am I correct Minister?'

'Yes, that is correct,' Jamie confirmed, moving towards his camera, obviously amused by the interaction he was watching.

'The information I presented to the committee dealt with the historical incidence of shark attacks across the world. Similarly, Nick correctly described the pattern of behaviour of this shark that we, in the UK, had seen up to that time. When you asked him if the shark represented a danger to the public, all he said was that the shark had been tracked off the US for a number of years and that the people over there had no record, at all, of this shark interacting in a threatening or dangerous manner. Or, for that matter, showing any behavioural traits that would lead them to conclude that she represented a danger.'

The other attendees looked on, fascinated by what was unfolding in front of them.

Andrew Wallace continued. 'It was actually *you*, Mr LeGrand, who concluded that the shark was not a danger to the UK public. At no time did either of us suggest that to be the case. We are not being paid for our advice and we are thus not here in a professional capacity. Therefore, both Nick and I expect an apology from you for maligning us in front of the other members of the committee and for suggesting *we* were at fault when it was *you* that made the incorrect inference.'

LeGrand was clearly unaccustomed to being challenged in this way.

'We are waiting,' Andrew said, staring intently into the camera. 'If I don't hear your apology in the next ten seconds, I will walk away from this meeting. And, believe me, you will not want to hear what I shall have to say to my contacts in the press about the way I was treated.'

LeGrand looked apoplectic with anger.

'Five seconds.'

Jamie Stoddard interrupted. 'Nigel, please apologise.'

Silence.

'Nigel, I won't ask again,' Jamie said firmly.

LeGrand looked everywhere but at the screen as he whispered through gritted teeth, 'I apologise.'

Andrew and Nick smiled inwardly but were brought back to reality by the firm voice that came through their speakers.

'Right, let's get this meeting back on track,' Jamie said, decisively. 'I'll take the chair for the rest of this meeting. I think it's obvious to us all that we need to take swift action to ensure that no further lives are endangered.'

All the participants muttered their agreement.

Jamie paused, checked his notes and continued. 'First of

all though, I think we need a better understanding of the potential threats. Andrew, I think this is an area that you have done a lot of work on. Please could you give us your thoughts about what behavioural changes might have brought about the attack on the surfer by the great white?'

'Of course. I'd be delighted,' Andrew said leaning back in his chair as if in deep thought. Then, with a mannerism familiar to those who knew him well, he lifted his glasses from his forehead and absent-mindedly placed the tip of the arm in his mouth before continuing.

'Mistaken identity is frequently cited by the media to explain shark attacks on humans; however, it's now thought to be just as probable that such human-shark interactions are the result of a shark's curiosity. Considering the majority of attacks on humans are hit and run, i.e. non-predatory, it seems unlikely that the surfer was mistaken for a potential meal. Many ichthyologists…'

'What's an ichthyologist?' Jamie asked.

'Sorry - someone like me who studies fish,' Andrew responded, momentarily caught out. 'As I was saying, many ichthyologists consider that because sharks don't have hands, they use their highly dextrous jaws and sensitive teeth and gums as a substitute. Unfortunately for us, humans have a high density of blood vessels very close to the skin, so an investigatory bite that would do little more than wound a seal, can have considerably more distressing results for a human. '

Andrew surveyed the faces of the other participants on his screen. He was pleased to see they were all listening intently.

'This theory is borne out by what happened this morning. The shark hit the surfer hard with an investigatory bite, realised that the texture of the board didn't match its memory experience of what constituted edible prey, and let go.'

'Can I just add something to Andrew's assessment?' Nick said. 'The time of the attack is also important – sharks tend to hunt for their prey in the hours just after dawn and those preceding sunset. The attack on the surfer was early morning and, in fact, the Praa Sands attack was also pretty early. I think we should take this into account when considering what action to take.'

'Good point,' Jamie said. 'Andrew, thanks for your analysis. It's obvious that the second attack at Praa Sands was by a very different fish from the great white that has been worrying us so far. Nick, can I ask for your thoughts on what kind of shark we may be talking about in this case?'

'Yes, of course, Jamie,' Nick replied using the Minister's forename, deliberately emphasising his close relationship with him and hopefully upsetting LeGrand even further.

'I actually discussed this in a brief phone call I had with Andrew before the meeting, and interestingly, found we'd independently reached the same verdict. Namely, if this attack had occurred off the US or African coasts, we would have concluded from the nature of the attack, i.e. in shallow water, that it had almost certainly been carried out by a bull shark. Unfortunately,' Nick paused for effect, 'since bull sharks have not been found within thousands of miles of our shoreline, we must consider other possibilities.' Nick continued. 'The problem we have is that only a few sharks are potentially dangerous to humans. Until now, none of the, has ever been reported in British waters. There's also only been one unprovoked shark bite in British waters since records began in 1847, and that was in 2022. And that was in deep water off Penzance. So we must work with the species we know to be here.'

'And what do we know?' Jamie asked.

'Well, after a great deal of consideration, I think there are two likely possibilities. Most sharks found in our waters are pelagic, in other words, they prefer deep water. Of those that have been spotted in British shallow waters, the Blue shark and the Nursehound Shark, perhaps better known as the spotted dogfish, are the two I would suggest. But, as Andrew said, to our knowledge, no one has ever been attacked or bitten in British *shallow* waters by either of them so, until we have better evidence, I'm afraid this is just speculation. Sorry not to be able to given a more specific answer.'

'I completely agree with Nick's assessment,' Andrew said. 'But I must emphasise that just because we have no past experience of this sort of incident, it doesn't mean that the recent attacks won't be repeated, so we must plan accordingly.'

'Thank you both for your frank appraisals of both incidents,' Jamie, said nodding his thanks at the camera. 'Now, I need to inform you all that I had a phone call from the Prime Minister, only an hour ago, and he's taking a personal interest in the decisions we reach today.' LeGrand's expression suddenly changed from sullen distraction to serious interest. 'In fact, he told me that *nothing* is to be done without his prior approval. I, therefore, have to send over a summary of our intended measures straight after this meeting. I trust that we will get an immediate response so that we can then brief the news services for their evening broadcast. These can then be implemented from tomorrow first thing.'

'In that case,' Nick said, 'I suggest that Peter Williams from the Coastguard Agency quickly recaps the proposals he put forward at our last meeting. It seems to me that they comprehensively cover the immediate situation in north Cornwall and, with a few small adjustments, can also be adapted to the new development on the south coast.'

'I think that's an excellent suggestion,' Jamie said. 'Peter, could you remind us of the proposals?'

The expression on the Coastguard's CEO's face showed that he was clearly gratified to have his ideas given support from such distinguished members of the Committee.

'Thank you for giving me the opportunity to revisit my proposals,' he said and he once again launched into a presentation on the measures that were about to affect the lives and holidays of hundreds of thousands of tourists to the region.

CHAPTER TWENTY-NINE

WEDNESDAY, 11TH JULY
Department for Transport,
London

The announcement of the restrictive measures was made, in person, by Nigel LeGrand on the steps of the Department for Transport building in London. It was also released simultaneously to the news and wire services.

LeGrand was surrounded by TV cameras, reporters and freelance photographers whose whirring camera motors provided the soundtrack for his announcement. After a brief introduction, he thanked all the members of the Advisory Committee (at Jamie's insistence) for their expert help and advice. He emphasised the importance of safety for implementing the restrictions with the priority on the prevention of endangerment to life.

He then moved onto the measures themselves.

'From midnight tonight, all beaches within twenty miles of Newquay on the north coast of Cornwall will be closed to the public *before* the hours of 9 a.m. and after 6 p.m. We have been informed by experts in this field that the hours of closure are those during which sharks prefer to search for their prey and are therefore more likely to come into contact with humans. *Between* the hours of 9 a.m. and 6 p.m., those who wish to swim, use inflatables, or partake in any water based activities must do so *within* 20 metres of the shoreline. We regret this will, in all probability, preclude those wishing to surf in these particular waters. Those wishing to launch any powered craft from these beaches, for example, speedboats, dinghies or jet skis, will not be permitted to do so.'

He paused for effect, and looked out across the gathered entourage. Fifty cameras immediately clicked away. This was *his* moment in the national spotlight and he was going to make the most of it. The journalists merely bristled against the man's arrogance.

'In order to ensure these measures are enforced, police patrols will be put in place on all major beaches in the defined areas. These will not only involve officers in cars and on foot, but they will also be supported by boats, ribs and hover-skis operated by the police themselves, the Coastguard Agency and the RNLI. Drones will also be employed, not only to help to ensure the restrictions are observed on smaller and less accessible beaches, but also for spotting any possible signs of a shark approaching a beach.'

He paused for effect once more. This time the journalists groaned audibly.

'The same restrictions will also apply to a defined area on the south coast of Cornwall. In terms of the area to be covered this will be for a distance of twenty coastal miles from Praa Sands, where this morning's attack took place. However, there is one further difference. Due to the nature of that particular attack, i.e. in relatively shallow waters, the restriction for venturing from the shoreline will be limited to ten metres only.'

A car drove past honking its horn. The passenger opened his window and screamed 'wanker' at LeGrand. The assembled press were all highly amused. LeGrand, however, remained unmoved. It would take more than this to burst his bubble of pomposity.

'Full details of the restrictions, together with maps delineating the exact parts of the coastlines covered by these, have been released across all the normal channels to ensure ease of access for media and the public alike. Signage will be put in place overnight to keep locals and visitors informed, and announcements will also be made on both national and local television and radio. There will be no excuses for people to breach these restrictions. Does anyone have any questions?'

A female reporter at the front got her question in quickly. 'Minister, please can you tell us what punishments are in place for those who breach these new rules?'

LeGrand's chest puffed out as far as his waistcoat would allow. 'The full weight of the law will be brought to bear upon any transgressors,' he said, fixing the questioner with a steely stare. 'There are already numerous sanctions available under existing legislation and bye laws, ranging from community service to heavy fines and even imprisonment for repeat offenders. Who knows,' he said, a crooked smile appearing on his face. 'The ultimate sanction may be applied by Mother Nature herself in the form of a bite from a curious shark.'

This attempt at levity drew mutters of disbelief from the journalists. It seemed inappropriate that the minister should make light of the subject when victims lay seriously injured in hospital. Their reaction took LeGrand aback. He studied their faces and it suddenly dawned on LeGrand that he had spoken unwisely.

'Minister, please can you explain why you couldn't be

bothered to travel down to the south west of England to make this announcement to the people affected instead of appearing to issue a proclamation from London to the *poor* people in Cornwall.'

All eyes turned towards LeGrand who could *feel* their eyes upon him. He stared out across the faces, desperately searching for a quick response or witty put down. But for once in his political life, nothing came to mind. LeGrand's thick veneer of confidence was beginning to be pierced as he started to realise that responsibility came at a very heavy personal cost.

CHAPTER THIRTY

THURSDAY, 12TH JULY
Great Western Beach,
Newquay, Cornwall

'Good morning sir,' PC 'Mack' Mackay said to the middle aged man walking his dog on the beach. 'Would you mind explaining to me exactly which part of the sign "**No Entry – Beach Closed 6.p.m. - 9 a.m**." you didn't think applied to you?'

'Well, I'm a local and I walk my dog here every morning,' the man replied indignantly. 'I thought those signs were just to stop the holidaymakers from entering the beach.'

'Well sir, I'm sorry to burst your own personal bubble of exclusivity, but these rules apply to everyone. So, since it isn't 9 o'clock yet, please can you leave the beach immediately by the closest exit,'

'But can't I just walk to the far end of the beach and leave there?' the man pointed to the steps concerned.

'You can, of course do that sir,' the policeman said in a calm voice. 'However, if you choose to do so, then I will be obliged to take you into custody and it would then be up to the magistrates to decide your fate. Your choice sir but I know which option I'd prefer.'

'I don't know what this country's coming to,' the dog walker muttered to himself as he headed for the nearest steps. 'Bloody nanny state. A man isn't allowed to think for himself anymore.'

Mack smiled as the dog walker continued to mumble to himself and headed towards the nearest exit. He looked up as, further along the beach, a police Land Rover towed an orange rib down the slipway, shortly followed by another vehicle with a Lifeguards' jet ski in tow.

Mack watched the cars drive two hundred metres across the beach to the shoreline, where the tide was now on the turn, the waves starting to increase in height. He walked over to his colleagues and exchanged greetings as they prepared the sea craft for launch.

'Lovely day to go playing around on the water, Mick,' he joked to one of his mates who was untying the ropes that secured the rib to the trailer.

'Not so good when the temperature's going to hit twenty-eight degrees and we have to wear all this ridiculous survival gear,' Mick replied. 'Elf n' Safety gone bloody mad if you ask me.'

'You sound just like the bloke I had to turf off the beach a few minutes ago. His problem was he didn't think the new restrictions applied to locals!'

'Yeah, I can imagine. I reckon we're going to spend most of our day turning back people and reminding them about the rules. It's amazing how once they get in the water, all concept of distance disappears. I bet we'll be so busy that the bloody shark could swim right behind us and we wouldn't even notice it!'

'Don't expect any sympathy from me mate. I've got to

work an extra shift today, so I won't get away until seven tonight. No doubt the most exciting thing that will happen to me will be telling people where the toilets are!'

'Mr Cardy, Mr Mackay. Nice to see you again.'

The two policemen turned round as a tall, athletic, younger man approached them from the jet ski trailer.

'Sorry, I should have introduced myself. I'm Sam Moyle. I was at school with your two boys.'

'Well damn me, Sam. Sorry we didn't recognise you immediately, but you've grown a bit since we last saw you!' Mick said with a huge smile. 'What have you been doing with yourself for the last few years?'

'Well, I've just finished my engineering degree at Southampton Uni and I start a new job with an aerospace company in September.'

'Good on you. You always were one of the bright ones,' Mack said. 'And you've certainly taken after your dad. He's a big fella and I think you're even bigger. We had some good times on and off the rugby field with your dad, didn't we Mick?'

Mick laughed and nodded in agreement

'Did you know he's still playing?' Sam said. 'Only for the 5th XV now mind, but he still manages to get into trouble.'

'He was always a hard bastard. I remember club training nights. No one wanted to be tackled by him,' Mack said shaking his head. 'Bloody good bloke though, and he would always look after his mates. So what are you doing here?'

'I'm a trained lifeguard and I've also got my jet ski licence, so they want me out there patrolling and supporting you lot.' Sam delved into the pocket of his shorts. 'They've also given me this radio so I can keep in touch with you. Do you have a couple of minutes to show me how it works, Mr.

Cardy? Perhaps you should also tell me what you would like me to do?'

'My pleasure, Sam. We're delighted to have you on board,' Mack said. They all looked up as loud voices reached them across the sand.

'Well Mack, it looks to me as if the masses have decided it's time to invade the beach,' Mick said with a huge grin on his face

Mack watched as dozens of holidaymakers hurried down onto the beach to select their favourite spots. He groaned at the sight. His day had really begun in earnest.

CHAPTER THIRTY-ONE

THURSDAY, 12TH JULY
Dowrtreven,
Helford River, Cornwall

Nick's phone rang as he was going through his diary for the next few months with Jill. It was Jamie Stoddard.

'Morning, Jamie. That was a bit of fun yesterday.'

'Hmm, that's why I'm calling - to apologise for LeGrand's behaviour,' Jamie said. 'He really doesn't have a clue of how to relate to people. I hope that you and Andrew weren't too upset by him.'

Nick walked out onto the terrace.

'Not at all. In fact Andrew only pretended to be offended just to make LeGrand feel uncomfortable. I sat back and enjoyed what I was watching. Anyway, LeGrand got his comeuppance during the announcement, didn't he?'

Nick could hear Jamie laughing at the other end.

'Well that's for sure,' Jamie said. 'I was actually very happy to let him do the announcement because I knew it was going to be really unpopular. I have to admit I also secretly hoped that he would make a mess of it. And he did - big time. Have you seen the hilarious photograph they've used in all the papers? They caught the expression on his face when he was asked why he was making the announcement in London not Cornwall? He looks as though he has just trodden on a dog turd!'

It was Nick's turn to laugh.

'By the way, have you heard how the restrictions are going down on the beaches?'

'Actually, the early feedback we're getting is pretty positive,' Jamie said. 'There are always a few people who will always try to push the limits, but, generally speaking, people are acting pretty responsibly.'

'I think the pictures posted on the internet of the injured surfer and the huge wound on the second victim's leg, have helped people realise that there's a serious point to all this.' Nick bent down as Molly wandered up from the river and rubbed up against his leg. 'Urrgh, you're soaking wet, you horrible animal,' Nick said pushing Molly away.

'That's a bit harsh. Being called wet is one thing but…'

'Sorry, Jamie! Wet dog.'

'Ahh, dear Molly. Well, I'm looking forward to a relaxing afternoon with you and the family tomorrow. I think Sophie said around 4.30?'

'Come whenever you want. We're just going to do a simple BBQ for us and the kids.'

'If Pete has anything to do with it, there'll be nothing simple about it. I bet there'll be numerous sauces and meat that's been marinaded in the spiciest mixes you can imagine. Not complaining, by the way. The hotter the better for me.'

'Be careful what you wish for!' Nick warned as the minister ended the call.

CHAPTER THIRTY-TWO

THURSDAY, 12TH JULY
Royal Cornwall Hospital,
Truro, Cornwall

Colin and Gail Woodhouse arrived at the hospital unsure on which ward they would find Kris and whether they would be able to see him. However, Gail's nursing experience enabled her to start the search with confidence.

'Col, it's probably best if you wait outside while I try and find out where Kris is,' she said as they approached the A&E department.

'Good idea,' Colin said. 'I'll see you out here when you've found out'.

Gail felt a warm glow of familiarity as she entered A&E and approached the reception counter.

'I'm sorry to trouble you,' Gail said politely. 'But I wonder if you could tell me on which ward I'll be able to find the shark victim. He arrived yesterday by air ambulance, please?'

The receptionist's expression turned more serious. She told Gail to wait a minute and then disappeared into the room behind her.

After a minute, a blue uniformed nurse walked briskly out the office and into the reception to talk to Gail.

'Good morning,' the nurse said in a very serious tone. 'I'm the Senior Clinical Nurse here. How can I help you?'

'And good morning to you matron,' Gail said smiling broadly. 'I'm always delighted to meet a fellow nurse. I recently retired after thirty years working in A&E so I fully appreciate the work that you do here.'

The matron's demeanour softened and she broke into a smile. 'Well thank you and I hope enjoying your retirement. I understand that you're trying to find out about the shark attack victim?'

'Yes that's right. I was on the beach yesterday and I actually saw the attack. I then did the best I could to stabilise the poor man until the doctor arrived on the helicopter.'

'Oh, that was *you*!' the matron said. 'When they wheeled him in, the chopper boys explained he was lucky to get good initial care on the beach. That definitely made our job easier.'

'I'm afraid there wasn't much I could do in the circumstances. Anyway, how is he?'

'I understand that he's doing pretty well. We had to do a minor procedure for the hemopneumothorax, but he's responded well and hopefully will have no further complications. The main problem we had were the multiple lacerations. Some were really deep, but amazingly there was no major internal trauma. We also had that second shark attack victim brought in here. Not the same extent of injury but still very unpleasant. Both of them are very lucky men.'

'Or very unlucky men, depending on how you look at

it!' They both smiled. 'I've got my husband with me. He helped out on the beach as well. Is there a chance that we could have a couple of minutes with Kris – we're also looking after his dog, Ripper, for him and I'm sure he would like to know how his furry friend is getting on.'

'Let me see what I can do,' the matron said and went back into the office.

After a couple of minutes she returned with a warm smile. 'Good news. They're going to let you see him for just a short while. Go back outside, walk down to the next entrance on your left and then you'll see the signs for the ICU. When you get there, tell them Helen from A&E sent you. Look, I'm sorry for my frostiness when you first came in, but we've had lots of journalists creeping around and I was worried that you might be one as well. Couldn't have been more wrong, could I?'

Gail reached out and touched the matron on her arm. 'Oh don't worry. I'd have done the just the same thing in my time. Thanks for all your help Helen.'

'Not at all. It's been a pleasure to meet you.'

Gail and Colin made their way to the Intensive Care Unit and introduced themselves to the staff at the nurses' station, mentioning Helen's name.

'Ah yes, you're here to see our shark man,' the sister said. 'Officially you're outside visiting times, but I think we can make a special case for you. I must warn you that he's got a chest tube thoracostomy inserted so speaking isn't very comfortable for him.'

'Sorry, what's a chest tube thoracostomy, please?' Colin asked.

'Simply put,' the sister explained, 'it's a plastic tube that's inserted between the ribs into the area around the lungs. It drains off the air and blood that might leak out due to the perforation of his lung. Right, you can spend a short time with him but don't expect too much verbal response, okay?'

'Thank you very much,' Gail said. 'Don't worry, we'll do the talking and we won't stay long, I promise.'

'In that case, let's go through.'

There were ten beds in total on the ward but only six were occupied. Kris was in the furthest bed on the right. Colin was momentarily taken aback by the number of tubes and attachments that seemed to emerge from his body. Kris had his eyes closed but as they approached he opened them and turned to see who was there.

'Hello, Kris love,' Gail said. 'You look a bit different from when we last saw you.' Kris managed slowly to lift a hand in greeting and was about to speak, but Gail cut him short.

'No, don't say anything. We know how uncomfortable it must be for you. We just wanted to drop by and let you know that Ripper's settled in and made the house his own already.' Kris smiled and raised his eyebrows to indicate he understood what Gail meant. 'But there's one thing I bet you're not aware of – he loves cats. We've got an old Siamese who's seen it all, but I was amazed that she and Rip just accepted each other immediately.'

'I actually found them cuddling up together, asleep in Rip's bed when I went down this morning,' Colin added. 'I don't think I've ever seen such an immediate bond before. Quite extraordinary.'

Kris shook his head in disbelief. He motioned Gail to lean into him and whispered, 'He always chases cats, if any come in the garden.'

'Well, he might still do that with Simba because they haven't been outside together yet,' Gail said. 'We took him for a walk along Chapel Porth beach this morning. Understandably, he hasn't been his normal exuberant self but he was alright until we got to the spot where you were pulled out of the water. Do you know, he just stood there, perfectly still, looking at the sand and whimpering? We just let him stand there for a minute or so and then he suddenly sprinted off towards the sea and leapt into the surf. He must have played around in the sea for, what do you think Col, at least ten minutes?' Colin nodded. 'He was running in and out and swimming quite a distance away from the beach. I was a bit worried, but when he finally came out he seemed like a different dog, wagging his tail and wanting to play. It was almost as if he had gone through some therapeutic process and come out the other side.'

Kris smiled and mouthed 'thank you for everything'. Gail noticed he was struggling to keep his eyes open.

'Kris, we're going to let you get some rest. Don't worry about Ripper, he's welcome to stay as long as needs be. We also wanted to tell you that, when they let you out of hospital, we'd be delighted if you'd come and stay with us for a few days until you're back on your feet again. Anyway, have a think about it. Right, Col, let's be off. You get plenty of rest. And do what those nurses tell you. They really do know what they're talking about.'

Kris whispered, 'Thank you both,' raised his hand and waved goodbye.

As they passed the nurses' station on the way out, Gail stopped to thank them and to tell them about the offer they'd just made Kris. She also gave them her contact details and told them to call her at any time, if they needed to.

'Poor bloke,' Colin said as they walked across the car park. 'He had so many tubes coming out of him. Must be bloody uncomfortable.'

'I'm afraid it will be for a while, but as soon as his lung heals, he'll start to recover really quickly. I should think he'll be out of ICU and on to a ward in a couple of days. And then they'll want to turf him out as soon as possible to free up a bed, so we'd better get ready for a visitor in the very near future.'

CHAPTER THIRTY-THREE

THURSDAY, 12TH JULY
Great Western Beach,
Newquay, Cornwall

'I just don't see why I can't take this out a bit further.'
　　Out on the police rib, Sergeant Mick Thomas had by now stopped more than twenty people who thought it was acceptable to take their inflatables out as far as they liked. This one, a lad in his late teens, had clearly been drinking a bit, which only added to his stroppy attitude. Mick had had quite enough of these idiots.

'Right sir,' Mick explained. 'You know that people have been talking about sharks a lot recently, especially one that's spending time close to this beach?.'

'Yeah, course I have.'

'And you also know that they have a mouthful of these very sharp things called teeth.'

'Yeah, I've seen them on telly.'

'Well the fact is they are very attracted to colourful objects. Can you see anything colourful around here, sir?'

'Yeah, my inflatable dinghy.'

'Yes, well done sir. So, if this shark comes along with its pointy teeth and decides to have a nibble of your colourful dinghy, what do you think's going to happen?'

'It would burst it, durrr!'

'And what would happen then, sir?'

'It would sink and I'd end up in the water.'

'Correct sir, right next to this massive shark with teeth that can rip you apart in seconds with blood pouring out everywhere. Do you know what the worst thing is sir? I can tell you. They bite you in half, eat the bottom bit first and then come back to finish off the top bit where your head is. And you, sir, would be able to watch yourself being eaten alive.'

'Oh god that's gross,' the teenager shouted out, nervously scanning the surrounding sea for any signs of a shark's fin.

'Yes, sir, and *we* would have to collect up all the little bits that are left of you to hand back to your mother. In the bottom of a Tesco bag. So what's your plan now, *sir*?'

'I'm off,' the young man replied and started paddling for the far off shore at a rate of knots.

'You know, you can be a right bastard at times, Sarge,' said his colleague, Chris Smith.

'I'm afraid that's what morons like that deserve,' Mick said, wearily.

'Is that really what sharks do to you, Sarge?'

'To be quite honest, I've no idea, but if it causes idiots like that to think twice then I'm happy to make anything up.'

Mick looked out across the bay and spotted another rule breaker, this time a bikini clad woman on a paddle board.

'Oh, for god's sake, not another!' Mick said exasperated.

'Come on, let's go and see if this woman fancies doing an audition for *Jaws*.'

Mick's radio came to life.

'Don't worry, Mr Cardy. I've got this one.' Mick turned to see Sam hurtle past on his jet ski.

'She's all yours. Thank you, Sam,' Mick said, relieved he wasn't going to have to give yet another lecture.

'My pleasure,' came the reply. 'Always happy to give a helping hand to a lady in distress.'

BACK ON DRY LAND, PC 'MACK' Mackay has spent most of the morning wandering up and down the beach, reminding people not to go out more than twenty metres. On the whole, people behaved sensibly. Quite a few people responded to his humour. A bunch of attractive young women had tried to encourage him to 'get his kit off' and join them in the water. As much as that appealed to him, he pointed out that 'he'd lose his job if he did!'

He was now once more back on top of the sea wall, enjoying a cooling ice cream as he looked out across the beach.

'Enjoying that, are you Mack?' He turned to see his old friend Russell Prior standing next to him, binoculars around his neck and rucksack across his shoulders.

'I certainly am, Russ,' Mack replied. 'It's been bloody hard work walking up and down the beach in this heat.' Mack looked at Russ' binoculars. 'I hope that you aren't doing anything illegal with those? I know there are lots of pretty young things out there but there's a limit to what you can use them for.'

'Of course not,' Russ said, frowning at the suggestion. 'You know I'm not like that. We pensioners have a lot of time on our hands that we can put to use for the public good. So I've been walking along the coast looking out for any signs of that old lady out there that's causing all this fuss.'

'What old lady?' Mack asked as he turned to hear his friend's response.

'The shark, you daft pillock.' Russ said shaking his head.

'Oh yes, I see what you mean.'

The two of them stood and chatted for a bit longer. Mack announced that he'd better get back out on the beach.

'I'm on duty till seven tonight,' Mack said to Russ. 'So if you're still around later on, come and have a chat. Once we shut the beach, it should be very quiet.'

'Don't you worry, 'Russ replied, 'I'll be keeping a good look out till it starts to get dark. Nothing's going to get past me and my binoculars.'

CHAPTER THIRTY-FOUR

THURSDAY, 12TH JULY
Newquay, Cornwall

Jack Sherwood looked up at the clock on the office wall - not quite 3 o'clock – and groaned at the thought of another two hours stuck in the hot, airless offices of Young & Son, Accountants.

Jack had left school the previous summer with straight A's at A-level. However, instead of going to university like so many of his school friends and 'having a jolly for 3 years', he'd decided to go straight into work. He lived with his mother, who was delighted when he'd been accepted as a trainee accountant in one of largest accountancy firms in the south west.

A first year spent mainly in the auditing department had not exactly been an exciting one, but Jack believed he had a future with the firm. He committed himself to studying for his professional exams and signed up for an online course, paid for by the firm. They also allowed him a study afternoon off each week, and so far, he hadn't found it too difficult to keep up with the demands of work.

The sound of his phone vibrating on the desk brought him back to reality. The screen displayed a message from Grubber, an old friend from his earliest days in primary school. He opened the message.

Can you talk for a mo?

There was no one in the office so he rang back immediately.

'Hoody, how are you my old mate?' Hoody was Jack's school nickname, arrived at by the connection of his surname with Robin Hood.

'I'm good, Grub. Hurry up because I'm not meant to make calls during office hours.'

'Yeah, okay. Look a few of the gang are going to head down to Great Western beach after work and swim out to the diving platform.'

'But the beaches will be shut, mate.'

'Look, once they've got everyone cleared off, they're not going to keep checking all the beaches. We'll just creep down, jump in and away we go. We can go for a few pints afterwards. Tammy's going to be there.' Grubber knew that Jack really liked Tammy and that would guarantee he showed up.

Jack's interest was piqued when he heard this. 'Yeah, okay then. What time?'

'Good man. We're all going to try to be there around 6.45. See you then,' and, with that, he was gone.

At last, he thought. Something to look forward to. And Tammy was going to be there, too!

Jack smiled to himself as he looked again at the clock, willing it to move faster. Five o'clock could not come fast enough.

CHAPTER THIRTY-FIVE

THURSDAY, 12TH JULY
24, Marine Terrace, Newquay, Cornwall

Jack stood in the kitchen quickly putting together a cheese and tomato sandwich.

'Where are you off to in such a hurry?' Jack's mother, Faye, asked. Jack's father had died three years earlier and his mother now doted on him.

'I'm meeting a few people on the beach and then we're going for a drink somewhere,' Jack said, pouring himself a glass of milk.

'The beach?' Faye said. 'But they're all closed.'

'Yeah, but no one's going to bother checking after everyone's gone home, are they?'

'But you're not going for a swim are you?'

'Only out to the diving pontoon and back.'

The change in expression on Faye's face betrayed her concern. 'Is that safe? Do you think it's a good idea after what happened to that surfer yesterday?'

Jack swallowed his mouthful and gave his mother a big hug.

'Oh, come on, that was just a one off. Anyway, he was a surfer and everyone knows that sharks can confuse them with seals. The shark just made a mistake. If it had really wanted to, he could easily have ripped him to bits,' Jack said.

'Don't say that,' Faye chided Jack and banging her fist playfully on his chest. 'Well I wish you wouldn't. It just seems foolish to take the risk. Look, you promise me you'll be careful and won't swim out too far. You never know what might happen.'

'You silly old thing,' Jack said, giving his mother a kiss on her cheek. 'You still worry about me as if I was a small boy. We'll all be careful. I promise.'

Jack grabbed his rucksack 'Sorry, got to go, I'm late already. Not sure what time I'll be back, so see you in the morning.'

He went out the back door in a rush. As he passed the kitchen window, he waved to his mother. She raised her hand in reply, shaking her head and then watched as he made his way around the side of the house and across to the bus stop.

Fifteen minutes later, Jack was walking along the sea wall to the far end of the beach. It was strange to see it completely empty of holidaymakers at this time of day. He bumped into an old man who was looking out towards the sea with a pair of binoculars.

'Oi. Watch where you're going,' the old man said.

'Sorry about that, mate,' Jack replied, continuing along the path.

The warm rays of the evening sun bounced off the glass on the shop windows and Jack had to screw up his eyes against the glare. He finally reached the point above the beach where he knew he would find the others.

'Oi, Hoody, come on mate. We've been waiting ages for you.'

Jack looked down to see Grubber surrounded by a bunch of his friends, both boys and girls, already changed into swimming costumes. Why he was called Grubber, Jack couldn't remember. He'd always been called Grubber and that was that.

As he made his way down, Jack picked out Tammy in the crowd. She was wearing a pale blue two piece which perfectly set off her dark tan.

'Oh god, she looks beautiful,' he thought as he walked down the steps.

There were a few girls there that Jack didn't recognise. Grubber had no problem attracting girls and they stood around him, laughing at his jokes. It had always been like that - even when they were early teenagers, Grubber had always been the biggest boy, the best at sport, the one who made the girls laugh. And now he had the good looks and physique to help keep up his image.

'What the hell kept you, Hoody?' Grubber asked in an unnecessarily loud voice, intended to get the attention of the girls in front of him.

'Sorry, mate. I got nabbed by my boss just as I was about to leave and I couldn't get away. I won't be a minute,' Jack replied and took the rucksack off his back, placing it with the others' belongings.

He had just started to undo his shirt when Grubber shouted. 'There you go ladies, your own live Chippendale act.' All the girls and boys started laughing, including Tammy.

Jack self-consciously turned his back to the crowd as he took off his shirt, revealing a rather white, skinny body.

'Okay, last one out to the pontoon gets eaten by the shark!' Grubber joked. They all raced down the beach to the shoreline, shouting and kicking up large sprays of water as they ran through the smaller waves.

'Hold on,' Jack shouted, getting his foot stuck in his trouser leg in his rush to join them. He'd already put his swimming costume on at home, so having got his leg free, he folded up his jeans and sprinted off down the beach and into the water. By now the others were well ahead of Jack. The tide was in and, as he ran into the shallows, he reckoned the pontoon was probably about fifty metres out from the water's edge. The pontoon was simply a basic low level diving platform, with ladders front and back. It was anchored to the sea bed and covered in a non-slip, green material.

The rest of the group had almost reached the platform. Each had their own version of the crawl or breaststroke, some more effective than others. Grubber, and two more boys were already hauling themselves out of the water and shouting encouragement to the girls not far behind them.

Jack was not a strong swimmer. He'd developed his own laboured attempt at crawl. It involved slapping the water with each stroke, and making more noise than movement. He progressed at a snail's pace, and he seemed to expend an enormous amount of effort just to gain the smallest forward momentum.

The pontoon seemed a long way off.

CHAPTER THIRTY-SIX

THURSDAY, 12TH JULY
Great Western Beach,
Newquay, Cornwall

PC Mackay looked at his watch. Only another quarter of an hour to go before the end of his shift. He had to admit he was knackered. Twelve hours patrolling in a hat and with sleeves rolled down to protect against the hot sun would leave anyone feeling exhausted.

It had been surprisingly easy to clear the beach. A couple of people had complained, but even they had walked off once he had explained the rules. As he looked down on the empty beach, he watched Mack's rib making its way to the shore, and fifty metres behind, Sam was steering his jet ski slowly towards the beach.

'You know there's a bunch of young people over by the pontoon, don't you?' Mack looked up to see Russ, binoculars in hand, peering down the beach.

'What? We cleared everyone off,' Mack said, leaning over the metal railings to get a better look.

'Here, use these,' Russ said, handing the binoculars to Mack.

Mack looked out towards the pontoon. Sure enough, a group of young people were on the beach and stripping off ready for a swim.

'Thanks Russ, I'll call it in.' Mack handed back the glasses and started speaking into his radio.

Russ rested his binoculars on the rail in front of him and cleaned the front and back lenses with a cleaning cloth. He then put the strap around his neck again and focused on a point out in the bay. He couldn't be certain but he was sure he saw movement in the water.

Mack was still speaking into his radio as Russ brought up the glasses once again. He scanned the water's surface until he found the same spot. Yes, it was there. Something was moving fast through the water, occasionally breaking the surface and heading towards the beach over to the left. Oh God, he thought, the pontoon.

'Mack, forget that. There's something large moving in the water out there and it's heading towards the pontoon.'

'Oh shit!' Mack said looking out to sea. 'Are you sure?'

'Of course I'm bloody sure. It's a large fin. About three hundred metres out. Get onto those boys on their boats, tell them to turn around and head towards the pontoon as fast as they can. If they don't, we might have a disaster on our hands.

Mack held down the send button on his radio.

'Mick, Sam, can you both hear me? Over.'

A moment later both voices came clearly.

'Yes, what's the problem Mack?' Mick said.

'Russ Prior's here next to me with some powerful binoculars. He says there's a large shark's fin cutting through the water about three hundred metres out and it's heading for the pontoon. Over.'

'I just heard your report about the kids on the beach. Right we're on our way. Just hope we're not too late.'

Mack started to run along the path next to the railings. As soon as he got within range he waved his arms and shouted down to the group, most of whom were now on the pontoon.

'Shark, shark, get out of the water!' He pointed across the bay to the shark's fin moving quickly through the water. He shouted again and was relieved to see they were now looking up at him and appeared to be responding to his call. He felt a wave of relief as he watched the last two preparing clambering onto the pontoon.

Leaning further over the railing, he spotted a lone figure making desperately slow progress, midway between the shoreline and the pontoon. Oh God, oh God, he thought, please hurry up.

He continued running and shouting, his voice becoming more and more desperate.

'Shark, SHARK! Get out of the water!'

ON THE PONTOON, the group looked up to see who was shouting. The words themselves became clearer. Suddenly the mood changed. They strained to see what the policeman was pointing at.

'Shit, I can see it,' one of them shouted.

Grubber shouted at Jack.

'Hoody, Hooddeee. Faster mate. Swim bloody faster.'

Then they all joined in, desperately urging Jack to swim faster.

'Shark, mate, there's a bloody shark. Faster Hoody, swim.'

Jack felt the panic rise within him as he desperately tried

to increase his pace. He kicked as hard as he had ever done and moved his arms quicker than he thought possible. Then, as he pulled his arm over he forgot to breathe out. Instead, in his panic, he breathed in drawing a huge mouthful of water. He stopped swimming as he choked, coughing and flailing in the water. He tried desperately to get his breath and draw oxygen back into his lungs.

Christ, he thought. *I'm going to die.*

CHAPTER THIRTY-SEVEN

THURSDAY, 12TH JULY
Great Western Beach,
Newquay, Cornwall

When the message came through on the radio, Sam was still on the water preparing to beach his jet ski. He heard the desperation in PC Mackay's voice, and spun the jet ski round, opened up the throttle and headed off as fast as the craft could go. He scanned the water, desperately trying to spot any sign of the shark. And then, he saw it in front of him to the right. The tip of the fin was just breaking the surface and heading straight for the pontoon.

He could see the group on the pontoon, shouting and pointing at something in the water. There was a swimmer frantically trying to make it to the pontoon. It was clear that the shark would get to them. And then, for some reason, the swimmer stopped altogether and starting flailing around in the water.

'No, no, no!' Sam shouted in desperation. He looked at the shark and tried to calculate if he could get there in time.

There was a chance, a very small chance, Sam told himself, *he couldn't, mustn't fail.*

The shark seemed to be moving ever more quickly through the water, attracted by the noise of the struggling swimmer transmitted through the water.

Sam was standing as he drove, urgently making a new calculation with every second that passed. *I'm going to make it, I must,* he told himself, but he knew the reality might be different. *God, it's going to be touch and go.* His forearms cramped in pain as he gripped the handlebar tighter and tighter.

Fifty metres, forty metres. *I can do it.* Thirty, twenty. *'Please God, please God.'* He briefly glanced at the figure in the water. The swimmer was only a dozen metres from the pontoon, but the look of terror on this face showed that he knew he wouldn't make it.

The screams of girls on the pontoon pierced the air. Fifteen metres. *Get between the shark and the swimmer.* Ten. Five. *NOW!* Sam threw the jet ski hard left and cut the throttle. As he did so, the side and bottom of the jet ski glanced the shark and it turned sharply away, under the pontoon, disappearing into the sea beyond. As the craft righted itself, Sam leant down to pull the straggler out of the water. He was clearly in shock but he managed to whisper, 'Thank you,' to Sam.

Sam hauled the swimmer safely on board and headed slowly towards the beach.

On the pontoon, the group burst into spontaneous applause, clapping and shouting and hugging each other. The sense of relief they all felt was enormous. The euphoria quickly dissipated, though, when an orange rib pulled up alongside, with two policemen aboard.

'You should all be ashamed of yourselves.' Mick shouted at them. 'A man could have easily died this evening. One of your friends could have been killed in front of your eyes. If it hadn't been for the quick thinking of that brave lifeguard, your mate could have been just a bloody mess floating around in the water.'

Mick let his words sink in. 'And for what? A bit of a laugh, a little breaking of the rules.? Well aren't you all the brave ones. For goodness sake, just stop and think about it.'

Guilt and remorse covered the faces of the entire group.

'Right, we'd better get you to the beach. Oh, and by the way, don't imagine for a moment this is the end of it. You're all going to be taken in for questioning and may be charged with a number of offences. So that might well mean a criminal record. Think on that for a while. Now, four ladies first please, into the boat as fast as you can.'

On the beach, PC Mackay picked up a couple of towels and wrapped them round the shoulders of the shivering, rescued swimmer.

'You'll be alright, mate. I suggest you dry yourself off and get some clothes on.'

He then took his notebook out, ready to record the names of everyone involved. He wasn't going to be finishing at 7 p.m. tonight, but somehow it didn't matter. The day could have ended far worse than it did. He wasn't a particularly religious man, but Mack said a small prayer of thanks under his breath.

CHAPTER THIRTY-EIGHT

THURSDAY, 12TH JULY
Dowrtreven,
Helford River, Cornwall

'That was absolutely delicious,' John said. Sophie's brother in law pushed his chair back an inch or two from the table.

'We're all in agreement with you there,' Alice said. 'Beth and Sophie, you make a great mother and daughter team. Fabulous food. I fear that I am not going to be able to move for a week!'

'Our pleasure,' Beth said and turned to Alice. 'And I'm pleased to hear that *you* won't be able to move for a week because you've barely sat down for a minute the entire time we've been here. *You* deserve a rest.'

'I hope you're taking this on board, John?' Alice said, looking down the table at her husband.

'Of course, darling,' John replied. 'You'd better get off to bed now and start that resting regime!'

'Ha, fat chance,' came the reply.

Nick's phone vibrated in his pocket. He took it out and looked at the screen. The message was from Jamie:

There's been a serious incident involving our favourite lady. No casualties, but serious nonetheless. There's a report on the BBC News page. Please could you have a look at it and give me a quick ring? Thanks. Jamie.

He quickly found the page and read the report. The concern on his face was evident as he read.

'What is it?' Sophie asked.

Nick looked up. 'Jamie has just texted me. There's been an incident on the beach in Newquay. Apparently, a bunch of young people decided to go for a swim after the beach had been closed. It seems our old lady was attracted by the sound and the movement and made a beeline for them. They were swimming out to the diving pontoon… Hold on, I need to catch up.'

He continued to scroll through the report, reading it aloud for the others to hear.

When he'd finished, John said. 'I can imagine the proverbial's going to hit the fan in the morning. The police are going to get some real stick for this.'

'Yes, you're right,' Nick said. 'There could easily have been a dead body on that beach tonight if it hadn't been for that quick thinking lifeguard.'

Emma was looking at her own phone. 'Nick, if it's possible, I'd really like to go over there in the morning and try to have a word with some of the people involved. Get a bit more background research for the shark project.'

'Good idea,' he replied. He stood up and moved away from the table, dialling Jamie's number at the same time. 'Excuse me, but Jamie has asked me to call him. I'll see what he can arrange for us Emma.'

As he walked the steps to the lower terrace, the dialling tone was interrupted.

'Nick, hi. Thank you for calling. My apologies for disturbing your evening,' Jamie said. 'Have you had a chance to look at the BBC report?'

'Yes I have. Looks like a disaster was narrowly avoided tonight.' Nick replied, gently shaking his head as he walked down to the beach.

'Absolutely. I'm afraid you can put in place as many controls as you want, but there's no accounting for idiots who will simply ignore them. I know that people are going to have a go at the police. But, to be honest, we just don't have the resources to patrol all the beaches across north Cornwall after hours.'

'Does this mean you're going to have to move the controls up to another level? Perhaps stop people from entering the water altogether?'

'I think that would be impossible to police.' Jamie said. 'I have just discussed this with Angela Myers, the Police and Crime Commissioner for Devon and Cornwall. She is obviously very upset by what happened tonight and is keen to do everything she can to ensure everyone's safety in the future. She thinks, and I agree with her, that we should bring the restrictions for both north and south coasts into line and tighten them.'

'So what does that mean in practice?'

'From midnight, all beaches would still be closed between the hours of 6 p.m. and 9 a.m. During the daytime, no one would be allowed to move more fifteen metres of the shoreline and inflatables and sea craft would be banned altogether. What do you think?'

Nick stood by the water's edge and watched as a fish broke the surface to catch a fly.

'Well, people are bound to be upset by any regulations, but what happened tonight should help to get some perspective. I agree that you have to allow people to have some access to the water because that's the main reason people go on beach holidays.'

'Good, we'll get those restrictions put in place immediately,' Jamie said. 'And what do you think about the part the shark played in all this? Should we be more worried about further attacks?'

'Jamie, this wasn't an *attack*,' Nick replied, picking up a stone and threw it skimming across the water. 'The shark was drawn to the spot by the noise of the individuals on the pontoon and the splashing sound made by the swimmers - especially the swimmer who had got into difficulties.'

'But how far away would the shark have been to be attracted by the noise?' Jamie interrupted.

'Look, sharks can detect sounds up to two miles away. It was probably moving past the entrance to the bay when the change in the sound waves reaching it from the beach drew it in. It had no intention of attacking a human, but was merely investigating the sound. So, yes, we should be concerned that there is always the possibility of another incident, but if there's nothing making noise in the water, there's nothing for a shark to be attracted to.'

'Understood, thank you,' Jamie said. 'By the way, we're all looking forward to joining you tomorrow. I think it will be nearer five, if that's OK?'

'Yes, perfect. There's just one favour I'd like to ask,'

'Ask away.'

'You may remember me telling you that Emma, the kayaker involved in the Scottish incident, is now working for us, and is staying down here?'

'I do indeed. I look forward to meeting her.'

'Well, she is currently working on a project bringing together all the experiences and developments linked to the sharks. We'd really like to go to Newquay tomorrow morning and meet some of the people involved. Could you possibly have a quick word to check Angela Myers is okay with this?'

'I'm sure everyone in Newquay would love the chance of meeting you! But, yes, I'll have a word with Angela.' His tone suddenly changed. 'Sorry, got to go, I've got the Prime Minister's office waiting on hold.'

'Good luck,' Nick said and ended the call.

Nick climbed back up to the house to join the others, who were now having coffee.

'How was Jamie?' Sophie asked.

'Hassled, by the sound of it,' Nick said, sitting down at the table. 'The PM was calling just as we were finishing.' He shook his head in sympathy for his friend. 'Poor devil. Who would want that level of accountability all the time?'

'Clearly, he does,' Alice pointed out. 'That is, if he really wants to be PM himself one day.'

'Fair point, Sis,' Nick said and turned to Emma. 'Jamie's going to warn the Police Commissioner that we're going over to Newquay tomorrow. If it's alright with you, we need to leave by 7.30 a.m.? Oh Sophie, Jamie said they'd be with us around five tomorrow.'

'That's fine,' she replied. 'A perfect time. The children can have an hour or so in the water to work off some energy before we eat. It's going to be a wonderful day tomorrow.'

CHAPTER THIRTY-NINE

FRIDAY, 13TH JULY
Helford Passage,
Helford River, Cornwall

Simon Harris sat on the deck of his 30-foot yacht, *Lovebird*, sipping his first cup of tea of the day. He loved the peace of the river at this time of morning. The only the sounds to break the tranquillity were the water lapping up against the hull and the rigging moving gently in the breeze. The soft, mesmeric chorus was repeated on the many boats moored nearby.

He shielded his eyes against the low, early morning sun. Another hot day, he thought, as he got up and walked across the deck before momentarily disappearing into his cabin to fetch his sunglasses.

Simon was now sixty-four years old. He and his late wife had bought the boat almost twenty-five years earlier and they and their two children had enjoyed many summers sailing along the Cornish coast. The children still occasionally came down to join him for a few days during the summer. However, they both had young families now and the boat wasn't the ideal playground for toddlers. Anyway, Simon was used to having the boat to himself and being able to do what he wanted, when he wanted to do it.

He picked up his laptop and opened the home page of his favourite national newspaper. The headline about yet another shark incident near Newquay immediately caught his eye. He read the article and thought, 'I'm pleased we're not on the north coast. Too many people and too many sharks.'

He scrolled down the page and read another article about water shortages in the south east. It was like that fifty years ago and they still haven't sorted the bloody problem out, he ranted to himself.

Had he lifted his head at that moment and looked a few feet to his left, he would have seen a small fin cutting through the water and glide past the side of his boat. But he was too engrossed in his laptop and the fin, unseen by human eyes, slipped below the water and continued its slow, silent journey upstream.

CHAPTER FORTY

FRIDAY, 13TH JULY
Great Western Beach,
Newquay, Cornwall

Nick hadn't appreciated just how busy the approach roads to Newquay would be, nor what a nightmare he was going to have finding somewhere to park.

'I wonder if last night's incident has brought the rubber-neckers out of the woodwork and that's why it's so busy?' Nick commented.

'That would include us then,' Emma pointed out. 'To be honest, I think this is just typical July holiday traffic. That, plus the fact the weather is still wonderful.'

They eventually found a space in a car park some ten minutes back from the beach. They joined the other holidaymakers, filling the pavements en route to the seafront. The sun was already hot. Emma sensibly wore cut-off jeans shorts and a white T-shirt. Nick was wearing a polo shirt and shorts but had added a baseball cap and sunglasses, in the hope that he wouldn't be recognised so easily; however, he still found that he had a few people staring at him. They both heard one woman, with a perfect Cornish accent, wondering aloud to her friend if Nick might be that 'bloke off the telly, you know, the one who does the dog food adverts.'

To Nick's horror, Emma laughed when she heard this. The woman turned to see who'd laughed at her.

'Sorry!' Emma, said holding up her hand in apology as Nick gave her an admonishing stare.

The women turned back to her friend muttering 'no need for that, was 'ere?'

Nick gently pulled back on Emma's arm so the woman and her friend could get well ahead of them.

'Dog food adverts, for god's sake,' Nick said as they continued along the pavement. 'Dog bloody food? She could at least have chosen an expensive perfume or aftershave. Has it come to this already?'

'To be fair,' Emma said, 'you're wearing a cap and big sunglasses. I don't think I'd have recognised you in the street wearing those. I suggest you remove the cap on the beach, or someone might mistake you for a sad, old rock star!'

'Okay, let's stop this now.' Nick immediately removed his cap. He looked over the heads in front. 'Good, here's the seafront.'

Emma glanced up. The view of the beach, and the sea beyond, opened up in front of them.

They reached the railings overlooking the beach. Although it had only been open for half an hour, it was already filling up with people claiming their spot.

Nick looked down at his phone. 'Angela Myers, the Police Commissioner, has kindly texted me. She said we're to look out for a police constable called Mackay, who'll be patrolling the beach. Apparently he'll be expecting us.'

They scanned the beach and Emma spotted a figure in a lightweight fluorescent waistcoat over a uniform shirt.

'Over there, by the bottom of the slipway. Let's make our way down.'

A couple of minutes later they found themselves on the sand and approached the policeman.

'Ah, Mr Martin and Ms Warren, I presume?' PC Mackay greeted them with a broad smile and a local burr to his voice. 'Welcome to sunny Newquay where the sun shines 365 days a year. If you believe that you'll believe anything! I'm Mack and I'm delighted to meet you both.'

'Delighted to meet you too,' Nick said shaking his hand. Emma followed suit. 'Please call me Nick and this is Emma.'

'Well it's not often I get to meet a celeb in this job, and not just one, but two. My wife won't believe me when I tell her – she'll just say I've had too much sun!'

'Forget all that celeb stuff, Mack. We're just two people having a nice day out,' Emma said, returning his smile. 'Have you got a few minutes to chat with us?'

'I've been instructed to give you as much of my time as you need, which suits me just fine. Do you mind if we head over to the coffee shop and find a bit of shade? I'm afraid I'm already boiling in this outfit?' They could see beads of sweat forming on his face.

'Yes, of course,' Nick said. 'I'm sure we could both do with a coffee anyway.'

AFTER QUEUING FOR SEVERAL MINUTES, they eventually got their coffees and found a small table and three slightly rusty metal chairs in the shade.

'Thanks for my coffee,' Mack said. 'Now, how can I be of assistance?'

'Well,' Emma said, 'we, actually mainly me, are planning a retrospective programme looking back at all the shark events that have occurred – and still might occur – this summer. I want to talk to everyone who has been involved or affected in some way. From what we've been told by your police commissioner, you might have a story to tell us.'

'I'm not sure it's as good as she might have been told.' Mack took a sip of his coffee and winced. 'Ooh, bloody hot! Okay, I'll start with the moment I met an old friend of mine, just up there by the side of the road.' He pointed to a spot about half way along the railings overlooking the beach. 'That's where it started, up there. The police launch was just coming into land on the beach and the Lifeguard's jet ski was about fifty metres behind, following it in…' Mack recounted his story from the moment he met his old friend Russ Prior and how everything 'went mad from that point'.

Five minutes later, he reached the end of his involvement in the evening's events.

'Christ, *that* was one hell of an evening,' Emma said, shaking her head in disbelief.

'I suppose you could say that.' Mack's understatement amused his visitors. 'But the only thing that really mattered was that no one got injured. I'm not saying the shark would definitely have gone for that swimmer, but you can only imagine what might have been the result if it had. Thank god for Sam's quick thinking on his jet ski. I reckon he saved a man's life out there.'

'You could well be right there,' Nick said. 'But, as you said, thank God we'll never know. The one thing that's certain though, is your actions saved those swimmers just as much as the jet ski operator. If you hadn't made the decision to call to the boats as quickly as you did, he wouldn't have got there in time. So, PC Mackay, *you* played a vital part.'

'Oh no,' Mack said, shuffling in his chair, clearly embarrassed. 'I just did my job. Thankfully, others did theirs too. If only those idiotic young people had used their brains and thought about what they were doing.'

'Well I think you're a hero,' Nick said.

'And so do I,' Emma added. 'I hope that, at some time in the near future, you'll allow me to come back and do a proper interview. I want everyone to hear your story.'

'Emma, for you, of course!'

'In that case, sir, I'll be in touch,' Emma said and took out her phone. 'Would you mind entering your mobile number for me so I can get in touch again, nearer the time?' She handed her phone to Mack.

'Shall I enter my email as well?' he asked.

'Yes please.'

As he handed the phone back to her, she asked, 'Do you know where we might find the jet ski guy - Sam, was it?'

'Of course, no problem,' Mack said, checking his watch. 'I know he wasn't starting till 10 a.m. so your timing's perfect. We'll just head back down to the beach and I'll take you to meet him.'

They left the coffee shop and headed down the slipway. Once they reached the beach, they turned right and walked to the lifeguard station, where a large red awning was flanked by two banners. A few sunbathers raised their heads and pointed when they recognised Nick

Nearing the awning, they noticed a female reporter and cameraman talking to a very tall man who had his back to Nick and Emma.

'Just hold on a minute,' Nick said. 'Let's give the reporter enough time to finish her interview.'

'That's Anita Dhami from South West News,' Mack said.

'Yes, so it is,' Nick said, suddenly recognising her. 'I did an interview with her a couple of years ago about my Cornish heritage.'

'Well, it looks like they're finished now. Come on, let me introduce you to Sam,' Mack said. He headed off in Sam's direction and the others followed closely behind.

Anita was checking her phone and looked up just as Nick approached the tent.

'Well, just look who's here,' she said to her cameraman. 'Only the most famous Cornishman on the planet. What are you doing here, Mr Martin?'

'Come on Anita, less of the *Mr*. It's Nick to you.' He bent down to give her a peck on the cheek. 'We're just here to do what you're doing – meeting the people who were involved in last night's events. Let me introduce…'

He turned to introduce Emma but she had walked over to the tall, bronzed lifeguard who had just been interviewed.

'Sam Brodie! What the bloody hell are you doing here?' The lifeguard turned to see who was speaking to him. His face lit up when he realised who it was.

'Emma!' He walked up to the unexpected visitor and gave her a quick hug. 'God, it's great to see you,' he spurted out. 'How've you been? What are *you* doing here?'

'I'm working with Nick Martin.' She pointed back at her colleague, who, along with Anita, was staring in surprise at what had just happened. 'We're here to do some background research on yesterday's events.' She was then hit by a sudden realisation. 'Oh my god, *you're* the Sam, the jet ski man they're all talking about! You're a bloody hero!'

'You know that's a load of bollocks,' he replied, slightly embarrassed but also rather pleased.

'Excuse me for interrupting,' Nick said. 'How come you two know each other?'

'I'm sorry. How rude of me. Sam this is Nick and vice versa,' Emma said awkwardly. 'Sam and I were at uni together. He captained the men's rugby team and I was women's' captain, so we saw a lot of each other. I'd completely forgotten you lived down here. Nick, Sam is the jet ski hero.'

'I gathered that.' He held out his hand. 'Good to meet you, Sam, and well done on the rescue yesterday. That was really good work.'

'Very kind of you to say that.' Sam replied modestly. 'Much appreciated'.

'So, we seem to have "Shark Girl" meets "Shark Boy",' Anita said, seeing the opportunity to ease her way into the conversation. 'Hello, Emma, I'm Anita Dhami. You seem to have got the dream job I'd have loved - working with Nick Martin.'

'Oh it's not such a big deal, honestly,' she said in a deliberately flat voice, teasing Nick. 'Don't believe the public image he portrays. Underneath it he's horrible to work with - he's a real slave driver and insists that *he* gets all the recognition. I really don't know what I'm doing here.'

Nick laughed and the others smiled, as well.

'The fact that he can laugh at your micky taking proves he's alright,' Anita said. 'I'll tell you what, Nick, would you mind doing a short piece to camera about this shark? I think it could do with someone to speak up for it.'

'Delighted to,' Nick replied. 'But I think Emma should also be involved.'

'Great,' the journalist said. 'The more the merrier as far as I'm concerned.'

They all turned as a voice behind them said, 'I can see you've all hit it off perfectly so I'll get on my way.'

'Mack, my sincere apologies,' Nick said, horrified at his oversight. 'Look, Anita, this is PC Mackay and *he* is the hero who alerted everyone about the shark. Because of him, a possible disaster was averted. You really should get him in front of the camera.'

'Nick's absolutely right,' Sam said. 'His early warning meant I was able to reach the swimmer just in time. A few seconds later and who knows what might have happened.'

'Well, PC Mackay,' Anita said. 'Could you spare me five minutes of your time? I've just got to interview Nick and Emma briefly, and then I can come to you.'

'I should really be getting back on my beat,' Mack said, reluctantly.

'I'll tell you what, Anita,' Nick said. 'Why don't you do the piece with Mack now, and then us afterwards? We're not in any rush.'

'Perfect, thank you,' Anita said and beckoned her cameraman over. 'Let's do it here with the sea behind you, Constable. Is that okay?'

While Anita was prepping Mack, Nick walked across the tent to where Sam and Emma were deep in conversation.

'Nick come and join us,' Sam said with a welcoming smile. 'Emma was just telling me about her good fortune in meeting you.'

'I'm not sure she regards being tossed into the water by a great white to be particularly lucky,' Nick said, smiling. 'You're right, serendipity played a major role, but Live World are the ones who have benefited most from it. We all think she's going to be a big star one day.'

'Emma, see, I always said you were going to make it big, didn't I?' Sam said and smiled at her. 'The thing is though, will you still talk to me when you're famous?'

She punched his arm. 'Stop that right now, Sam Brodie. Of course I'll still talk to you. You'll be my chauffeur!'

Nick realised that the young couple had a bit of catching up to do. 'If you'll excuse me for a few minutes,

I'm going to walk down the beach and stretch my legs. I'll come back when Amanda's ready for us.'

'Yes, okay,' Emma said. 'See you in a while.' She and Sam then spent the next few minutes talking about their old friends from Uni and what they were all up to now.

They were interrupted by Anita's loud voice from the side of the awning.

'Emma, sorry to trouble you but I'm ready to do the interview if that's okay? Do you know where Nick is, please?

'He said he was just nipping down the beach to stretch his legs,' Emma said, looking round. 'I'm sure he'll back in a moment. No, look he's here, right behind you Anita.'

'Hi all,' Nick said as he approached the awning. 'Where do you want us, Anita?'

'Exactly where you are, please, with the sea as the backdrop.' She turned to her cameraman. 'Jo, good for you here?' Jo nodded. 'OK Nick, can you just say your name and what you do so that we can get the sound level right?'

'Hi, my name's Nick Martin and I bore people for a living.'

'I certainly hope not if I'm going to interview you!' Anita said. 'Emma, can you do the same please?'

As soon as the sound levels were right, Anita began.

'Right, here we go……. I'm very lucky to have not only Nick Martin, one of Cornwall's finest sons, here with me today on Great Western beach but also Emma Warren, who I'm sure you'll all remember is the kayaker who was tipped into the sea by the shark in Scotland.'

'To be accurate, *off* Scotland!' Emma said and smiled.

'So, what are you both doing here today?'

'Well, Emma's now joined us at Live World Films,' Nick explained. 'We're working on producing a retrospective of all the events linked to sharks that have taken place this summer - and that may yet happen before the summer's out.'

'We all know that you have made that you have a special affinity with sharks. Can you tell us why you think this great white has chosen to spend so much time in Cornish waters? After all, there's an awful lot of the British coastline that she hasn't visited yet!'

'I think it says a great deal about the huge steps that have been taken to improve both the quality of the sea water off the south west coast and its bio diversity.' Nick turned to include Emma in the conversation. 'Would you agree?'

Emma nodded. 'Yes, exactly that. The fact that every year we're seeing such large numbers of humpback whales off our shores proves that there's now an abundance of life that can sustain these large mammals. The creation of Marine Conservation areas all around the south west coast has been instrumental in achieving that.'

Holidaymakers were now crowding round, wanting to hear what was being said.

'Okay,' Anita said, 'So we've got clean seas and a rich, diverse marine environment, but why is the so-called "Grim Reaper" staying here, right off our shores?'

Emma noticed Nick grimace at the use of that name.

'Let's avoid using names like that.' Nick said, firmly. 'They're purely for tabloid headlines not serious discussion. The reason that remarkable old shark stays around is that the diverse environment attracts the exact prey that great whites hunt – porpoises, seals and dolphins - and there are now plenty of those in the seas off our coast. I suppose it's a case of staying where the food is easiest to find.'

'So what danger does this "grand old lady" pose to the public and the beaches on our coast?'

Emma could see Nick was starting to warm to his

subject. She envied the ease with which he performed in front of the camera.

'Look, we've all got to understand that the world's oceans remain the shark's natural habitat and that *we* are the ones who are intruding upon it. Sharks don't set out to attack humans, they investigate what has entered their territory. That's when incidents, like those that happened to Emma and to the surfer, occur. If we can stay out of that habitat for at least a few days, then that old queen of the oceans won't feel the need to stay around.'

'So you're in favour of the restrictions'

'Yes, but on a short term basis only. Look, I know how tough it is, especially when these are the only weeks of the year that most people can take their holiday, but we must all place personal safety above everything else.'

Behind Nick, a number of heads nodded in agreement.

'Nick Martin, Emma Warren, thank you very much for talking to us today.'

'Our pleasure,' Emma said.

'That was brilliant, thank you both,' Anita said. 'My apologies for the Grim Reaper reference,'

'Don't worry about it. It gave me the chance to get that particular bugbear off my chest.' Nick said as he and Emma were both suddenly surrounded by people wanting to take selfies with them.

After a few minutes of pleasing the crowd, he said. 'Emma, I think we should head back to the car.'

'Okay, won't be a moment.' Emma went to the back of the tent where Sam was leaning over a table to writing something on a piece of paper. As she approached, he stood up and handed it to her.

'Here Emm, that's my mobile number. Give me a call sometime if you've a got a free weekend. It would be great to have the chance to catch up properly.'

'That would be great.' Emma gave Sam a hug. 'And I'd also love to interview you for the programme we're making. Would that be okay?'

'I'll look forward to it,' Sam said, a big smile lit up his face.

'In that case, I'll be in touch soon. Good to see you again Sam. Byee,' Emma said as she walked out of the awning. She joined Nick who had just finished another round of selfies and autograph signing.

'Bye Sam,' Nick said with a wave. 'I hope we'll see you again soon. Come over to Helford sometime.'

'I'd really like that, thanks. Have a good journey back.'

CHAPTER FORTY-ONE

FRIDAY, 13TH JULY
Dowrtreven,
Helford River, Cornwall

On the way back from Newquay, Nick and Emma visited the site of the surfer incident at Chapel Porth, to get a feel for the landscape. They then continued their journey back to Dowrtreven to prepare for the arrival of their guests.

They'd spent much of the journey talking about the shark project and what further input from Nick, Jill and the rest of the team might be required. Emma made copious notes for future reference and they agreed to sit down with Jill on Monday to go through it in greater detail.

They arrived back at Dowrtreven just before 4 o'clock. As they entered the kitchen, they were greeted by Sophie and Beth, both hard at work creating salad dishes for the evening's BBQ.

'Ah good, you're back. How did it go?' Sophie asked.

'Really well, I think,' Emma said. 'We met up with a

couple of the key people who'd been involved in last night's incident. Then we were grabbed by Anita Dhami and her cameraman for an interview, which seemed to go okay. After that we were mobbed by Nick's fans and ended signing autographs and do lots of selfies.'

'Sounds like my idea of hell,' Sophie said, then looked at Nick. 'But I bet you loved the adoration, darling!'

'I wasn't the only one enjoying the adoration,' Nick said smiling at Emma. 'It also turned out the jet ski hero is a bronzed, rugby playing Adonis who was very good friends with Emma at university.'

'Lucky you,' Beth said taking Emma's arm in of sisterly support. 'Wish I'd been there, he sounds just my type!'

'Did you once have the body of an Adonis, Nick?' Sophie asked, teasing her husband. 'I can't remember that far back'

Emma smiled as Nick pretended to be hurt.

'Come on,' he said looking down at his stomach. 'It's not that bad. Well, okay, I suppose it could do with a bit of toning.'

'A bit?' Sophie said in a gently mocking voice. 'Don't worry darling, there are clearly loads of people out there who still worship the ground you stand on!'

'Is there anything I can do to help, Sophie?' Emma said, gently changing the subject.

'Well, Pete and Jill spent most of the morning creating various marinades and sauces for the BBQ,' Sophie said, looking at numerous bowls of delicious food lying on the large pine kitchen table.

'I know what's missing,' Beth said. 'Emma, would you mind making a green salad, like the delicious one you made the other night? That would be wonderful. You'll find most of the ingredients in the pantry fridge.'

'No problem,' Emma said and set to work.

'Nick, please can you go outside and clear up any mess the children have left and check everything looks alright out there?' Sophie asked. 'Could you also grab the clean towels off the washing line so they're ready for the children to use tonight?'

'Yup, I'm on it,' Nick said and walked through the sitting room and out onto the terrace.

He picked up various toys, clothes and clutter and took them inside for sorting later. As he moved down to the lower terrace, he saw Pete setting up his camera on the concrete hard standing above the beach.

'How's it going?' Nick asked, walking down to join his friend.

'Good, thanks, mate,' Pete said. 'At the start of the holiday Sophie asked me if I could film the children at various times so you'd have a bit of a visual record of our time here. So, with the Stoddard children coming over later for a swim, I thought I'd set the camera up out here on a stand. That way I can just leave it running while we get on with other stuff.'

'That's a great idea,' Nick said. He pointed to the rib lying on the beach, a few metres above the water line. 'Did you manage to fix the outboard?'

'Yes, it's running smoothly now. I thought I might take some of the children for a quick ride up the river.' Pete hesitated for a moment before continuing. 'Can I check, is there going to be any problem doing that or the children swimming in the river afterwards?'

'No,' Nick replied, bending down to pick up a plastic bag that had washed up on the shore. 'Rivers aren't covered by the restrictions and, anyway, the sharks we have around our coasts couldn't survive in freshwater rivers, including great whites. Those that can are found thousands of miles from the Cornish coast.'

'That's good. I just wanted to check since we've got a government minister coming over. What time are they due here?'

'Sometime in the next half hour, so I'd better get a move on and finish tidying up or I'll be in trouble'.

They climbed the steps to the upper terrace.

'I'd give you a hand but it looks like you've pretty well done the job already.'

'I think you're right, not much left to do here. Would you mind just fetching the towels off the line and I think we're ready.'

CHAPTER FORTY-TWO

FRIDAY, 13TH JULY
Dowrtreven,
Helford River, Cornwall

The Stoddard family, Jamie and his wife Bella, Georgie, thirteen, Ben, eleven and Tom, nine had arrived shortly before 5 p.m. and the children had immediately split up into the four older girls and the five younger boys.

The boys had gone out with Pete on the boat while the girls had retired to the sitting room, playing on their phones and watching television.

The adults watched from the terrace as Pete brought the boat load of excited boys back to the shore. He jumped out, holding the boat at the edge of the sand as the boys slipped over the side into the shallow water. They ran up to join their parents, competing to tell them all about their trip. Pete, meanwhile, dragged the rib up onto the hard standing.

'I think it would be good if all the children spent some time in the water,' Sophie suggested. Bella agreed. 'In the meantime, John can start up the BBQ and we can get the tables ready.'

'I doubt you'll get the girls to join in,' Nick said and Jamie nodded his agreement across the table. 'Once they're on their phones, nothing can shift them.'

'Oh, I don't know about that,' Emma said confidently. 'Just give me a minute,' and disappeared into the house.

After a short while, Emma reappeared on the terrace in her swimsuit, followed by all the girls, similarly attired.

'How on earth did you manage, that Emma?' Alice asked, surprised.

'In the olden days, I think they used to call it *Girl Power*,' she said and turned to the girls behind her. 'Isn't that right, girls?'

They all shouted 'Girl Power' and laughed as they sprinted to beat Emma into the water. The boys, not to be outdone, shouted 'Boy Power' and jumped into the water splashing wildly, producing screams from the girls.

'I think there's a lot I can learn from that young lady,' Bella said, full of admiration for what Emma had just achieved. 'Now, Sophie, what can I do to help?'

AFTER TEN MINUTES of playing in the water and getting the girls to take part as well, Emma made her way out of the river onto the beach, grabbed a large towel and started to dry herself off.

'Well done Emma.' She looked behind her to see who had spoken. Pete was standing by the camera a few metres away, Nick next to him. 'You just achieved what Nick and the other parents have failed to do for the past year,' Pete joked. 'That is, getting the girls to do as they've been asked!'

'All I did was tell them I was going in and I expected

them to support their fellow woman. No different from captaining a rugby team.' Emma smiled at the two men, shrugging her shoulders as if the whole thing was really very simple.

Suddenly, a scream cut through the air, piercing every adult's heart.

CHAPTER FORTY-THREE

FRIDAY, 13TH JULY
Dowrtreven,
Helford River, Cornwall

Emma span round to see who the scream had come from and immediately spotted a fin above the water. At the water's edge, Tom, the nine year old Stoddard boy, was being dragged back through the shallows by a small shark that had its jaws clamped around his leg. In trying to pull the boy away, the shark had momentarily stranded itself on the sand and started to thrash about in the water in attempt to free itself.

It took only a split second for Emma to react and, without a thought for her own safety, threw herself into the water. She somehow managed to grab hold of the shark's flailing tail, aware that at any moment it could let go of the child and turn on her instead. But her focus was only on rescuing the boy. It took all of her strength to hold on as she tried to stop the shark dragging the child out into deeper water. Pete realised what she was trying to do, and he too leapt forward, grasping the thrashing tail and helping to keep the shark in the shallows. All the children were screaming as Nick rushed into the water and jumped onto the shark's back. He dug his fingers into the shark's eyes with such force that the shark released its hold on the boy's leg.

Immediately, he leapt off the shark, staying clear of its mouth as it writhed around in agony. He grabbed the sobbing boy from the water and carried him to the safety of the beach. Jamie ran down the steps to meet him.

'It's okay, Nick, I've got him now, thank you,' Jamie said calmly, taking his son in his arms. As he did so, the terrified child whimpered 'Daddy, daddy'.

'I'm here now, Tom, don't worry, I'm here,' he said as he started to carry the bloodied body up the steps to the house. Tom's mother, Bella, met him at the top and looked in horror at the blood streaming from the jagged cuts on the young boy's leg.

'Oh my poor little thing,' she said as Tom cried out for her. 'We're here darling. Mummy and Daddy are both here and everything's going to be alright.' She stroked Tom's head as they walked quickly across the terrace and into the house.

Nick's brother in law, John, had immediately moved into professional caring mode and was laying out clean towels on the sofa.

'Can you put him down there so I can take a look at that leg,' he asked. The severity of the injury was immediately obvious. The shark's teeth had shredded the flesh down to the bone.

John turned to his wife and quietly said.

'Alice, darling, please can you get my medical bags from the car? The keys are in the kitchen.' He then continued to wipe away the worst of the blood with a clean hand towel and was able to inspect the wounds more closely.

John stood and spoke quietly to Tom's father. 'Right, Jamie. We need to get him to hospital urgently. In addition to the bleeding I think he might also have a broken leg. Can you call 999 and explain that time is of the essence. They need to get the Air Ambulance here immediately?'

For a moment, Jamie just stood motionless in shock. Then, suddenly, he seemed to return to reality, took out his phone and dialled the number.

NICK LOOKED BACK to the river as he ran up the steps to the house. Pete and Emma had, together, managed to drag the shark out of the water. It was still thrashing around, but going nowhere.

The children had wrapped themselves in towels and moved onto the terrace, away from the shark. They were clearly shocked by the suddenness and ferocity of the attack. Emma put her arms around some of the younger children, pulling them together in a huddle.

In a soft voice she said, 'That was a horrible thing for anyone to have seen. I know that it's going to take some time before you can come to terms with it. But we've got do everything we can to keep it together for all your mums and dads, so they can get the best treatment for Tom. Georgie, Ben, I'm sure your brother is going to be alright. Uncle John will take good care of him before they can get him to hospital. So let's allow your parents the space to do what they can. Okay?'

The children all nodded.

Emma was mindful they were probably treating Tom in the sitting room.

'Milla, please could you take everyone round to the

back of the house to watch television in the playroom? I've got to help out down here for a while, but I'll be with you as soon as I can. There are lots of rugs in there, so wrap yourselves up nice and warm and we'll get some clothes for you.'

Milla immediately understood what Emma was thinking. She and Heli helped to guide everyone away from the back of the house to the playroom. As they did so, Nick emerged from the front of the house and down to the beach.

'How's Tom?' Emma asked.

'John's managed to stop the bleeding but I think he's going to need some fairly major surgery.' Nick shook his head. 'Poor Bella's beside herself. Jamie's just about holding it together. He's called it in and I understand they're going to land the Air Ambulance in the field at the top of the lane. Fortunately, there's a paramedic nearby. He's been treating a patient about five miles away and should be here any minute.'

Nick looked at Emma and Pete and realised what he should have said.

'Oh god, I am so sorry. Emma, what you did was amazingly brave. You acted without any thought for your own safety. That shark could easily have turned on you. If you hadn't stopped it from dragging Tom out into the water, who knows what might have happened. You, as well, Pete. Thank you both for everything that you did.'

'Look, I did nothing,' Pete said with typical humility. 'Emma had already done the hard work. And what about you, Nick? You took one hell of a risk. Never seen anything like that before.'

'We all just acted on instinct,' Nick said. 'And, thankfully, those instincts proved to be right.'

Nick looked at the shark, which had almost stopped

breathing and studied it closely. It was about five feet long, but very thin and clearly very under nourished.

'If this is the same shark that attacked that man two days ago, then our first impressions were right. That is definitely a juvenile bull shark.'

'That's what I thought it was,' Emma said looking at Nick. 'But what the hell is it doing thousands of miles away from its natural habitat?'

'I think that's something only a post-mortem examination will tell us,' Nick said and jumped back as the shark suddenly started to wriggle around. 'Talking of which, I'll give Andrew Wallace a call and see if he can arrange for a CSIP Team to come down.'

Pete looked confused. 'What's this CSIP Team?' he asked.

Emma got in first. 'It's the Cetacean Strandings Investigation Programme. They travel round the UK mainly doing post-mortems on stranded mammals, but mainly whales. When I was a student, I attended one on a sperm whale that got stranded on the Norfolk coast. Absolutely fascinating, but bloody smelly!'

'I'm not surprised,' Nick said and smiled. 'Most of those carcases are so full of decomposing gases they are about ready to explode!'

They heard footsteps coming across the terrace and turned to see Jamie coming down to join them.

'How's Tom?' Nick asked.

'The paramedic's here now and he's stabilised Tom. He's putting some type of support around the leg. John did a great job as well.' Jamie looked drained, clearly finding it hard to keep himself together. 'We're just waiting for the Air Ambulance which is due any minute now.'

Jamie moved next to Emma and Nick.

'Look, I just want to thank you all for what you did

earlier. Emma, I already knew that you're brave, but what you did was truly remarkable. Thank you.'

Jamie stopped for a moment, his emotions welling up. He composed himself and continued.

'Nick, what you did was equally remarkable. You read about people repelling sharks by digging their fingers in the shark's eye, but you always wonder if it's true. Well, today you proved it works. Thank you.'

Jamie turned to Pete who was standing by the shark.

'And, finally, Pete. I saw how it took all of your incredible your strength to help Emma drag that shark away from the children and onto the shore. Without all your brave acts, my son may not be alive now. So thank you, with all my heart.'

Nick noticed the tears welling up in Jamie's eyes and instinctively gave his friend a hug. Jamie wiped his eyes and looked up, slightly embarrassed.

'Sorry about that,' he said. 'I hadn't realised just how much this had got to me.'

'Well,' Pete said, walking over to Jamie and putting his around his shoulder. 'I'm just pleased to see that our next Prime Minister isn't afraid to shed a tear in front of his friends. You'll get my vote.'

Jamie managed to smile. 'Thank you Pete. Much appreciated.'

The throbbing whirr of helicopter blades could suddenly be heard in the distance.

'I must go and help to get Tom up to the landing spot,' Jamie said, looking up skywards to spot the incoming aircraft.

'I'll come in with you,' Nick said, heading up the steps.

'Good luck. Hope everything goes well,' Emma shouted at the retreating figures. Jamie waved back in acknowledgement, before disappearing into the house.

As they entered the sitting room, the paramedic, with John's help, was preparing to lift Tom out to a vehicle to transfer him up the hill. Bella was clearly still in shock, but she managed to hold the drip to one side as the two men carried the boy out to the cars. Alice had folded the rear seats down in their 4x4 and Tom was laid on blankets already placed there. The medic climbed in beside Tom. Bella sat with her feet hanging out the back, still holding up the drip and ensuring it didn't get tangled.

Jamie climbed in the front passenger seat. John drove gently up the drive. Nick and Sophie followed in their car.

They arrived at the field just as the helicopter was arriving. Alice had previously driven up to the field to obtain the GPS location that had guided the pilot to the exact spot.

Within minutes of landing, the on board trauma specialist had done a quick assessment of Tom's condition. Satisfied that he was stable, they transferred him carefully onto the helicopter's custom built stretcher. The pilot said they could take two adults with them. Nick made sure that both parents were able to accompany their son.

'We'll drive across to the hospital and join you as soon as we can. And don't worry about Georgie and Ben. We'll make sure they know you send your love and will be in touch later,' Nick assured them.

As soon as all the passengers were secured on board, the engine started and the Air Ambulance took off on its twelve minute journey to the hospital. By car, the journey would take an hour longer.

Back at the house, Nick stood out on the terrace and called Andrew Wallace.

'Nick, how are you? Andrew asked.

'Could be better,' Nick replied and explained what had happened.

'God that's awful news. Please send my best wishes to Jamie. I hope his son's recovery is a very swift one.'

'Sophie and I are going to drive to the hospital in Truro once we've got everything sorted out here,' Nick said. 'Andrew, a couple of things. I think we need to do a post mortem as soon as possible on this shark. Do you know if there's a CSIP team around here at present?'

'I don't think there will be, but Rob Burton, the lead vet on many strandings, lives near you. I'll call him and see if he can get over tomorrow.' Andrew sounded excited by the prospect of a post mortem. 'One thing's for sure, I definitely want to be involved. I'm going to get up early and be with you around 9 a.m. if that's okay?'

'That would be perfect,' Nick said, grateful for his friend's offer. 'I'll send you our address.'

'Good. I'll let you know if Rob's available. You said there were two things?'

'Yes. I'd be very grateful if could you let all the other members of the advisory committee know about this attack. I would imagine that LeGrand will need to tell the PM.'

'No problem, leave it with me. I'll be in touch shortly. Bye.'

Nick pocketed his phone and went to find the children.

'They're in the playroom,' Beth said, carrying the dirty towels round to the laundry. 'Emma's with them. By the way, you should know she did a great job in calming them all down after the attack. She also made sure they didn't come into the house while Tom was being treated. Not only was she so brave in dealing with that shark, but she's also made sure that Georgie and Ben have been cared for.'

'Thanks for letting me know.' Nick said as he turned and left the room.

As expected, he found Emma in the playroom, sitting on a sofa, her arms around the Stoddard children.

'Hi Nick,' Emma said, looking up as he walked in. 'We were all just saying feel like something to eat now. Shall I have a word with Sophie?'

'Yes, please do.' Nick replied as Emma got up and walked to the door.

Nick joined Georgie and Ben on the sofa.

'Your mum and dad have gone off in the helicopter with Tom to the hospital. I'm afraid they didn't get the chance to come to say goodbye as it was all a bit frantic. They asked me to tell you they love you both very much and will call you as soon as they have more news about Tom.'

'He's not going to die is he?' Ben asked, tears welling up in his eyes.

'No, Ben,' Nick said and gave him a hug. 'The injury to his leg was pretty bad, so once they've treated it, he'll probably have to spend a few days in hospital. But I bet he'll be back home with you really soon.'

'Will we be allowed to visit him in hospital?' Georgie asked.

'Yes, of course you will. Mum and Dad will be back tomorrow and they'll be able to tell you about it.'

Emma put her head round the door.

'Right, dinner's going to be served shortly on the terrace, so come on everyone, let's go.'

Milla was the last to make her way out and Emma stopped her as she went past.

'Nick, your eldest daughter was a star earlier.' Milla, looked embarrassed by the praise. 'Even though she was upset herself, she unselfishly spent a lot of time making sure Georgie and Ben were okay. You would've been very proud of her.'

Nick gave his eldest daughter a huge hug. 'Thank you, Mills. It's a very hard thing to take care of others when you are suffering yourself. Recognising those two were having an even harder time than you and helping them as best you could just shows what a special young woman you are. I'm so very proud of you.'

Milla wasn't sure whether to laugh or cry. She did both.

'Oh, Daddy,' she said, leaning into Nick and wiping her eyes on his shirt.

She then pulled back and looked at Nick's shirt. 'Daddy, you're covered in blood!'

'Yes, I know. I'm going to do a quick change and then Mummy and I are off to join Tom's parents at the hospital. We might be there most of the night.'

Milla nodded. 'Okay. Please send my love to them, and to Tom. Poor little boy.'

Nick looked at his watch. 'I should think they'll be there by now and I imagine the doctors will get Tom into surgery pretty quickly. But don't mention that to the others, please. We don't to worry them more than necessary.'

'Of course,' Milla said and started to move out of the door. She paused for a moment. 'We're all very proud of the way you jumped onto that shark. That was so brave. Well done, Daddy.' And with that she walked off to join the others.

He watched her go, astonished by his daughter's words. After a few moments, he said, 'Well, I wasn't expecting that.'

Emma smiled. 'She's just like her mother - strong, beautiful and intelligent. You are right to be proud of her.'

'And you are a very good role model, not only for Milla, but for all the girls here. We're all very grateful.'

'Oh, stop this otherwise you'll have me crying too,' Emma said. 'Right, I'm going to get some food. Please send my best wishes to the Stoddards.'

Nick's phone buzzed in his pocket. It was a message from Andrew.

Rob Burton is free tomorrow. We'll both be with you around 9.

Please send location details. Have sent email to committee members. Best wishes to Jamie and his wife. Hope the little boy is OK. Andrew.

Nick texted his address as he headed towards the sitting room entrance. Just as he was about to go through the door, Emma walked out carrying two plates of freshly cooked meat.

'In case you're interested,' Nick said, stopping her before she walked over to the table. 'Andrew Wallace is coming over early tomorrow along with one of the specialists from the CSIP team to do the post mortem. Would you like to help out?'

'Yes, please,' Emma replied, her eyes lighting up with excitement. 'I can't wait to see the Professor again. Do you know who the other person is?'

'Yes, it's Rob Burton.'

'Really? He was the lead on the autopsy I attended in Norfolk. That's great, I can't wait. Look, I'd better get this food over to the children. Beth cooked it all in the oven rather than messing about on the BBQ. See you later.'

Nick smiled to himself. He couldn't imagine there would be many twenty-one year olds who would get excited at the thought of cutting up a dead shark.

Before he went in to change, Nick went down to the beach for a last check on the shark. He met John walking up the steps, an old fashioned leather bag in his hand.

'I euthanised the shark while you were getting Tom into the helicopter,' John said and held up the bag. 'This is a captive bolt unit I was given years ago by our senior partner when he retired. It may be old but it does the job perfectly. It puts the animal out of its misery immediately. Like you, I don't like to see any animal suffer.'

'Thanks, John,' Nick replied, relieved. 'I was going to ask you if there was anything we could do.'

John shrugged his shoulders. 'It's done now. Look, I'd

better put this device back in the car, well out of the way of inquisitive boys.'

Nick continued down to the beach. Pete was there, dismantling the camera. He'd pulled the shark all the way up to the concreted hard standing by himself and covered it with a green tarpaulin. Nick never failed to be surprised by his strength.

'Thought I'd get it onto hard ground ready for the post mortem,' Pete said as he folded up the camera tripod.

'Thank you, mate. They're going to be here about nine tomorrow.'

'Hmmm, I might just give that a miss. Never did like cutting animals up, especially smelly ones. I'll have a look at this film later tonight and do a bit of work on it. I'll send it to you as soon as I'm finished,'

'Great, thanks Pete. Sophie and I are about to head over to the hospital. No idea what time we'll be back. Before I forget, there's some food up on the terrace if you want some.'

'I'll be right there.' He looked at Nick and screwed his face up. 'Can I suggest you change your clothes before you go to the hospital? You look a bit like a mass murderer!'

'Don't worry, about to do it,' Nick said and set off up the steps.

'By the way,' Pete called out. 'You did bloody good today mate, and so did Emma. Top work, both of you.'

Nick stopped for a moment and looked back, unaccustomed to praise from his friend. 'And not too bad yourself, Pete. Not too bloody bad at all.'

He hurried up the steps to the house.

CHAPTER FORTY-FOUR

FRIDAY, 13TH JULY
Royal Cornwall Hospital,
Truro, Cornwall

After spending ten minutes searching the hospital, and having asked several members of staff staff for directions, Nick and Sophie eventually found the right ward. As they walked through the doors, they saw Jamie and Bella sitting on a couple of plastic chairs in the corridor. Jamie had his arm around Bella. They could see the tears in the distraught mother's eyes.

'Hi, you two,' Sophie said as they gave their friends a welcoming hug. 'What's the news on Tom?'

'We think he's still in surgery,' Jamie replied. 'We hoped we might have had a bit of news by now.'

A door opened a few metres down the corridor. A doctor wearing blue scrubs appeared and looked uncertainly at the four adults.

'Mr and Mrs Stoppard?'

'That's us,' Bella said taking Jamie's arm, desperately hoping for good news.

'Hello. I'm Chris Perks. I've just operated on Tom. Could you possibly join me for a moment and I'll update you on his condition?' he said and smiled reassuringly as he ushered the parents into a separate room.

After a few minutes they reappeared, shook hands with the surgeon and thanked him. They joined their friends in the corridor.

'How is he?' Nick asked.

'Well, he's only just come out of surgery but he's okay,' Bella said, still shaken but relieved to have had some positive news about her little boy. 'The surgeon said the bite wounds were deep but they were able to clean them out and sew or staple them back together.'

Jamie continued. 'What took so long was that they discovered two fractures in the leg. The major one is in his tibia. They've had to use screws to hold it in place. There's also a hairline fracture in the fibia. He'll need to wear a cast for quite some time - and that will drive him mad.'

'Oh, poor boy,' Sophie said sympathetically. 'How long before you can go in to see him?'

'The surgeon suggested we give him half an hour to come round from the anaesthetic,' Jamie said, checking the time on his watch.

'In that case, why don't we see if we can get a coffee?' Sophie suggested, thinking the distraction might help the time pass more quickly.

'That would be good,' Bella said, sighing. 'We could do with stretching our legs for a few minutes.'

Sophie put a comforting arm around Bella as they led the way down brightly lit corridors that smelt faintly of disinfectant. Nick and Jamie followed a few paces behind.

'Before I forget,' Nick said, pulling a bunch of car keys

out of his pocket. 'I found these on the table on the terrace, so I drove your car over and Sophie brought ours. At least it gives you a bit of flexibility about when you go home.'

'That's brilliant, thank you Nick,' Jamie said. 'I must admit I was wondering how we were going to arrange it. One big problem solved.'

As they followed their wives, they were passed by busy nurses and medical staff, several of whom smiled when they recognised Nick. He duly obliged and smiled back.

'I also asked Andy Wallace to let all the advisory group members know about the attack. I thought LeGrand might need to keep the PM informed.'

'Yes, of course, thanks Nick,' Jamie said. 'With all that's been going on, I hadn't had time to think about the wider consequences. I suppose the media are going to have to be told at some stage.'

'Look, I'm sorry to trouble you with this,' Nick said, seeing the concern on his friend's face. 'Perhaps later on you should give LeGrand a quick call and then you can control when a statement is made. Just so you know, Andy Wallace and another specialist are coming over to do a necropsy on the shark first thing tomorrow.'

'Okay. It'll be interesting to see what that reveals,' Jamie said, trying hard to concentrate on what Nick was saying. 'The problem is that word will definitely have got out about the attack. Unfortunately, we both know the fact that it was my son who was injured will attract a lot of attention. Similarly, I'm sure your involvement will guarantee increased media interest.'

'Don't worry about me, I'm used to it,' Nick said and smiled as he placed a reassuring hand on his friend's arm.

Sophie and Bella had stopped further up the corridor.

'Oh no,' Sophie said, standing outside the shutter of the closed coffee shop.

'Don't worry, there's a drinks machine here,' Nick said, pointing out a large dispensing unit behind them. 'It's one of those big brand machines, so the coffee ought to be drinkable. Is Americano with milk okay for everyone?'

They all nodded. Jamie joined him at the machine.

'Did you get a chance to look at the film Pete recorded?' Jamie asked as they waited for the machine to perform its task.

'Not yet,' Nick said. 'Pete did say he was going to work on it and I'm sure he'll send it over as soon as he's finished.'

'I'm not going to enjoy watching it, but at least it will prove that the steps we're taking are necessary. Please could you make sure I get a copy as soon as he's able to do it.'

'Of course I will. Apologies, I haven't told you – it turned out to be a juvenile bull shark.'

'Just as you and Andrew predicted. Isn't it a long way from home though?'

'Absolutely. We're hoping that the post mortem will help to explain that for us.'

Nick passed round the cups when the machine finished its cycle.

'Here you are,' Nick said. 'Enjoy, if that's possible!'

'Thank you,' Jamie said, raising an eyebrow, and turned back to Nick. 'I suppose we should possibly consider removing the restrictions on the south coast now. That is, as long as you and Andrew are satisfied this shark was probably the culprit of the Praa Sands attack.'

'I think that's a move too far at this stage. I understand how keen you are to ease the restrictions, but I think we ought to wait for the results of the post mortem before making any further decisions.'

'Of course,' Jamie said, agreeing with Nick. 'We must be sure before we take any further steps.'

Bella looked anxiously at her watch. 'I know we've only

been gone ten minutes, but would you mind if we headed back to find out if we can get in to see Tom? I'd hate for him to wake up and not have us with him.'

'Yes, of course, let's make a move,' Sophie said. They all hastened back down the corridor, spilling the odd drop of brown liquid as they went.

CHAPTER FORTY-FIVE

SATURDAY, 14TH JULY
Dowrtreven, Helford River,
Cornwall

Sophie watched the white van pull up outside the kitchen window. The lettering on the side of the van said *University of Southampton*.

'Nick,' Sophie shouted through the kitchen door. 'Your visitor's here.'

'Yes, seen him, thanks,' Nick replied and went out to greet his old friend.

Andy Wallace was climbing out of his van as Nick approached.

'Surprised you can move after driving that thing all the way down here,' Nick said shaking Andy's hand. 'Welcome to Dowrtreven. Good trip?'

'Considering it's July and I was driving that old thing, it went surprisingly well,' Andy replied with a smile pointing at the van. 'Lovely place you've got here. Pity it's so far from Southampton - I had to leave before dawn. By the way, thanks for sending the film of the attack. The quality was so good I thought you must have had a film crew here.'

'That's all down to Pete Higham. I think you'll have met him with me before,' Nick said. 'Look, come on in and have a coffee before we get to work.'

As they began to walk towards the house, Emma appeared round the corner.

'Professor! How lovely to see you again,' she said, walking up to Andy and shaking his hand.

'Emma! I'd totally forgotten you'd be here,' Andy replied, delighted to see his former, high achieving student. 'And please call me Andy.'

'Thank you,' she said. 'I'm looking forward to seeing you help perform the necropsy.'

'Come on, let's go inside and get Andy a coffee,' Nick said directing them towards the kitchen, where he introduced Andy to Sophie and Beth. He then steered Andy outside while they waited for the coffee to be made. John appeared from the lower terrace and Nick once more made the introductions.

'John is actually an equine vet,' Nick said. 'But he's very keen to lend a hand, if needed.'

'I'm not sure I'll be much use with a fish,' John said. 'So just treat me like one of your students.'

'Well, the more the merrier, as far as I'm concerned,' Andy said. 'Now, is this fish anywhere nearby? I'd love to see it.'

'Yes, just down there,' Nick said, leading the way.

They walked across the terrace, down the steps and arriving at the hard standing where the dead fish lay.

'Pete covered it with a tarpaulin overnight to prevent the gulls having a go at it,' John explained.

Andy bent down to look at the shark carefully. 'You were right Nick, that's definitely a *carcharhinus leucas*, or bull shark.

It's a juvenile male and I'd bet you it's got African origins. But we'll be able tell that from the DNA tests. I'm so excited about the chance to work on this fish.'

Emma came down the steps carrying a tray of coffees, accompanied by an athletic looking man in his mid-forties.

'Rob. Good to see you again,' Andy greeted his colleague. 'Can I introduce Nick Martin? I'm sure you recognise him. This is his brother-in-law, John, who's an equine vet. And last, but far from least, Emma Warren, a former student of mine who's now working with Nick. This is Rob Burton, who's taken the lead in the majority of necropsies for CSIP.'

'Delighted to meet you all and, of course, Emma and I have met before,' Rob said shaking hands with everyone. 'Andy, you may remember that you kindly allowed her to assist me on a stranding I dealt with on the Norfolk coast a year or so ago. And John, I hope you're going to join in, too?'

'I'd love to, as long as that's okay with you all.'

'Of course. It'll make quite a change from your normal patients. Now, as soon as you've finished your coffees, we'll make a start,' Rob said. 'Can I suggest you wear wellies if you've got them? Please don't wear any clothes you're not prepared to throw away. I've got some white Tyvek overalls in my van you can wear if you'd prefer.'

FIFTEEN MINUTES LATER, dressed in white overalls and protective gloves, they all stood round the sharks' body. Rob had laid out a number of sharp instruments and plastic trays in preparation for the autopsy. He'd also put a set of scales nearby.

'Right, let's get started,' Rob said. He selected up a large knife and made an incision from the gills all the way along the body to the anus. This immediately revealed the shark's liver.

'That's a huge liver,' John said, surprised by what the opening had revealed.

'Yes,' Andy said. 'It can be up to twenty per cent of the shark's body weight. But this one won't be. It's actually relatively small and the colour just supports the observation that this wasn't a healthy shark.'

Rob removed the liver and placed it onto a large plastic tray for weighing. 'Andy, you're right. This shark was seriously malnourished. It's remarkable it even made it to these waters.'

'Rob, would you mind explaining to me how a bull shark can survive for long periods in fresh water when other sharks can't?' John asked.

'Of course,' Rob replied. 'The bull shark's a member of what we call a diadromous species, meaning it can comfortably move from salt to fresh water, and back. They're able to do this thanks to several organs which maintain the balance between their *internal* salt and water. The rectal gland,' Rob pointed to an organ at the base of the tail, 'kidneys, liver and gills all work together to achieve this. The rectal gland is used to excrete excess salts – in freshwater, they simply excrete less of it. Does that make sense?'

'Thanks,' John replied. 'It certainly does.'

When Rob cut into the intestine, it was almost devoid of the fish remains he would normally have expected to find. It did reveal a large quantity of plastic and tapeworms. He removed the rest of the intestine and used a bucket of water to wash through the contents.

'Look at this,' Rob said excitedly as he pulled a small mass of flesh from the rest. 'I think this could be human flesh. If it is, it would almost certainly give you the proof you need that this shark was involved in the first attack, Praa Sands was it?' Andy nodded. 'DNA tests should provide the definitive proof you need. Emma, please can you put it in the sample pot with the purple label and seal it? Thank you.'

After removing the key organs from the carcass, Rob moved to the head, eventually revealing the brain. He removed the bolt John had used to euthanize the shark.

'I'm afraid that belongs to me,' John explained.

'I haven't seen one of those in ages. Old fashioned but very effective,' Rob said and smiled as he handed the bolt back to John.

Rob made further incisions to free the brain. A huge pink tumour was revealed attached to the surface of the brain.

All the onlookers drew their breath as the tumour was exposed.

'Bloody hell, I don't think I've ever seen a glioblastoma multiforme that size before,' Andy said, looking on in astonishment. 'That would almost certainly account for the shark's wholly untypical journey to these shores. A tumour as large as that could have played havoc with its innate navigational ability.'

'Absolutely,' Rob agreed. 'It could also account for its lack of natural fear of humans and thus the attacks.' He continued to cut into the brain and held it up for the others to examine. 'You can see here how the tumour grows by sending these tendrils out into the surrounding brain tissue. The poor creature would have basically lost control of its own natural function.'

After another twenty minutes of weighing the organs and taking samples for DNA testing, Rob announced that he had finished.

'Nick, could we use your boat to dispose of the carcass

and the organs? We need to tow it out into the estuary, nearer the sea, before we release it and throw the rest in the water.'

'Of course,' Nick said. 'I'll ask Pete to go with you just in case there's any problem with the engine.'

'I'll come along as well,' Andy offered. 'We'll need to make sure the rope holding the carcass doesn't get caught up in the prop.'

'Thanks, Andy. That would be a great help,' Rob said to his colleague. He picked up a coil of rope lying on the floor next to the carcass. 'Nick, John, could you tie that rope securely round the shark's tail? Emma, please can you give me a hand wrapping those remaining organs in this plastic sheet before we get them on the boat?'

PETE CAREFULLY MANOEUVRED the boat onto the water. The sheet containing the waste organs was safely transferred to the boat. As Rob and Andy climbed aboard, Pete started the engine. The others watched from the shore as the boat headed downstream, the shark's carcass carefully towed behind.

Steps could be heard on the terrace and they turned to see Jill walking briskly down the steps.

'Have you finished?' she asked, anxiously.

'Almost. Just got to finish clearing up down here. What's up?' Nick asked.

'I think you need to come and see what's happening in the real world,' Jill said. 'Jamie sent Pete's edited film clip to the other members of the committee with the express orders that nothing be published until you had contacted him after the autopsy. It appears that your favourite minister, Mr. LeGrand, has already released the video to the press.'

'Bloody idiot!' Nick said angrily, shaking his head in disbelief. 'I presume the media have gone beserk?'

'To put it mildly,' Jill said nodding her head. 'Your phone has been ringing non-stop, and yours as well, Emma. Apparently, reporters are turning up in droves at the hospital harassing the staff. It's all over the TV, radio and online. And that's not all - we now have a gang of them at the end of the drive.'

'Oh God,' Emma said. 'Poor Jamie and Bella. That's the last thing they need.'

'Exactly,' Nick said, turning to Jill. 'Do you know if they're still planning on collecting Georgie and Ben this morning, or have plans changed because of this?'

'Sorry, I'm afraid I haven't heard. Perhaps you can give him a call.'

Nick nodded his agreement. 'Okay. I'll be up as soon as we've cleared up here.'

'Don't worry about that,' John said. 'Emma and I can finish up here, it won't take a minute. You go and deal with the mess that the moron LeGrand has caused.'

Nick thanked them and ran up towards the house. He was about to go inside when Sophie appeared at the door.

'Don't even think about coming in wearing that outfit,' she said. 'You smell like a fish processing factory. Come on, strip off!'

Jill smiled, enjoying Nick's embarrassment as she walked past into the sitting room.

CHAPTER FORTY-SIX

SATURDAY, 14TH JULY
Dowrtreven,
Helford River, Cornwall

Fifteen minutes later, after showering, Nick walked into the office, joining Jill who was working on her computer.

'You certainly smell better,' Jill said. 'I'm afraid that eau de shark's guts is *not* going to win any prizes. Have a look at this.'

Nick looked at the headline on the *Daily Globe*'s website.

TV nature star Nick Martin in heroic boy's rescue from shark attack.

Kayak girl hero as she throws herself at shark to rescue Minister's boy!'

'And there are a dozen more like that across the internet, together with the video. You and Emma especially, and Pete to a lesser extent, are being treated like national heroes whether you like it or not.'

'I'll give Jamie a call,' Nick said, angered by the fallout

from LeGrand's interfering blunder. He picked up his phone and dialled Jamie's number. After half a dozen rings, Jamie answered.

'Nick, hi. I'm so sorry if you're getting a load of hassle as a result of that film. It shouldn't have been released. God knows what that idiot LeGrand thought he was doing. Just wait till I get hold of him.'

'I can handle it,' Nick said. 'More importantly, how are you both and how's Tom getting on?

'We spent the night at the hospital. Tom's doing well. Bella's still there but I got back to the house half an hour ago to freshen up and put some clean clothes on. There are TV crews and loads of reporters outside. I've agreed to go out and make a statement in about five minutes. The police are helping out.'

'Last thing you need, heh?' Nick sympathised with his friend, having been in the media spotlight himself on too many occasions.

'True – but I'm afraid it goes with the territory. I understand Bella called Sophie a few minutes ago to confirm that I'll be over to pick up Georgie and Ben after I've dealt with the media scrum outside. Thanks for looking after them.'

'They've been brilliant,' Nick said and noticed Jill nodding in agreement. 'And they're desperate to see Tom.'

'Right, I'll be over as soon as I've done my bit outside.'

'I'm afraid you're also going to have to go past a group of media people at the end of our drive. Anyway, just to let you know, Andy confirmed that it was a juvenile bull shark. The autopsy also revealed what appears to be a small amount of what could be human flesh. So, as soon as we have the DNA results back, hopefully tomorrow, we'll be able to make a decision about relaxing the restrictions on the south coast.'

'That's great news, thanks. Look, I'd better get off.'

'See you soon. Have fun!'

'If only,' Jamie said and finished the call.

'Poor man,' Jill said. 'Having to deal with the media when his son is lying in hospital with awful injuries. Life just isn't fair sometimes.'

A thought suddenly struck Jill. 'I bet his media statement will be live on television.'

'Good point,' Nick said, suddenly feeling energised and moving towards the door. 'Let's go and see. I'll make sure his children are there, too, if it is.'

As it happened, all the children were already in the sitting room having a quiet moment watching a music programme on the TV.

'Sorry to interrupt,' Nick said. 'Georgie and Ben, we think your father's about to make a statement to the press outside your house. Do you mind if I check to see if it's being shown live? Where's the remote, please?'

There was a general murmur of agreement and Heli handed the control to her father.

Sure enough, it was being shown on the twenty-four hour news channel. The screen showed the assembled press and TV outside the Stoddards' house, where two policemen stood guard. The rolling news ticker at the bottom of the screen announced the minister was expected to make a statement in front of the cameras in the next two minutes.

Nick shouted to let the rest of the family know and they quickly joined the children in front of the television. Emma appeared with a towel wrapped round her wet hair

'Sorry about the towel,' Emma said laughing at herself. 'I heard you shouting as I was climbing out of the shower and rushed down.'

Just as she spoke, the screen showed Jamie walking down the drive of his house. He stopped at the gate in front of the TV cameras and various other media representatives. He was casually dressed in a sky blue shirt and navy chinos. He carried a natural air of authority about him and an easy charm, which his good looks only added to.

'Daddy looks smart,' Georgie said, as she and Ben stared at the screen

'Good morning, everyone. Sorry to keep you waiting. As you're all no doubt aware, my son, Tom, was severely injured yesterday while playing in the Helford River. He was attacked by what we now know to be a bull shark. Our scientific advisors believe it was probably the same shark that attacked Mr Neal at Praa Sands earlier in the week. During the attack, my son suffered severe lacerations to his leg, a badly fractured tibia and a hairline fracture to his fibia. He underwent lengthy surgery last night, but we've been assured he should, in time, make a full recovery. I am pleased to say when I left him this morning, he was sitting up in bed and smiling. I think he was just beginning to realise what an interesting answer he would be able to give at school to the question, *'What did you do in your summer holidays?'*.'

The assembled journalists and camera crews smiled with Jamie.

'My wife, Bella, and I would like to thank *all* the wonderful staff at the Royal Cornwall Hospital for their tremendous skill, care and understanding. I cannot praise them enough. Please can I ask for your cooperation in one respect. We would ask all the news outlets that still have people camped outside the hospital, to withdraw them and please leave the staff in peace. There is nothing they can tell you that I won't have said this morning.'

Jamie paused, gathering his thoughts and looked directly at the cameras.

'There are three more remarkable people to whom I must say a *very special* thank you. You will have seen in the film of the attack, the immediate and extraordinarily brave actions of Emma Warren, Nick Martin and Peter Higham. Without their selfless and courageous intervention, it's unlikely that my son would still be alive today. I've already thanked them all personally but I want to repeat that front of the cameras, so that everyone recognises the vital part that they played. Once more, to all of them, Bella and I cannot ever thank you enough for what you did.'

Jamie paused, unable to continue as emotion stirred within him. All the adults watched sympathetically, fully understanding the emotional turmoil he had gone through. He quickly got himself under control and carried on.

'Right, that's all I wish to say today. Sorry, I won't be answering questions on this occasion. Please can you direct to the Minister of Transport any further questions you may have about the remaining restrictions on the north coast. He will be delighted to answer them in depth. Finally, please can I ask that you allow my wife and me the privacy to spend time uninterrupted with our son and our family over the next few days. Thank you all for coming and for your good wishes.'

And with that, Jamie turned and walked back down the drive, accompanied by the odd shouted question from a frustrated journalist.

'Georgie, Ben,' Nick said. 'Your father is a kind and generous man. I hope the media leave you all alone to look after Tom and enjoy a great holiday together. You will come round here again, won't you?'

'We would love to,' Georgie said, her brother nodded in agreement. 'Though I'm not sure I'll be going swimming for a while!'

Everyone laughed and Nick replied. 'Georgie, I'm glad to see you've inherited your mother's sense of humour. Now,

I think we can expect your dad to be here soon and then you'll be off to see Tom.'

'I can't wait to see the size of his plaster cast,' Ben said excitedly. 'I'm going to draw a stupid face on it like I did on Chris Grange's cast last term.'

'So, that will be your face then,' Georgie said, giving Ben an affectionate punch on the arm.

CHAPTER FORTY-SEVEN

SATURDAY, 14TH JULY
Dowrtreven,
Helford River, Cornwall

Twenty minutes later, Jamie arrived to collect the children. Everyone praised his performance. For his part, he apologised modestly for having been unintendedly emotional. 'But once more, thank you all for your help and support yesterday. In circumstances like these, you soon find out who your friends are. And ours are most definitely here.'

Ben had no time for all this. 'Come on Dad, stop making speeches and let's get off to the hospital. I can't wait to ask Tom what it felt like to be half-eaten by a shark.'

Jamie looked horrified. 'Ben, that is *not* what you're going to ask your brother. Right you two, have you got everything? OK, let's be off and give these kind people a break. By the way, there's quite a gathering at your gate. I'm afraid I didn't stop to have a word. I just smiled and waved.'

'I don't blame you,' Nick said. 'I think Emma and I are

going to have to have a walk up there and face the music, otherwise they'll never go.'

It took five minutes for the Stoddard family to leave. Everyone wanted to say goodbye and send their best wishes to Bella and Tom. Eventually, the family stood and waved as the Stoddard car made its way up the drive.

Jill took Nick and Sophie by the arm and said quietly. 'Can we have a quick word in the office?'

Nick and Sophie knew better than to ask what it was about in front of everyone and they allowed themselves to be steered in the right direction. Once inside the office, she explained the reason for her furtiveness.

'I popped back in here whilst you were saying goodbye to Jamie and looked at the emails that were coming through. I wanted to speak to you two first and get your thoughts.' Jill scrolled though the messages on her screen. 'First up, they want you and Emma to do the Ed Norton Show a week on Saturday.'

Nick looked mystified. 'Ed Norton? But that's a show for actors, celebs and rock stars.'

'You've got it!' Jill said, laughing at Nick's reaction. 'Also, among many other numerous requests, two of the Sunday papers want to do separate interviews with you both. But the most interesting ones are for Emma on her own. *Vogue*, want to feature Emma on the cover of their *Women and the World* edition in a couple of months.' Sophie's eyes lit up in surprise.

'Also DigDag, the upmarket clothes brand, want to talk to her about becoming a brand representative.'

'Oh my God,' Sophie exclaimed.

'And then there's Women's Hour. They want Emma to do an in depth interview sometime next week!'

'Jill, I think you and Sophie need to have an honest, business like conversation with Emma about temporarily acting as her agents,' Nick said, as the two women looked at him questioningly. 'I'm being serious. She has no idea what all this will entail. You two, on the other hand, have always handled that side of my life and you have the experience and knowledge to guide her through it all. She's got no idea what sort of money she should expect for commercial opportunities like this.'

Nick looked at them both, waiting for their response.

'She really needs guiding through all the offers and opportunities that are coming her way,' Nick stressed.

'I know you're right,' Jill replied. 'She's an attractive, intelligent, twenty-one year old woman who approaches life like a stuntwoman. She is a godsend for all types of industries.'

'Exactly,' Sophie agreed. 'But, as Nick said, this is going to be a whole new world for her. Given half a chance, these people won't hesitate to take advantage of her inexperience. Jilly, for the time being, you and I are going to have to be stand in mothers and mentor her through this tricky time.'

'OK, let's do it,' Jill said, nodding enthusiastically. 'We need to go through all these offers with her.'

'Let's see if she's got time now,' Sophie suggested. 'I'll go and find her. Nick, if you don't mind, this needs to be a women only meeting.'

Nick held his hands up in surrender. 'Fine by me. I expect Andy and Rob will be back soon. By the way, would it be alright if I ask them to stay for lunch?'

'I'm sure that will be fine,' Sophie said. 'Just check with Mum first. Right, I'll go and find Emma.'

It took longer to dispose of the shark than Nick had expected. Over half an hour later the boat appeared and

Nick helped Pete pull the boat clear of the river and onto the beach.

'Sorry we took so long,' Andy explained as they climbed out of the boat. 'But we got the shark tangled up with a bloody great branch that had fallen into the river and it took ages to get it free. Anyway, after that it all went well and we had a lovely journey from the estuary up the river. It's a good job we had Pete with us because I'd forgotten how tidal the Helford is.'

'Yeah,' Nick agreed. 'Some people get caught out by it. It can be hard to make it up river when it's at its worst. Would you like to stay for some lunch?'

'That's very kind,' Rob said. 'But I've got to get back. My wife's brother and family are due anytime now.'

'Count me in, though, please,' Andy said enthusiastically. 'I'll need to set off straight afterwards if that's okay? I'll get back to the lab tonight and start the DNA test on the sample we think might be of human.'

'No problem at all,' Nick said. They helped Pete secure the boat and headed up to the house.

Andy left after lunch having said goodbye to everyone and getting a big hug from Emma.

Before he got into the van, he said quietly to Emma, 'I hear big things might be opening up for you. I'm not at all surprised, you were always destined for a successful career. But just take a word of advice from me. Before you do anything, just take a moment to think what your mother would have done and you'll never go wrong! Take care and I hope to see you soon.'

He drove off waving his hand wildly out of the van's window.

Nick stood next to Emma and watched as the van turned the bend in the drive and disappeared.

'How did the chat with Sophie and Jill go?'

'Oh, they were wonderful,' she said, her eyes lighting up. 'It's like having two extra mums. So easy to talk to and giving me so much good advice. I think you and I need to talk soon and see what you will be happy for me to do.'

'Well, there's no immediate rush for that. Let's find time to discuss it next week?'

Emma suddenly found herself wiping away a tear. 'Thank you so much. You've all been so kind to me.'

'Well, the probation period's coming to an end. We start to get nasty soon,' Nick joked as they went into the house. 'I'm afraid part of the job's dealing with the media. That means you and I will have to talk to the crowd at the end of the drive. Shall we go now and get it over with?'

'I understand. If we don't, they'll just hang around until we give in. Can you just give me a couple of minutes to make myself look presentable and I'll be with you.'

'Of course,' Nick said, 'not a problem. Let's meet outside in, say, ten minutes.'

'That's fine, see you then,' replied Emma as she disappeared upstairs.

Shortly afterwards, they walked up the main drive. As they reached the top bend, they could see, for the first time, the large media group that had assembled, and a number of TV cameras.

'Bloody hell,' Emma said. 'I wasn't expecting as many as that.'

'Don't worry. Just smile, keep your answers short and we'll get through this in no time'.

Emma watched in admiration as a smile immediately appeared on Nick's face.

'Good morning, everyone, and thank you so much for being here today,' he said, confidently. 'Emma and I are here to answer your questions as best as we can, so let's get started!'

Half an hour later, Nick and Emma arrived back at the house. Jill was waiting for them on the terrace.

'How did that go?' she asked.

'Very well,' Nick said and turned to look at Emma. 'Though I'm not sure I really contributed much – it was Emma they wanted to talk to!'

'Oh come on, Nick,' said an indignant Emma. 'You were asked just as many questions as me.'

'Well, one thing's certain,' Nick said, 'you were completely at ease in front of the cameras. Also, the calm way you dealt with badgering reporters was very impressive. You're a natural presenter. It's going to save us a fortune in training fees!'

CHAPTER FORTY-EIGHT

SUNDAY, 15TH JULY
Dowrtreven,
Helford River, Cornwall

Nick returned from walking Molly. He had walked back across the fields and was delighted to see that the entrance to the drive was now devoid of media representatives . He had just rejoined the driveway nearer to the house, when a text message from Andy came through on his phone.

Been up all night. Can confirm that the sample is human. We still need to get a DNA sample from the Praa Sands victim for confirmation. Confident this is the same shark involved in both attacks, Can thus recommend the end of restrictions on the south coast. Best. Andy

Nick replied with his thanks and immediately called Jamie.

'Jamie, how are you, or, more to the point, how's Tom?'

'We're all fine, thanks. As for Tom, well, the doctors are really pleased with his progress. They just want to make sure that the antibiotics are working. As you know, shark bites contain lots of nasty stuff. All being well, they're going to allow him to come home with us tomorrow.'

Nick slipped off Molly's lead and she ran on ahead of him.

'That's fantastic news. He's clearly a toughie, is Tom. Takes after his father!' he said as he followed Molly down the drive to the house.

'I think we both know that's a load of bollocks!' Jamie replied, smiling.

'Well, I've got some good news for you.' He then described the text he had just had from Andy.

'Oh, thank God for that,' Jamie said. Nick could hear the relief in his voice. 'The PM's office has asked if he can call me in ten minute's time. He'll say that he was ringing to ask about Tom, but what he really wants is to discuss whether it's safe to remove some of the restrictions on both coasts. Obviously, the news on the south coast will please him but I'd be grateful if you could tell me your thoughts about the north coast?'

'Gosh, that's not going to be easy to answer,' Nick said, considering his response. 'On the one hand, you could say the restrictions are working because there haven't been any incidents reported in the past forty-eight hours. In fact, to my knowledge, there haven't even been any *sightings* in that time either. So you could either argue that the shark seems to have disappeared from these shores entirely, or that the reason there haven't been any sightings is that all the protective activity around the beaches has been effective as a deterrent.'

'Those are the exact arguments I've been considering with my departmental staff,' Jamie said. 'But I'm afraid the PM will just tell me to take the responsibility on board and make a decision. The reality is he's being influenced by some less than favourable opinion polls we've had from the south west.'

'I can see your problem. So why not, initially, try removing the ban on jet skis and on boats launching from the beaches. To be honest, I didn't really understand that restriction in the first place – but, for safety purposes, you'd have to keep a ban on water skiing. You could perhaps also allow people to use paddle boards and inflatables, but not beyond fifty metres of the shore from where they launched. You've got to state that otherwise, you'll get people disappearing round headlands. If there's still no sign of the shark in a couple of days, you could then consider lifting the ban altogether. The key thing is still to minimise the opportunities for humans and shark to interact.'

'That sounds like a reasonable solution,' Jamie said. Nick could hear the relief in his voice. 'Thanks for your help. I'm afraid that my brain hasn't been at its sharpest in the past few days.'

'That's what I'm here for and, don't worry, anyone would understand you've had a pretty tough couple of days,' Nick said. Approaching the house, he saw Sophie wave through the kitchen window. 'I'd better get off the line in case the PM calls. By the way, why isn't LeGrand taking the lead on this?'

'Well, after his cock ups with the first announcement and then again yesterday's releasing of the film of the attack, I was advised by the PM's office that LeGrand no longer "entirely enjoyed" the PM's confidence. They also told me the PM would be grateful if I could possibly take the lead on this once again.'

'Sounds like LeGrand's buggered,' Nick said walking onto the terrace, raising his fist in celebration

'Couldn't have said it better myself. Thanks again my friend. Speak soon.'

Pete and Jill were sitting at a table on the terrace.

'Who's buggered?' Pete asked.

'Our friend LeGrand,' Nick said, pulling up a weed from between the flag stones. 'It appears that he no longer has the PM's confidence. More work for Jamie, I'm afraid, but at least he's about to have the more agreeable task of announcing a relaxation of some of the rules. That's going to make a lot of holidaymakers much happier.'

'Now *that* is good news,' Jill said. 'I presume that was him on the phone?'

Nick nodded.

'How's Tom?' she asked

'All being well, he'll be out of hospital tomorrow.'

'Sorry,' Sophie asked. 'is that Tom you're talking about?' She joined them at the table.

'Yes. It'll be a huge relief for his parents,' Nick said.

'It's going to be a lengthy healing process,' Sophie said. 'But children of Tom's age are so resilient and they heal quickly.'

Having been forewarned by text, Nick watched the lunchtime news. Jamie announced the changes to the coastal restrictions . The station switched live to a reporter interviewing holidaymakers on Newquay's beaches to get their reactions. They all welcomed the news. Many offered thanks and sympathy to the minister for the injuries to his son.

'People aren't going to forget the horror of Tom's attack any time soon,' Nick said to Sophie as they watched. 'Jamie's had to live through a nightmare, but on the positive side, the good news about the lifting of restrictions, combined with his son's recovery, can't do any harm for

Jamie's PM campaign at some stage in the future. Politics works in a funny way.'

'Let's just hope there aren't any new incidents from now on. If there are, that makes today's decision look a bit premature,' Sophie said. 'I think we're all hoping the old girl just disappears.'

'It would be sad to see her go, but I couldn't agree with you more,' Nick said. 'It's time she moved on.'

CHAPTER FORTY-NINE

SUNDAY, 15TH JULY
Trevose Head,
North Cornwall

The two paddle boarders now had a clear view of Trevose Head Lighthouse. It had taken them almost an hour to reach this point from Booby's Bay. They had overcome the choppier waters of the headland and now were able to move in towards the calmer, protected waters of Stinking Cove. There, before them, was the small colony of grey seals they had come to see. The seals inhabited the rocks and the water around Trevose Head in considerable numbers.

Zeb and Trina Jameson always considered themselves a little rebellious. They weren't married (an unnecessary concept in their eyes) although most people thought they were. Instead, Zeb had changed his surname by deed poll to Trina's. They were leading lights in the local environmental and conservation movements and proudly lived a mindful and sustainable vegan lifestyle. As a result, they often deliberately acted against any in authority who might limit their choices. This trip on their paddleboards was in direct contravention of the new restrictions.

They'd planned this day a long time before the ban. As far as they were concerned, the ban only applied to holidaymakers and intruders who inflicted their jet skis on their shores, spoiling the idyll of Cornish coastal life. And as for the shark, there were thousands of square miles of sea and the chances of it turning up at Trevose Head were too small to consider.

The sea was calm and the skies were perfectly clear. They'd set out early to ensure that they would be back before the real heat of the midday arrived. For now, though, they were happy to sit peacefully on their boards watching the seals playing in the water, oblivious to their presence.

THE SINCLAIR FAMILY had left their car in the National Trust car park on the cliffs above where Zeb and Trina now relaxed on their boards. They walked along the cliff path, peering down into the bay. The children excitedly pointed at the seals and then they noticed the two paddle boarders on the water.

'Daddy, why are those people on their paddle boards?' asked Laura, the youngest. 'I thought you said the police had ordered everyone to stay near the beaches.'

'Yes, you're right, they did,' Edward, her father, replied, lifting his binoculars to take a closer look at them. 'I'm afraid there are always some people who think they're above the law.'

'Well, it's just not fair,' said Fiona, his wife, looking down at the bay. 'We've had to make sacrifices, even if they spoil our holiday. It's not right that some don't follow the rules. I hope they get caught and find themselves in trouble.'

Edward switched his focus back on the seals. He thought he could count six in total enjoying the peaceful waters of the cove. Fiona was about to urge him to move on along when she noticed him looking intently at something in the water.

'What is it Edward? What are you looking at?'

'I don't know, but I think that couple might already be in big trouble . I'm sure I saw a large fin about a hundred metres further out from them. It looked to be heading their way,' Edward said. He looked again. 'Oh my lord, look, you can see it even without binoculars.'

He pointed at the sea about sixty metres behind the paddle boarders. The triangular fin was cutting through the water towards them.

'We've got to warn them.'

Edward screamed, 'Shark!' at the couple who remained oblivious, sitting peacefully on their boards, absorbed in watching the seals in front of them. They didn't seem to respond at all. He turned to the rest of his family. 'Come on, everyone together, let's wave our arms and shout shark as loudly as we can. One, two, three, SHARK!'

Zeb and Trina heard the distant shouting and looked upwards. They could just about make out the word 'shark' but the waving of the arms suggested something more urgent.

Zeb, puzzled, looked to his side and then behind him. Twenty metres away, a large dorsal fin cut through the water directly towards them. His heart went into his mouth and he froze, barely able to warn his partner.

'Shit, Trina, watch out, behind us!'

She turned just in time to see the dorsal fin slip below the water. They both looked down into the clear water, terrified, as the huge bulk of the shark's body passed between their boards and moved swiftly towards the seals playing in the water.

The shark struck the nearest seal with unbelievable force, throwing it clear of the water. As the seal fell back into the water, the shark grabbed it again in its massive jaws, its teeth tearing into the body. It tossed the body from side to side while ripping the flesh from the now dead seal's body.

The attack lasted for no more than a minute until the shark lost interest and turned, diving deeper into the sea below.

Zeb and Trina sat motionless on their boards, trembling. Shock hit them. They had been afraid for their own lives but were even more appalled by the slaughter of one of their favourite creatures. The water all around them had turned a dark red. The remains of the seal's carcass still floated on the surface. A gull landed on the water and started to peck at the fresh meat remaining on the seal's bones. Trina, repulsed by the attack and the blood in the water, turned and vomited into the discoloured sea. Zeb stared at the carnage that surrounded them, tears rolling down his cheeks. The traumatic death of such a precious animal was more than he could bear.

After a few minutes, Zeb managed to compose himself and turned to Trina,

'Are you okay to continue?' he asked.

'Let's get away from this place as soon as we can,' Trina said. 'I never want to come here again.'

MEANWHILE, up on the cliff, the Sinclair children couldn't believe what they'd just seen.

'That was incredible,' said thirteen year old Jem. 'Just like a scene from a nature film. They must be two of the luckiest people alive. I really thought they were done for, Dad.'

'So did I,' Edward said, shaking his head in astonishment at what they'd witnessed. 'I'm going to call the emergency services. They need to know that the great white shark is still around our coast. We don't want any other idiots risking their lives like that.'

HIGH ABOVE THEM, unnoticed by everyone, a drone hovered almost silently capturing the action. A mile away, PC Monica Singh watched the events on the drone operator's screen and called it in. She opened up an app on her phone giving her access to the pictures that the drone was sending back. Then she and her colleague, PC Dan Hoskins, climbed into their car and set off towards Booby's Bay, where they guessed the paddle boarders were heading.

THE SHOCK of what they'd experienced, coupled with increasing fatigue, meant that it took Zeb and Trina an extra fifteen minutes to return to the beach. They pulled the boards out of the water and sat on them silently for a while, exhausted, just looking out to sea.

'That wasn't much fun was it?' Zeb said eventually.

But it was not his partner who answered.

'And the rest of the day isn't going to be much fun either,' a voice said behind them.

They turned to see two police officers standing a couple of metres away.

'Mr Jameson?'

Zeb nodded. 'How do you know that?' he asked.

'There's only one car in the car park with a roof rack large enough to carry your boards and that's registered in your name,' PC Singh replied. 'I presume that you're fully aware of the legal restrictions in place on this coast. If not, you must be blind, because there's a large warning notice right next to your car.'

'Yes, of course we know about them,' Zeb said, disdainfully turning his head away from the constable and staring back out to sea. 'We're a true Cornishwoman and Cornishman born and bred. Those rules are for the outsiders not for the likes of us.'

'I see,' PC Singh said walking in front of the couple to examine their faces. 'So the reason that great white chose not to have you two for breakfast is that it doesn't attack locals. Is that right?'

'How do you know about that?' Trina said, standing up.

'Oh that's just the eye in the sky,' PC Dan Hoskins said with a grin. 'But I'm afraid that you two are going to be coming with us to the station, where you will find yourselves facing a number of charges'

Dan recited the Miranda warning to the pair.

Zeb jumped to his feet, ready to look the police officer in the eye - but found he was talking up to a 6ft 6inch giant. '*We* are going nowhere,' Zeb shouted at the officer and then moved towards him aggressively, arms out in front of him, to push him away.

But Dan Hoskins grabbed Zeb's arm, twisted it sharply behind his back and slammed him face down on the sand.

'Oh dear, sir,' Hoskins said, reaching for the handcuffs on his belt. 'You've just added the rather serious charge of attempting to assault a police officer to the list of charges. You really are in deep trouble now.'

'Get off him,' Trina shouted. She jumped onto Hoskin's back, trying to pull him off the prostrate Zeb. 'This is police violence and intimidation.'

Before she knew it, she also found her arm wrenched up agonisingly behind her back and also thrown down on the sand.

'You can't do this,' she screamed as Monica Singh knelt on her back and handcuffed her. 'We'll sue you for police violence.'

'I'm afraid you won't be succeed,' Hoskins said. 'You see, there's a drone that's been filming everything you've done for the past couple of hours. It's currently flying right above us recording all this. So, sue away.'

'Get up please,' Monica Singh asked the couple, more of an order than a request. 'And don't make it any more difficult because we can tighten those handcuffs if needed.'

The couple stood up and reluctantly began to accompany the police officers to their car.

'What about our boards?' Zeb asked.

'Well, if you ask politely,' Monica Singh said, 'Officer Hoskins may carry them to your car for you.'

Zeb said nothing.

'Last chance, sir.'

'Please will you carry them to our car,' Trina asked through gritted teeth.

'That wasn't hard was it,' Hoskins said, picked up both boards and dragged them across the sand. 'Pity that you're going to be in the cells on a Sunday. The food's always rubbish. Do you like burnt chicken?'

The vegan Jamesons groaned. Life had just got much worse.

CHAPTER FIFTY

SUNDAY, 15TH JULY
The Atlantic Pearl,
3 miles off Newquay,
North Cornwall

Ricci Taylor sat back in a leather seat on his Fairline Squadron 78 luxury motor yacht, *The Atlantic Pearl*, delighting in the company of his girlfriend and her two closest friends. Ricci had made his money in the scrap metal business and now, aged sixty-two, he was finally enjoying the fruits of his labours.

At the wheel was his skipper, Jonny Bullen, who together with wife Diane, were the only crew needed. Diane was a professional cook and was currently down in the galley cleaning up after having produced another fabulous lunch.

Ricci had bought *The Atlantic Pearl* as much for his girlfriend, Chaud DeTouche, as for himself. A pop singer from New York, Chaud had recorded two top thirty hits in her early twenties. Now, aged forty-eight, she mainly appeared on what Ricci called 'golden oldie' tours. *She's still got the body and the voice*, thought Ricci, staring at her over his glass of champagne.

Ricci looked out towards the coast and could make out the faint outline of buildings. 'Jonny, what's the town on the starboard side?'

'That will be Newquay,' Jonny said, looking across the water. 'I'm sure you will have spent some time around there in your youth.'

'Some very happy times, Jonny, some very happy times, but don't tell Chaud!'

'Don't tell me what, babe?' Chaud said walking onto the aft deck. She was followed by her beloved golden retriever, Sapphire, who travelled with them everywhere.

'How much fun you can have in Newquay, love,' Ricci said and laughing at the idea of Chaud in Newquay. 'You'd look great in a "kiss me quick" hat, eating a hot dog.'

'Get thee behind me Satan,' she said, laughing. 'You ain't getting me anywhere near that hellhole!' She held up her empty glass and tipped it upside down. 'A girl could die of thirst on this boat.'

Ricci struggled to his feet and topped up Chaud's glass with ice cold champagne.

'We'll be needing another bottle soon.' He started to move towards the drinks fridge when shouts of delight could be heard coming from the swim platform at the rear of the boat.

Ricci and Chaud walked along the boat and down the steps to the platform.

'What is, it ladies?' Chaud asked.

'Look, porpoises. Four of them,' one of her friends, Rhiannon, said pointing to the four large fish jumping in and out of the boat'swake.

'Are they porpoises or dolphins?' the other female guest, Lauren, asked.

'They're too small for dolphins,' Ricci said. 'Yeah, porpoises is right.'

Sapphire joined them on the swim deck and stood barking at the fish.

'Do you want to go in, Saff? You've not had any exercise today have you,' Chaud said. 'Ricci, could you get Jonny to stop for a while and then you can throw a ball for Saffie? You know how much she loves it. She must be bored, poor thing.'

Ricci returned to the skipper's chair and repeated Chaud's request.

'No problem at all,' Jonny said and slowly brought the boat to a halt.

The porpoises disappeared as quickly as they had arrived. The sea was flat calm, so the guests could stand on the aft deck and swim platform without any difficulty.

Ricci returned to the swim deck, took out an old tennis racket and a tube of yellow tennis balls from a storage compartments. Sapphire started running round in circles, anticipating what was to come.

'Just a moment please, Ricci,' Jonny said, appearing alongside his boss. Jonny lifted the seat of the large transom bench and pulled out a set of steps. These had been custom made for Sapphire, so she could climb out of the water more easily. Jonny fixed them to the side of the swim deck.

'All ready to go, sir' Jonny said and stood well to the side.

Ricci was always impressed by the fearless way in which Sapphire threw herself full length into the water. Once again, as he smashed the ball with a swing of the racket, the dog leapt out, landing several feet away from the boat, swimming strongly and confidently towards the ball.

Chaud and the other girls shouted encouragement. But then, as Sapphire got half way to the ball, she turned and started to swim back to the boat. Reaching the boat, she climbed up the steps and shook herself vigorously to get rid of the excess water off her thick coat.

'No, Saffie, No!' Chaud screamed as she got soaked by the dog.

Lauren and Rhiannon were standing higher up on the aft deck, and laughed as they watched their friend get an unwanted shower.

'Quiet, you two, or you'll be joining Saffie!' Chaud threatened, though she couldn't help but laugh as well.

'Come on Saffie, what's up?' Ricci said as the dog stood perfectly still, staring out at the sea. 'You can do this,' and he launched another ball only twenty metres out this time.

Sapphire didn't move, but just stared up at Ricci.

Ricci, with alcohol in his veins, was getting angry at what he saw as the dog's disobedience. 'Saffie get in there now. Bloody well go!'

Clearly fearful of what might happen if she didn't obey her master's command, Saffie jumped into the water, but without any of her usual enthusiasm. She started to swim slowly out towards the ball, looking nervously around as she moved.

She was about ten metres from the boat when, without any warning, the water erupted as a giant shark's head burst through of the surface and wrapped its huge jaws around the hapless dog.

'Saffie!' Chaud screamed.

The shark made two violent shakes of its head, foaming water flying everywhere. Then, realising its prey was mere skin and bones, lacking the fatty coating of its normal prey, it released the dog and slipped away again into the depths.

All the women were screaming uncontrollably.

Blood surrounded the crippled dog as it desperately tried to swim back to the boat, but her rear end had been crushed and her head slipped below the surface.

Without hesitation, Ricci ripped off his shirt and dived into the water, surfacing almost next to the dog. He grabbed Sapphire's collar, pulled her head clear of the water and held her front legs as he swam back to the boat.

'Get some towels out,' he shouted and Jonny reacted immediately, pulling several large bath sheets onto the platform.

As Ricci approached, Jonny ran towards him, holding out a large towel so that no one could see the catastrophic injuries the dog had suffered. He took the dog from Ricci, wrapping her in towels and walked across to Chaud. She was kneeling on the deck and took her treasured pet into her arms.

Sapphire was whining softly. Tears fell from Chaud's eyes as she held her tight, whispering, 'My baby, my poor sweet baby.'

Behind her, her two friends stood with hands over their mouths, in shock at what they had just witnessed.

Ricci knelt down next to her and watched as Chaud held Sapphire until the dog stopped breathing a minute later.

'I'm so sorry you had to see that, Chaud darling. It was horrific,' Ricci said.

Chaud looked at him, her eyes wet with tears but burning with hatred.

'*You* killed my precious Saffie. *You* made her go back in the water when she knew there was danger. *You* bullied her to go back in. Y*ou* killed her. Get out of my sight. I can't bear to be near you.'

Ricci Taylor felt humiliated. He had never seen Chaud express such hatred and disgust. At that moment he wanted to be anywhere but on board that boat. He knew the next hours, days and weeks were going to be a living nightmare.

CHAPTER FIFTY-ONE

MONDAY, 16TH JULY
Prime Minister's Office
10, Downing Street, London

'It's not looking good, is it?' the Prime Minister said as his PPS walked into the office. He was referring to headlines of the 'red tops' lying on his desk:
Cornish holidaymakers held hostage by a fish
Jaws, jaws, jaws and NO action!
We fought for the freedom to use our beaches

'No, Prime Minister, and I'm afraid the latest opinion polls don't make good reading either. Only 32% think you're showing strong leadership over this shark situation, and that drops to 12% in the south west. In terms of voting intentions, only 18% of voters in the south west say they'll be voting for you and your party. That would mean you wouldn't hold a single seat south of Bristol.'

'This is turning into a major problem,' the PM said and stared out the window deep in thought. 'Right, we need to act now to stop the rot. Get me the Secretary of Transport on the phone, please. It's time for serious action.'

CHAPTER FIFTY-TWO

MONDAY, 16TH JULY
Dowrtreven,
Helford River, Cornwall

'Good morning everyone,' Emma, said, as she joined the others at the breakfast table. 'Have you seen the reports of yesterday's sightings?'

'We were just talking about them,' Sophie said. 'The dog attack was particularly strange.'

'Yeah, wasn't it?' Emma said, pouring herself some coffee. 'And how lucky were those paddle boarders? I mean, a great white actually passing *between* your boards? And then to get the opportunity to watch a kill close up. If I were them, I'd definitely be doing the lottery this week!'

'Couldn't agree more,' Sophie said watching Emma help herself to some bircher muesli. 'There's more fruit in the kitchen if you'd like some.'

'No, this is great, thanks. Is Nick around?'

'He was up ages ago,' Sophie said. 'I presume he's in the office.'

'Okay. I'll pop in on him as soon as I've finished this.'

Emma knocked on the office door and opened it. Nick was on the phone but waved her in and pointed to the seat opposite him. She sat down and waited for him to finish his call.

'Yes, that's great Sean. Many thanks and we'll see you later. Bye.'

Nick put his phone down on the desk top and looked across at Emma. 'Hi, how are you?'

'Fine, thanks, 'Emma said. 'I apologise for barging in on your call.'

'Don't worry about it.' Nick said. 'I'm glad you popped in. About half an hour ago, I had a call from Jamie. He'd just come off the phone with the PM.'

'Good or bad news?' Emma asked, leaning forward in her chair.

'Not good news, I'm afraid. Apparently the PM has been spooked by the way public opinion has turned against the restrictions and, more importantly, against him in particular. His ratings and those of the party have plummeted and he believes that the shark is to blame.'

'God, who'd want to be a politician?'

'The problem for us is that he is moving into panic mode. He told Jamie that if the shark hasn't moved out of British waters in the next 48 hours, he'll issue an order under emergency powers legislation for the shark to be hunted and destroyed.'

'That's a bit extreme, isn't it?' Emma sat back shaking her head.

'Not, it appears, if you are the PM and your professional reputation is at stake.'

'It's a tough decision whichever way you look at it.'

'I agree but it got me thinking. For too long we've been sitting back and waiting for interactions with this shark. I think it's time that we got off our bottoms and went out to try to meet her in her own territory.'

'OK,' Emma said. 'But what are you proposing?'

'I just came off the phone with Sean Howell. He's the skipper of the fishing boat that had the shark stolen by our friend. He had a family charter booked for today but a couple of them have got flu, so they've cancelled. I asked him if we could do a late afternoon charter, finishing after sunset. He was delighted and gave me a really good price.'

'So we're going out tonight?'

Nick nodded.

'That's a brilliant idea. I can't wait.' Emma sat back in her chair, smiling.

'Of course, the chances of us seeing her are minute,' Nick said, introducing a note of reality to the situation.

'Look, it'll be great just to get out there and to know she could be around.'

'In that case, we'll leave here at three. I think I'll ask Pete and see if he'd like to come.'

'Good idea.' Emma stood up and walked over to the door. Reaching the door, she stopped and turned to speak to Nick. 'By the way, I thought I'd give PC Mackay a call and see if I can get the contact details of that bloke Sam rescued. I know it's all a bit raw at present, so perhaps I'll leave it a couple of weeks and then see if he's happy to talk. What do you think?

'Yes, good. I'm sure Mack will be delighted to help you.'

'Ok. By the way, I've come up with a name for the documentary - *The Summer of the Shark*,' Emma said as she walked out of the office.

CHAPTER FIFTY-THREE

MONDAY, 16TH JULY 4.30PM
The Shore Thing,
Newquay Harbour

Sean Howell welcomed Nick on board his boat with his customary, bone crushing handshake.

'God, it's been a long time since I took you out on my boat,' Sean said, standing back to give his old friend the once over. 'You're still a good looking bugger though.'

'Well clearly your eyesight's got worse in that time,' Nick responded. He turned to his friends behind him on the gang plank. 'Can I introduce Emma Warren and Peter Higham.'

'It's a real pleasure to meet you both,' Sean said as he shook their hands. 'I saw what you both did with that shark. And you, too, Nick. That was really good work.'

'Thank you, Sean,' Emma said and Pete agreed. 'Very kind of you.'

'Praise where praise is due, that's what I always say.' Sean stood aside to allow his guests onto the deck. 'Right, as soon as we've stored your gear in the cabin, we'll get under way.'

Two hours later, they were well out at sea trailing Rubby Dubby over the sides of the boat. Sean was impressed that Emma hadn't even batted an eyelid when he'd brought the bags of stinking chum out of the cabin. He mentioned this to Nick.

'She's done autopsies on week old dead whales. Your Rubby's nothing compared to the gases she'd have experienced.'

Sean smiled. 'You wouldn't get me cutting one of those open. Bloody things can explode if you're not careful!'

The two men had been talking loudly and Emma had overheard what they had been saying.

'Don't be such a wimp, Sean. It's only a dead fish,' she said.

'Well, I'll stick to catching live ones, if it's alright by you,' he said, giving Emma a big smile. 'Talking of which, we've got a visitor. Look over there.'

He pointed to a small fin breaking through the water a few metres off the starboard side. 'I'm afraid it's not your old lady. That's a blue. Lovely colour isn't it?'

Pete had his camera out, filming the shark as it passed close to the boat.

'How common are they?' Pete asked.

'We've caught literally dozens this year and done a lot of tagging work on them, too. They normally stay a few miles further out, but this heat seems to be bringing them closer in.'

'How big can they get?' Pete asked as he followed the shark with his camera.

'They've been recorded at well over nine feet and in excess 120kgs.'

'Crickey, that's really big,' Emma said as she watched the beautifully streamlined shark glide through the water.

'Maybe,' Sean said, leaning over the side of the boat. 'But when you see one in the mouth of a great white, you really begin to understand what a big shark looks like!'

He pulled up the bag of Rubby Dubby. 'That needs a bit of a top up'.

He walked into the cabin and refilled it from the sealed container in the corner.

'Do you want me to bring the other one?' Emma asked, pulling up the bag on the other side to check. 'It's about half full.'

'Yeah, can you bring it through ,'

Emma carried the chum bag to the cabin and Sean handed her the refilled container. 'Swap you. Now that's a perfume I'm sure all the men would go for!'

'Sexist bastard,' Emma said dismissively, but smiling, as she walked to the side of the boat, restoring the bag of rubby to its original position. She noticed a pair of expensive swimming goggles hanging from the rail.

'I didn't know you did pleasure cruises, Sean,' Emma said, holding up the goggles.

'Oh, yeah,' Sean looked out of the cabin and saw what Emma was holding. 'It was my wife's birthday a couple of Sundays back so we had a few friends on board. One of them must have left the goggles behind. You have them if you want them.'

'Thank you very much,' Emma said putting them in her pocket.

Over the next hour they were visited by three more sharks and, more excitingly, a pod of four common dolphins. They played around the slow moving boat for several minutes before getting bored and moving away towards the coast.

And then nothing for the next half an hour. The sun was getting lower in the clear blue sky and they had to shield their eyes when scanning the sea to the west.

'What do you think, Nick?' Sean said, eagerly looking through his binoculars for movement in the water. 'Give it another 30 minutes? The sun will almost be down by then. Don't worry, I'm not trying to push you. I'm happy to stay out as long as you want.'

Nick turned to Emma and Pete. 'Another 30 minutes?' They both nodded in agreement and continued to scan the water.

'I know you're close,' Emma whispered to herself. 'Come on, old lady, show yourself.'

Twenty minutes later, Emma was looking into the water next to the boat, convinced that they would be going home disappointed. Then, suddenly, a dark shadow emerged from the deep and the great white's massive body appeared within metres of the boat.

'She's here, she's bloody well here,' Emma shouted. The others rushed over to join her. Pete had his camera out, filming the shark as it began to slowly circle the boat.

'God she's a thing of beauty, isn't she,' Sean said shaking his head in disbelief that he'd had another chance to see this magnificent creature.

Emma was surprised by how emotional she'd become when the shark appeared and, even now, after watching it for a few minutes, she found she had tears in her eyes thinking this could be the last time they might meet. Then a crazy thought came to her.

As the others watched the progress of the shark, she moved a short way along the side of the boat, just out of sight, and pulled off her white T shirt to reveal a plain black swimsuit underneath. She put on the goggles, undid her shorts and as they dropped to floor, she climbed over the rail and slipped gently into the water.

'Emma, what the hell are you doing?' Nick screamed and unsuccessfully tried to grab her as she went under the water. They all rushed to the rail, looking on in horror as the shark reacted to the disturbance in the water.

Emma watched as the old lady turned and moved toward her. She felt no fear, just a feeling of intense euphoria. She was here, in the water, with the most amazing creature she'd ever seen. And she had never felt so safe.

The shark was now only a couple of metres away, barely moving, just suspended in the water. It turned its head to be able to look at Emma and she stared directly into its eye, not afraid but mesmerised.

Emma gently broke through the surface to take in a lungful of air and briefly heard screaming from above. Dropping below the surface once more she realised the shark had moved even closer. She felt a powerful urge to touch the shark. Ignoring the rows of razor sharp teeth, she reached out and placed her hand on the lower part of its snout where she knew the 'Ampullae of Lorenzini' could be found. Almost immediately, the shark became completely still as it went into sensory overload with Emma's gentle touch on this, the most sensitive part of a shark's body. Over stimulated and disorientated, the huge shark was temporarily incapable of movement.

Emma recognised a bond between them and didn't want it to end, but her lungs were bursting and she had to rise to the surface for air. As she took her hand away, the shark was released from its reverie and slowly turned away from the boat.

As Emma surfaced, she felt a hand grab her arm and drag her towards the boat. Then two strong arms lifted her clear of the water and through the gate in the rail which Sean had opened.

She stumbled onto the deck and looked up to see Nick staring at her.

'What on earth were you doing?' Nick shouted at her, as much from relief for her safe return as anything else. 'You had no idea if she would accept you, or kill you. You are stark, raving bloody mad!'

And then he started to smile. 'But you are also the bravest, most impulsive woman I have ever met and I'm really very envious of what you just had the guts to do.'

The men started to clap and, as a wave of emotion hit her, she burst into tears.

'That was the single most amazing thing I'll ever do in my life,' she said, laughing and crying at the same time. 'But, I'll tell you what, I'd do it again if I knew it was our old lady. Where is she now?'

They looked back down in the water but there was no sign of her. Then Sean shouted from the other side. 'She's here!'

They ran round to the port side, shielding their eyes as the last rays of the setting sun reflected off the water.

They watched as the shark bumped softly against the boat. Then, just as she had done in Scotland, she rolled onto her back, revealing her white underbelly and slowly began to move away from them.

'She's putting on a show just for us,' Emma said, as watching with delight.

Twenty metres out, the shark righted herself and turned

back towards the boat, slipping just below the surface. Two metres away from them, she stopped and lifted her head clear of the water.

'She's spyhopping,' Nick whispered.

The shark appeared to look directly at Emma for a few seconds.

'Go,' Emma whispered to the shark. 'Please go now.'

The shark turned slowly away from the boat following the last rays of the setting sun in the west.

'I think she's on her way home,' Nick said.

'Goodbye old girl,' Emma whispered, tears moistening her cheek.

They watched until the dorsal fin slipped beneath the water for the last time as the shark set out on the long journey back to the familiar waters of her birth.

THE END

ACKNOWLEDGMENTS

Firstly, my thanks must go to my wife, Jane, for having put up with me for so many years and also for her helpful input and advice.

Secondly, to my brother, Michael, for both his patience and his forensic editing skills, which ensured the book was reduced to an acceptable reading length!

My fascination with the 1916 Matawan Creek Incident was the catalyst for writing this book. The brilliant description of events in Michael Capuzzo's *Close to the Shore* helped to drive this interest. I would recommend it to anyone who might like to learn more, not only about this incident, but also the nearby New Jersey attacks which, of course, were a major influence for Peter Benchley's brilliant *Jaws*, the book that created a genre.

Printed in Great Britain
by Amazon